ANOTHER LUCKY NUMBER

NINA KAYE

For (my) James.

Chapter One

'Excuse me, madam? Would you like something to drink?'

'Ooh, a glass of champagne, please.' I quickly fold down the corner of the page I'm reading as the immaculate flight attendant places a flute of beautifully chilled fizz on the tray table in front of me.

'Hand cooked vegetable crisps or olives?' she asks.

'Can I have both?'

'Of course.'

'Greedy cow,' a voice mutters from across the aisle and I shoot the owner (my friend, Amber) a faux dirty look in response.

Once the flight attendant has served the rest of our row and moved on to the next one, I catch the eyes of my two friends and raise my glass.

'To an *amazing* holiday.'

'*Yay! Cheers.*' My bestie, Cat, thrusts her own glass in my direction while Amber surveys me with a bored look.

'This *is* incredible and all, Emma,' she says. 'But are you going to do that every time we're served a drink? You're starting to take the piss.'

'Aww, leave her alone.' Cat comes to my rescue. 'Neither of us have been in business class before. Don't spoil the fun because you're used to these perks from your job. And *remember*, it was Emma who made all this happen.'

'Hmm... that's not entirely true.' Amber taps her chin, wearing a pompous expression. 'I got us this business class upgrade... *remember?*'

'Right, Amber, *enough*.' I find myself bailing Cat out of her own failed rescue attempt. 'Let's compromise. No non-alcoholic toasts – but I make no apologies, I'm having the boozy ones.'

Amber simply rolls her eyes, allowing me settle back in my seat and enjoy my champagne. Closing mine for a moment, I bathe in the excitement and anticipation of what lies ahead, just several hours from now. This is what life should be about. Not stress. Nor heartbreak. I stretch out my legs, flexing my calves and wiggling my toes as recommended in the traveller advice I read. It feels nice, almost therapeutic.

Suddenly, there's a bump and the cabin shakes. I glance across at my friends, but they don't seem to have noticed. Giving my neck a stretch, I try to relax, but then there's series of bumps followed a huge jolt and the sound of the seatbelt signs being illuminated.

'Ladies and gentlemen, due to some unexpected turbulence, the captain has switched on the seatbelt signs. Please return to your seats and ensure that your seatbelts are securely fastened. The toilets and first-class bar are now out of use until further notice.'

My pulse quickens and I anxiously tug at my seatbelt to tighten it as the bumping and lurching in the cabin intensifies. Seeking reassurance, I make eye contact with Amber.

'*Relax*.' She chuckles at my terrified face. 'Happens all the time. Think about it like being on a bus on a bumpy road.'

'I don't think I like this bus,' I murmur.

'Seriously, it's fine. The flight attendants are still walking around. That's a sure sign there's no problem.'

The moment she says this, the cabin seems to drop a few feet, taking my stomach with it, and the captain's authoritative voice comes over the plane's PA system.

'*Cabin crew, take your seats.*'

'*Oh my god!*' I watch in despair as they swiftly leave the cabin.

The turbulence is now so heavy that my champagne is slopping over the sides of the glass.

'All right, I take it back,' says Amber. 'Bit worse than usual, but it's still fine. Maybe less bumpy road, and more... rollercoaster. They're fun though, right?'

'Not the time for it, Amber.' I down what's left of my drink in one go.

Clutching the arms of my seat for dear life, I glance helplessly at Cat, who's face has drained of colour. She's clutching her poker straight dark hair anxiously, and as her amber eyes meet mine, I can tell she's as petrified as I feel. We're being thrown around like rag dolls, kept in our seats only by our seatbelts, our belongings and refreshments now rolling around the floor.

Then without warning, the plane goes into a nosedive, the force of the acceleration pinning us to our seats as we scream in terror.

'*Cat, Amber...*' I call to them, tears rolling down my cheeks. 'In case we don't make it, I want you to know I love you both more than—'

'*We are not going to die,*' Amber yells back, barely audible above the noise of the plummeting plane.

'How can you know that?'

'*Because there's no effing way I'm missing out on this holiday...*'

My eyes fly open and I sit bolt upright. Everything is still shaking and bumping, but it's so bright I can't see a thing. I rub at my eyes, desperate to orientate myself, realising only after several seconds what's going on: Amber's in front of me, dragging my sun lounger across the concrete poolside – with me still on it.

'*Amber!*' I bark at her. 'What the hell are you doing?'

'You're getting burnt. I was trying to move you to the shade without waking you.' She states this as if it's obvious.

I look down at my reddening stomach and see that she's right.

'OK, well, you could have woken me up. Thanks to you, I just had a horrible dream.' I glance around self-consciously, noting that there's a growing audience enjoying this spectacle.

Amber, unmoved by my plight, carries on dragging me across the concrete. This includes some abrupt movements as she adjusts the lounger's direction, making me look like a poorly-trained circus performer.

'Look, stop, will you?' My face is now hot with embarrassment.

'Nearly sorted. Stay put.'

In my state of embarrassment, 'nearly' isn't good enough. Unable to bear being the centre of attention for a moment longer, I attempt a swift and graceful exit from the sun bed, but my foot gets caught in my towel, and before I know it, I've overbalanced and plunged head first into the swimming pool. Moments later, I emerge coughing and spluttering to raucous laughter and a shadow appears above me.

'What did you do that for?' Amber's incredulous face peers down at me. 'I told you to stay put.'

'But you were... Why would you even... *Oh, forget it.*' I haul myself out of the pool, grab my towel and furiously dry myself.

Cat bounds across to us from the bar, brandishing three ice creams, clearly oblivious to the drama that has unfolded in her absence.

'Here we are, ladies, thought you might... um... did I miss something?' She looks from Amber to me and back again.

'Everything's fine,' says Amber. 'Emma took a quick dip.'

'Oh, lovely,' says Cat. 'Was the water nice? It's so hot today.'

'It was *freezing*.' I seethe. 'I'm going for a shower. See you in a bit.' I quickly gather my stuff and stalk off in the direction of my room.

'Did I say something wrong?' I hear Cat ask Amber as I leave the pool area.

'Nah, don't worry, she'll be fine. Here, give me that extra ice cream. Shouldn't let it go to waste.'

Chapter Two

Back in my suite, I have a long, hot shower, partly to wash away my annoyance at Amber, and partly because it's the most amazing shower I've ever experienced: with body jets and massage settings and mood lighting. It's like being at a spa.

The spray works its magic on the tense knots in my neck and shoulders, while I sigh with bliss. Amber's antics aside, this holiday is the perfect wind down from a crazy-mad few weeks. In fact, it's almost impossible to believe that only days ago, my life felt like it was in tatters.

It was like something out of a movie. Dave, the man I thought I was going to marry suddenly dumping me, leaving me heartbroken, homeless and suffering from full-on anxiety and panic attacks – then discovering I'd won three-quarters of a million pounds on the lottery. I genuinely thought at the time that this was the answer to all my problems and boy did I have a rude awakening. After suddenly quitting my job because of a bullying boss, I'd embarked on a week of living like a millionaire, encouraged by my elderly adopted aunt Lottie to have some fun and create life-long memories – the kind she herself doesn't have because of a previous family tragedy. It should have been nothing but an indulgent pleasure, and it had started out like that, but it became one of the worst weeks of my life when I discovered Dave had been cheating on me with one of my best friends and I nearly lost Cat after thinking it was her (it wasn't, of course). Then on top of all that, Lottie ended up in hospital after a fall. It was *a lot*. It taught me an important lesson though: that money provides financial stability and creates new opportunities, but it most certainly doesn't buy happiness or solve the bigger issues in life.

But there was one huge plus that came from it all (aside from the money I won): James, the amazing man I met during that time – and coincidentally the travel agent who booked this holiday for us. I nearly fobbed him off for various unjustifiable reasons. Well, basically because he seemed to turn up *everywhere*, dripping with ego and trying to play the hero (that's what I thought anyway). But he's actually lovely – and totally gorgeous. Like, top quality boyfriend material and the opposite of my self-involved arsehole ex. It also turned out that I unknowingly used his mobile number to choose my lottery tickets when, during our first (not so successful) interaction, he was about to give me his number and dropped part of the scrap of paper he wrote it on. I had picked it up, unaware that it was his, and *'hey presto!'* I became a nearly millionaire. He doesn't know that bit yet though. Oh, and then there was the other big 'wow' moment that knocked me for six. His parents are Lottie's neighbours and they're currently supporting her with her recovery from her fall.

As I say, it was *a lot*.

Watching the bubbles from the resort's luxury aromatherapy shower gel disappear down the plug hole, the memory of my impromptu first date (and first kiss!) with James immediately before my departure for this very destination triggers a fizzing in my stomach. I could almost believe that it was fate. *Almost*. Maybe too soon to judge, but I'll certainly enjoy alleviating the holiday blues with his company when this trip is over.

After my shower, I'm towel drying my hair in front of the huge floor to ceiling mirror, when the doorbell rings, signalling a visitor to my suite.

'*Just a moment*,' I call out.

Throwing on the resort embossed silk bathrobe, I dash to the door, and on peeking through the spy hole, I see that it's Cat. She's still in her beach gear and she looks worried. I quickly pull open the heavy wooden door.

'Hi, Cat. Everything OK?'

Her expression morphs to one of confusion. 'I was about to ask you the same thing.'

'What do you mean?'

'You looked pretty hacked off when you left the poolside before. Did you have a fight with Amber? She kept saying it was nothing, but I know she's not telling me something.'

I feel a rush of guilt for making Cat worry. She had no idea what was going on, and Amber would never admit to being the instigator of my bad mood.

'Oh, Cat, no, I'm fine. It was a bit ridiculous, really, and I probably overreacted. Amber was her usual charming self, which of course, resulted in me looking like an idiot in front of half the resort. Sorry, I didn't mean to worry you.' I quickly fill her in on the poolside debacle.

'That must have been mortifying,' says Cat. 'And this is only day two. Are you sure it was a good decision bringing Amber on this trip?'

'I'm already questioning that myself, believe me.'

'Sorry honey, but at least I know you're OK.' Cat gives my shoulder a sympathetic squeeze. 'I'm off for a shower myself. See you in the cocktail bar at seven-thirty? Same as last night?'

'Perfect.'

We say our goodbyes and I resume my post shower

activities. For having arrived only the day before, my suite is already well lived-in, and I have to zig-zag across the refreshingly cool tiled floor, seeking items of jewellery, makeup and clothing which are strewn across the hard wood furniture and the cream fabric sofas. My idea of unpacking is clearly not how it's meant to be done.

After trying on about five outfits, I settle on a slinky low-back black evening dress paired with chunky wedged sandals that make my legs look long, slim and graceful (I love an optical illusion). Outfit sorted, I style my hair (though sometimes I wonder why I bother because it doesn't behave in hot and humid weather), then finish my makeup with a final volumising slick of mascara.

With half an hour to spare, I open the patio doors and step out onto the spacious balcony terrace, a wall of heat and humidity engulfing me as I leave my air-conditioned room. Leaning on the railing, I enjoy the feel of the warm sea breeze on my face while taking in the incredible view: the pristine white sand, luscious palm trees regally lining the shore, the sparkling deep turquoise water that hugs the coastline as far as the eye can see. All these visual treasures enhanced by the rhythmic crash of the surf and the cooing of the pretty Eurasian Collared Doves that have made the resort their home – the perfect habitat for an easy meal, just like Edinburgh city centre is to the less appealing urban pigeons back home. Never in my life have I experienced paradise like this.

I drink in the view for as long as I can, my normally busy, over-analytical mind astonishingly quiet. I promise myself that I will not – for even a second – take this experience for granted. This is a trip of once, maybe a couple of times, in a lifetime, and I'm going to make the most of it.

Prying myself away from the vista, I grab my handbag and room key, and head for the bar. I stride past the resort's cluster of boutique-style shops before whizzing by reception, giving a quick wave to Charnice, the remarkably friendly receptionist who checked us in the day before.

On arriving at the open-air cocktail bar, I can see that most of the tables are already occupied by a melange of hotel guests: from smooching young couples to families, middle-aged groups of friends, and travelling companions who have reached the greater milestones in life. I grab the last remaining table overlooking the pool and as soon as I've settled onto the comfortable outdoor sofa, Cat and Amber appear.

'Looking lovely, ladies.' I say, as a waiter materialises beside us. 'What do you fancy to drink?'

'Rum Punch, please.' Cat beams at the waiter.

'I'll have a Bahama Mama,' says Amber.

'And a Pina Colada for me, thank you.' I complete the order and the waiter disappears.

We sit quietly, taking in the atmosphere, enjoying our freedom from the everyday demands of being at home. The tasteful lighting on the terrace and the approaching dusk create a relaxed evening ambience that chases away the youthful vibrancy of the daytime. Even when our drinks arrive and we clink glasses do we stay quiet and contemplative.

Until Amber breaks the silence.

'Feeling refreshed after your dip earlier, Emma?'

Clear that this is an attempt to wind me up, I ignore her.

'I hear the water's *really* nice.'

'*Amber.*' Cat calls her out on her goading. 'You promised on the way along here—'

'It's fine, Cat,' I say. 'I'm over it. The more we react, the more she'll continue. Best thing to do is ignore her.'

Amber looks highly amused by my assessment of the situation, but says nothing further. I use the opportunity to savour my first taste of Pina Colada, which is delicious – and stronger than the cocktails I'm used to at home – and change the subject.

'Have you heard from Mike since we left?' I ask Cat. She's also recently met a new man and they've just gone exclusive.

'Yes, I have.' Her face lights up. 'We've been messaging loads.'

'That's amazing, Cat. He's obviously hooked. I can't wait to meet him.'

'I can't either. I think you'll like him. He's so kind. And generous. And patient.'

'Very much like you then.' I smile at her and she looks away, unable to accept the compliment.

'*Yawn.*' Amber makes it clear our U-rated 'fluff' is boring her. 'Tell us more about these messages, Cat. Were they juicy?'

I can see exactly where this is headed but unfortunately Cat fails to pick up on the true motivation behind Amber's question.

'Not really,' she says. 'It was just chat about...well, nothing, really. You know, just silly things... Jokey banter. It's hard to explain.'

'I bet it is.' Amber's eyes glint wickedly. 'Were there pictures too?'

'Pictures? No. Why would... Oh, you mean pictures of the resort. You know I didn't even think of that. I should—'

'*Dirty pictures.* I meant pictures of you both naked. *Come on*, you must be at the sexting stage by now.'

'What?' Cat looks a mixture of horrified and perplexed. 'Should I? Will he be expecting me to—'

'*No, he will not.*' I jump in, aware that Cat's relationship confidence is too fragile for this; last thing she needs is Amber playing unsolicited sex therapist. 'Mike is obviously a decent guy, and he respects you, so take things at your own pace. *That* is never a necessity. It's simply something *some* couples choose to do.'

Cat looks relieved. I shoot Amber a warning look.

'I was just asking.' Amber throws her hands up in spiritless surrender. 'What about you then, Emma? Have you heard from your hot man yet? Tell me you and James are at least hitting it hard.'

'No and no,' I reply. 'You really need to get your mind out of the gutter. We've only been on one date so he's hardly going to be pining for me – like Mike clearly is for Cat.'

Cat blushes and I can tell she's secretly pleased by my comment.

We finish our drinks and wander along one of the many meandering pathways of the resort gardens to a laid-back pan-Caribbean eatery which is housed in a white building with a beach house feel to it – one of eight restaurants on the resort. Even in the darkness of the evening, the balminess of the air and the noise of the waves crashing on the shore nearby reminds us that we're somewhere exotic and utterly fabulous.

A short while later, we're tucking into our mouth-watering mains of jerk chicken, barbeque pork with peas and rice and conch caesar salad in relaxed, satisfied silence, which of course, never lasts long when we're with Amber.

'So, Emma...' she says. 'What's the plan for when you get home?'

'Amber, please don't wish the holiday away,' says Cat. 'I expect Emma doesn't want to think beyond the next week or so of R&R. Let's just be present and enjoy every second of this experience.'

I look across the table and see Amber mimicking Cat in a rather unflattering way.

'*Hey*. Don't do that,' I scold her. 'Cat's looking out for me and it's very much appreciated.'

She stops and looks at me. 'Yeah, well, that plan sucks. If we're not allowed to talk about anything of any substance, we're going to run out of chat pretty damn quick. In which case – no offence – but I'm going to find better things to do than sitting around staring at each other.'

'I didn't mean we couldn't talk about anything of importance,' says Cat. 'But Emma's had a challenging time over the last few weeks and I expect she wants to switch off and recover from it.'

'It's not like it's a hardship thinking about what she's going to do next.' Amber puts on a voice. '*Oh, poor me, I won lots of money on the lottery, and I don't know what to do with it. Life is so unfair.*'

'Amber, you're exaggerating just as much as you claim Emma is.' Cat frowns at her. 'Emma's been lucky financially but you know fine well she didn't win enough to live the life of a socialite, and—'

'*Ding ding.* Let's call time on this.' I grab Cat's hand and squeeze it tight so she knows I've got her. 'Cat, thank you for your support, and Amber, *quit it*. I get where you're coming from but your delivery could use some work.'

Amber shrugs in apparent acceptance of this.

'I agree with Cat that I want to make the most of this down time...' Amber's about to protest and I hold up a hand to stop her. 'But... that can include a bit of chat about my next steps, and in particular, what I'm going to do career-wise. Because as you know, that's very important to me. It's been at the back of my mind anyway, and I've come to the realisation that I want to do something *totally* different.'

'You do?' says Cat.

'Yes. I just kind of fell into my career path because in Edinburgh, Financial Services is a core industry, but... sorry to say it... it's dull as dishwater – to me anyway. I don't want to wake up when I'm seventy and feel like I've wasted my life. The idea of that terrifies me. I also know it's a bit of a cliché, and probably unrealistic, but I want to be one of those people who doesn't see their job as work because they love it that much. And I know my mum thinks my idea to find my dream career is "codswallop" but if I don't try, I'll definitely prove her right, won't I?'

'That is true,' Cat concedes.

'So, maybe we could throw around some ideas during this trip and see where we get to.'

'All right, that I can work with.' Amber has perked up significantly. 'What are you thinking... voice over artist... air traffic controller?'

'Ha, neither of the above,' I say. 'I meant throw around some *realistic* ideas. And the answer is: I just don't know, but we have days ahead of us to figure it out, so get your thinking caps on.'

With this gauntlet thrown down, we fall into contemplative silence.

'What do you *think* you're looking for?' Cat asks eventually. 'I don't mean the job title, but the type of work, the skills it uses, the experiences it will give you?'

I quickly chew and swallow. 'Good question. I guess I'm open to learning a whole new skill set, even studying part-time, but it would be good if I could use some of the skills I've already got. I'd say non-corporate, or if it's an office-based job, one in an industry that's got a bit about it. Somewhere I'd be excited to show up to each day – whether virtually or in person. There wasn't much opportunity for that where I was previously.'

We continue to chat while we eat our meal, and contrary to Cat's concern, I find that I feel energised by the conversation. I'd never want the life of a socialite. It's just not me. But having a temporary financial cushion does really help because I won't feel pressured into taking the first job I can find when I get back. I have a bit of time to nail this down and find a career that's right for me. I know how lucky that makes me, and I'm not going to squander the opportunity.

As soon as we've finished eating, Amber's already onto what's next.

'Right, let's take this party down town. See what the nightlife's like.'

Cat and I look at each other.

'You don't actually mean *down town*, as in Nassau, do you?' I say.

'Yeah, why not?'

'Because we've got five bars here on the resort. We haven't been to them all yet, and as we're all-inclusive, everything's essentially free. Why would we want to go out?'

'Because it'll be fun. We need to experience this island properly and that's one way to do it.'

'I guess that's not such a bad idea,' I say.

Cat looks apprehensive. 'Is it... *safe*? I read on the gov.uk site that there's a risk of getting robbed or assaulted.'

'It says that about everywhere.' Amber throws Cat a condescending look. 'Happens to the absolute minority. Don't be such a wimp.'

'If we stick together and take a taxi there and back, I'm sure we'll be just fine,' I reassure Cat.

'Yeah, and if anyone tries anything, they'll have me to deal with,' says Amber.

Cat and I look our pint-sized, auburn-haired friend up and down, and share an unconvinced look. Though she's got a reasonable bark for a chihuahua.

'OK, then, why not.' Cat seems to relax a little. 'Could be fun.'

'*That's the spirit*,' hoots Amber. 'Let's go.'

We throw back the last mouthfuls of our drinks and head out of the restaurant.

Chapter Three

'*This is freakin' amazing!*' Amber is like an excited toddler as we emerge from the taxi near the waterfront in Nassau.

There are several bars around us, all brightly lit and filled to bursting point, a mix of music filtering across the tropical breeze, from more mainstream pop music to the heavy bass of reggae. The atmosphere is infectious and it's not long before we're mirroring Amber's enthusiasm.

'Didn't I tell you?' she calls over her shoulder. 'This is what it's about. The resort is awesome – *obviously* – but we have to do some of this too.'

'Agreed,' Cat and I reply in unison.

Happy for Amber to take the lead, we follow on as she checks out one bar after the next.

'I've been meaning to ask... How's Lottie recovering from her fall?' Cat asks me. 'Is she still in hospital?'

'She is.' I nod. 'I was chatting with her on FaceTime this morning. She's looking a lot better and she's even getting home tomorrow.'

'That's such good news. It could have been so much worse. She's staying with James's parents, right?'

'No, she's staying at her own place, in the downstairs bedroom and James's mum is supporting her with everything she needs. It's totally bonkers. I still can't believe my sort-of new man's parent are Lottie's neighbours.'

'*Score! Karaoke.*' Amber fist-pumps the air ahead of us.

'*Oh, no.*' I tune into the raw vocals coming from the bar. 'Anything but karaoke would have done.'

'Just go with it.' Cat smiles and puts her arm around my shoulder. 'We can pretend we don't know her.'

'We might have to.'

We enter the jam-packed open-air bar where there's a middle-aged woman standing in front of the karaoke screen bellowing out a faltering – but reasonably in-tune – rendition of *I Will Survive*. Despite her intense concentration, she's slightly off time, her vocals lagging just enough to make the whole performance sound a bit odd. Despite this, I can't help feeling a swell of respect. Rather her than me.

We grab a bench-style table, the previous occupiers of which vacated as we arrived, and I'm pleased to note that it's far enough from the makeshift stage that we can still have something resembling a conversation. Once we're settled, a cheerful waiter saunters across to take our order, and within minutes, two Bahama Mamas and a Mango Daiquiri are delivered to our table.

'What are you going to sing then?' I ask Amber.

'It's a surprise.' There's a slight glint in her eye, which unsettles me.

'Can I make a suggestion? Maybe go for something a bit more audience-friendly than your usual karaoke choices? They might be ill-matched to the chill atmosphere here.'

'I agree,' says Cat. 'How about some Bob Marley?'

Amber raises a defiant eyebrow and fixes us with her well-worn don't-think-for-a-second-that-had-any-influence-on-me-at-all look.

17

'Back soon.' She climbs out of her seat and skips off to the DJ box.

Cat and I sit quietly, soaking up the ambience while watching the brave and probably well-inebriated punters consecutively murdering or doing justice to the songs we know and love. There are now four American men singing a tuneless, but very lively, version of *Sweet Caroline,* arms draped across each-others' shoulders, forming a human chain. They manage to get the whole bar singing along with them, including me and Cat.

After a lengthy absence, Amber returns to our table, and after sitting impatiently for another half an hour, her turn finally arrives.

'OK, who do we have next...' The karaoke MC's voice comes over the PA system. 'Up you come... *Amber.*'

'Later, ladies.' She wastes no time in climbing back out of her seat and bounding across to grab the mic.

'Here we go,' I say to Cat. 'Cross your fingers it's reasonably clean.'

We watch as the song name and artist appear on the screen.

'Don't think I know this one,' I say. 'Do you?'

Cat shakes her head. 'I've never heard of *Limp Biscuit.*'

'It's *Limp Bizkit,*' I correct her, reading the screen.

Amber looks over, giving us a little salute as the intro starts to play and I hold my breath.

'Hang on, isn't this the Mission Impossible theme tune?' asks Cat.

'Ah yeah. I think it's a proper song that was featured in one of the films – quite good from what I remember.'

The lyrics appear on the screen and Amber starts rapping to the smooth melody.

'This is OK,' says Cat and I give an optimistic nod.

We sway to the music, relieved at Amber's acceptable song choice. However, it quickly becomes clear that we've relaxed too soon when the mellow verse culminates in a chorus of loud, shouty metal, and we watch in horror as Amber starts moshing on the stage, throwing herself around violently, while aggressively yelling the lyrics. Glancing around the bar, all I can see are slightly shocked and bemused faces. There's certainly no one clapping, cheering or singing along, like they did with the other songs.

The chorus comes to an end and Amber powers down, returning to the smooth rap: which now feels like a lullaby in comparison to what we've just witnessed.

'What on earth was that?' I say to Cat from behind my hands. 'I can't bear to watch it again.'

'Me neither.' She's sunk so low in her seat that she's almost under the table. 'The whole bar looks shell-shocked.'

I try to stifle an embarrassed giggle and accidentally let out a little snort. It's followed by more in quick succession as Cat and I are reduced to tears, irrationally howling our way through the rest of the song.

When Amber's moment of glory comes to an end, there's a stunned silence in the bar, interrupted only by Cat's and my failed attempts to get a hold of ourselves. Amber takes a proud bow, which prompts a smattering of applause that dies out almost instantly. At this point the *Sweet Caroline* guys take pity on her and start whooping and cheering – which only makes the lack of collective appreciation starker.

Amber doesn't seem to notice any of this though. She bounces off the stage and springs across the silent bar, a huge grin plastered on her face. Cat and I instinctively hide behind the drinks menu to avoid judgement by association.

'That was *awesome*.' Amber insists on a high five from each of us. 'I've never done that one before.'

'It was... different,' I say.

'Yeah, different,' agrees Cat. 'That's... a good way to describe it.'

Thankfully, Amber's victims (i.e. the entire bar) have recovered and are no longer staring mutely in our direction.

'I might try another one by that band.' Amber reaches for one of the song request slips on the table, and Cat and I share an unmistakable look: we have to get out of here – fast.

But before we're able to put our plan into action, things go from bad to worse.

'Well, that was a unique performance from Amber.' The karaoke MC's voice comes over the PA system after a crowd-pleasing filler of a music track, which I suspect was selected for therapeutic effect. 'Now, let's see who's next... *Emma*, you're up. Come and join us.'

Oh. Shit. My stomach lurches uncomfortably. I'm desperately hoping there's another Emma in the bar, but I know I'm not going to be that lucky.

'Why did you do that?' My steely eyes meet Amber's. Her smile is even broader than before.

'Your turn,' she says to me, then stands up and points at my head. '*She's over here.*'

All eyes turn to us once again.

'*Amber, I could kill you.* Go and tell him I'm not doing it.'

'Can't do that.' She resolutely shakes her head.

'Maybe you could go up again instead, Amber?' Cat suggests. 'You really enjoyed the last song.'

'Not my kind of music, Cat.'

While Amber sits there smugly, the karaoke MC makes another appeal, this time aimed directly at me. '*Emma*, up you come. Don't be shy, girl.'

I stay exactly where I am and pretend he's not there.

'My good people, are you thinking what I'm thinking?' The karaoke MC then appears to address the whole bar. 'That we have ourselves a Coconut Beach Bar virgin?'

'*Break her in!*' yells one of the crowd.

'This your first time here, Emma?' I'm asked over the mic,

causing me to squirm uncomfortably because everyone's now looking at me expectantly, some with amusement.

'Erm... yes, it is,' I call out in a strangled voice.

'Didn't quite catch that,' the karaoke MC booms playfully over the mic. 'Say again?'

'*I said... yes, it is.*'

'That explains it then. You don't know the golden rule. Everyone, shall we share it with Emma? Ready... and...'

'*If your name's put up, you gotta come up!*' the entire bar singsongs at me.

With my terror intensified by this unwanted attention, I throw a helpless look at Cat, who looks back at me with sympathetic eyes. This is my worst nightmare. It's a karaoke cult. And I'm not getting out alive.

'*Up. Up. Up. Up,*' the crowd continue their chanting.

Glaring at Amber, I climb out of my seat and head for the DJ box, prompting the chanting to turn into cheering applause and foot stamping. Not such a chilled crowd after all then.

'How you doing, Emma?' The karaoke MC gives me an inappropriate slap on the back when I reach him. 'The hardest part is getting out of your seat.'

Though I'm generally a pacifist (or more accurately, an avoider of conflict) I want to kick him in the balls for this. Hard. I'd also kick Amber in the balls if she had any.

He hands me the microphone and I shuffle over to the stage, where the song title materialises on the screen: *Rich Girl* by Gwen Stefani. Typical bloody Amber. She's intentionally added to my discomfort with her own private joke. I throw a you're-so-dead-if-I-make-it-through-the-next-three-minutes warning in her direction. Cat looks dutifully humiliated on my behalf, but Amber simply whoops: 'Sing like it's real, sister!'

Deciding it's best to ignore her, as well as everyone else in the bar, I fix my eyes on the screen. The intro starts and before I know what's happening, I'm tunelessly expelling the lyrics.

Similar to the woman who was singing when we first arrived, I'm faltering and off-time, but without the saving grace of being able to sing in key. My off-pitch warbling fills the bar, every inch of me consumed by humiliation.

As I reluctantly murder line after line, I become more aware of my surroundings, realising only when the second verse starts, that everyone is singing and clapping along. I dare a quick glance at the nearest tables, which to my surprise, are full of smiling, encouraging faces. Their support is like a drug. Now I've discovered it, I need more to keep me going.

Sweeping the sea of faces, I direct a brief cringing smile at Cat, who's cheering louder than anyone else. Then, while stumbling through a shockingly bad rendition of Eve's featured rap – holding out my hands in acceptance of my lack of talent – I inadvertently lock eyes with a man I didn't spot before now. He's older than me, maybe mid-thirties, tall, with mid-brown hair and a well-manicured beard. His fitted linen shirt perfectly defines his muscular physique and caramel tan.

In that one single look, I feel a surge of electricity between us: his smouldering gaze boring into mine, lips betraying his amusement at my performance, but at the same time, appearing to tease me with the slightest hint of a seductive smile. Flustered by this exchange, I lose my place and finish the song completely off-time, though this doesn't seem to bother my onlookers, who roar and cheer as if I'm Gwen Stefani herself.

Finally free from the jaws of humiliation, I scurry back to my friends and climb back into my seat, playfully cuffing Amber across the back of the head as I do.

'What was that for?' she complains.

'As if you need to ask. Thanks for making it even worse with your song choice.'

'You're welcome.' She breaks into a mischievous grin.

'You did great, honey.' Cat puts her arm around me, giving me a squeeze. 'The crowd loved you.'

'It seems they did. And I got a lot more applause than you did, Amber.' I fan myself with a napkin to cool myself down and disperse the residual embarrassment.

She ignores me and wanders off to the toilets.

Now back in a place of relative safety and calm, I remember about the mysterious man, but when I look around for him, he seems to have disappeared. And I'm surprised to find I'm a little disappointed.

'Hey, when I was up there losing every last shred of dignity, I spotted a majorly hot man.' I say to Cat. 'We made eye contact – and if I wasn't making a complete tool of myself up there – I would have said there was a moment between us.'

'Really?' Her face lights up with interest. 'Maybe there was. Point him out.'

'Well, that's the thing... He's disappeared, so I guess I'll never know. Probably a good thing anyway. I know it's early days, but I want to see what happens with James when I get home.'

'That makes sense. Although remember you've only been on one date. You're not exclusive – yet.'

'What are you two yapping about?' Amber says as she rejoins us.

'About moving on to a karaoke-free bar.' I climb back out of my seat. 'Drink up and let's go.'

'No bloody fun, you lot,' she grumbles as she trails out of the bar behind us.

Chapter Four

We check out another couple of bars before taking a taxi back to the resort. There's plenty of banter on the way, which seems to amuse the driver. Mostly playful sniping between Amber and myself, regarding our equally dismal karaoke performances – though in her head that's not how her moment of glory went.

'So, where to?' Cat asks, while we wander through the luscious resort gardens and circle the enormous lagoon-style swimming pool which is glowing invitingly. 'Cocktail bar? Beach bar? Bed?'

'*Bed?* Are you freakin' kidding me?' Amber shoots Cat a judgy look. 'We're on holiday, grandma.'

'I was offering *a range* of suggestions.'

'Let's go to the resort club. They've got a throwback night on.'

Cat's face falls. It's clear that she would have been quite happy to turn in for the evening.

'Why don't we leave that for another night, Amber?' I say. 'Thanks to you, I've had enough excitement for one day. What about the wine bar? We haven't tried that yet.'

'Ooh, great idea,' says Cat.

'Amber? You up for that?' I nudge her with my elbow.

'Suppose,' she huffs.

'We'll go to the club another night, I promise.' I slide my arm around her shoulders and she shrugs me off as she always does, not one for shows of affection.

We head along the pathway in the direction of the wine bar, eventually reaching a building that has the appearance of being an enormous rock. There's a metal sign above the entrance introducing it as *The Cave*. We walk inside and find ourselves in a small reception area where we're greeted by a young hostess.

'Good evening, ladies. Have you made a booking this evening?'

'No, did we need to?' says Cat.

'Not at all.' The hostess smiles warmly at us. 'But some of our guests prefer to do so to specify their table. Is it a table for three, or do you have others joining you? And would you like to sit inside or outside?'

'It's just us,' I say. 'And outside if possible.'

'Follow me, please,' she says.

We traipse behind her through the bar to an outdoor terrace, which is more secluded and intimate than the terrace of the cocktail bar. It has high tables, pretty feature lighting and a faux canopy roof that creates the cave-like ambience. Light jazz music floats seductively through the air at a low volume, and little more than twenty or so feet away from us, cloaked in darkness, is the vast, calm sea.

'Ooh, I love the twinkling lights,' I say, marvelling at our surroundings. 'And it really is cave-like, even though we're outside. Genius.'

We thank the hostess, who melts into the background and another staff member takes over.

'Welcome to The Cave.' The man hands us each a drinks

menu while we make ourselves comfortable. 'Please take your time and I will return for your order soon.'

After some toing and froing, we order a bottle of champagne and a dish of fresh chocolate-dipped fruit, which Cat claims is necessary because we didn't have dessert earlier.

'*Look*.' My attention is suddenly drawn to another feature of our environment. 'There are even those rock formations you find in real caves. The ones that point up and down. What do you call them again... salamites and salactites?'

Amber makes a face. '*Stalagmites* and *stalactites*, dipshit. Think you need to go back to school and re-learn the basics.'

There's a stifled chuckle from the table behind me. I glance round self-consciously, but I can't make out much more than the silhouette of a man sitting alone at a candlelit table.

'Yeah, well, I think being able to pronounce the words of rock formations is less important than being able to read a room, Miss Mosher,' I throw back.

Before Amber can retaliate, the waiter reappears with our champagne and discreetly releases the cork from the bottle. We watch silently, almost spellbound, as he pours us each a glass.

'Enjoy yourself, ladies. I will check with you again shortly to see if you need anything.'

We thank him and he places the bottle in the chiller and disappears.

Enchanted by our surroundings, we silently clink glasses. It's a moment that needs no words; only to immerse ourselves in the experience. But, as ever, the silence doesn't last long.

'So...' Amber fixes her gaze on me, her face almost ominous in the half-light. 'Any more thoughts about what's next for you, Emma? Your choice of career is only one part of it.'

'Amber, it's almost midnight,' says Cat. 'Would tomorrow not be a better—'

'It's OK, Cat.' I hold up a hand to stop her. 'This is

preferable to karaoke or any other mischief she might get up to.' My attention turns to Amber. 'That quite a broad question, isn't it? I sense you have an ulterior motive in asking it.'

'All right, I'll get to the point,' she says. 'You sacked off your last job rather than addressing the problem there: your conflict avoidance—'

'My problem was a bullying boss.'

'Who you didn't stand up because of your conflict avoidance.'

I narrow my eyes at her. 'What's your question?'

'My question...' She pauses and sips at her drink, looking thoughtful. 'Here it is: as someone with no backbone when it comes to dealing with difficult people at work – how are you going to grow one to land this dream career you're after – whatever it is? I meant it when I said I'd whip you into shape.'

'*Amber.*' I glance around self-consciously once more and lower my voice. 'Do you mind?'

'Not really, but thanks for asking.'

'You know what I mean. I don't want my private business shared around, and... there are people listening.'

'Where?' Amber looks around and shrugs. 'No one's close enough to hear.'

'*Him.*' I jab my thumb towards the man at the table behind me. 'He already got a laugh from your earlier piss-take.'

'Great. Someone who appreciates my humour. We'll get on well.'

'Amber, don't you dare—'

'Chill, would you.' She chuckles. 'There's no one there.'

Surprised, I look round and see that the man has gone. An empty champagne flute the only sign that he was ever there.

'OK, good. And to answer your – slightly o ensive – question—'

'You were the one who wanted me to be specific.'

'Well, whatever... I've already had some thoughts on this.

27

I'm going to invest in some personal development: a career coach. Someone I can work with to manage that issue and grow my assertiveness. They can also help me understand and build on any other weaknesses, as well as make the most of my strengths.'

'Honey, that's a great idea,' says Cat. 'A really sensible investment that should pay off – as long as you find the right person to work with.'

I beam at her. 'Thanks, yes, I think so too.'

I try to ignore the fact that Amber's eyeing me suspiciously.

'Where did that come from?' she asks. 'You were at a total loss just a couple of days ago, more than happy to sign up as my bitch.'

'I... um... gave it some thought on the plane.'

'You mean you were reading *Psychology Now* magazine on the plane and you've parroted from that.'

I flush. Cat looks and me and winces, obviously feeling my pain.

'Amber, please don't,' she says. 'What does it matter where Emma got it from? It's a great idea.'

'Yeah, maybe,' she says. 'I just love seeing the look on her face when she gets outed. Maybe that should be your first session with your new coach, Emma. How to keep a poker face. *That* you would get as part of the "School of Amber".'

'No offence, but I think I need to work with someone who's not going to teach me their bad habits.' I straighten my back defiantly. I don't really mean this. I know that Amber has a strong professional side and her devilish antics are strictly limited to pleasure, not business, but she's gotten under my skin.

'*Whatever.*' She rolls her eyes. 'I still suggest you do some work with me too. I'll give you way more value than any overpriced career coach.'

'I'll give it some thought...' I say, climbing down from my

seat to escape to the ladies toilets, having u-turned on my willingness to engage in this conversation.

After a quick breather, I make my way back to the table, noticing that the rude man from earlier has returned to his seat. I glower in his direction, and while I'm inelegantly clambering back onto my seat, he glances round, making eye contact and causing my breath to catch in my throat.

It's the hot man from the karaoke bar.

Chapter Five

The man does a double take, and his face breaks into the same amused – and slightly inviting – smile from earlier.

'*Alors...* what do we have here? It is the superstar from the karaoke bar.'

His accent is unmistakably French. And unmistakably sexy. Cat, Amber and I are goners the moment he opens his mouth. He may have offended me only minutes before, but my principles have already jogged across the terrace and dived into the sea.

'*Mesdames*, are you all right?' He athletically leaps off his seat and approaches our table, making it clear that we've been staring at him for way longer than what would be considered appropriate.

I clear my throat, triggering my friends to surface from their own trance-like states.

'Hi, I'm Cat.' My bestie thrusts an overenthusiastic arm forward to shake his hand.

'*Enchanté.*' He chuckles, giving it a squeeze. 'You British are so formal.'

Amber then introduces herself with a casual nod (much respect to that impressive turnaround).

'Pleasure to meet you, Amber.' The man pronounces it *Omber*, causing Cat to visibly swoon. 'And the superstar *chanteuse*?' The man's emerald-green eyes land on me.

I hold my hands up in a fanatical wave, then on realising what I must look like, quickly hide them behind my back. 'I'm Emma. And singing that song was *not* my idea.'

'I see. *Enchanté*, Emma.' He smiles warmly and Cat and Amber gape open-mouthed as he leans in and greets me French-style, with a kiss on each cheek, his fruity yet spicy aftershave wafting into my airways.

The whole experience leaves me a little faint, and I have to put a hand on the table to steady myself. I turn to my friends, speechless and wide-eyed.

'I see you've been sitting alone.' Amber immediately seizes the opportunity. 'That can't be much fun. Would you like to join us, *Monsieur...*?'

'Dumont.' He flashes Amber a heart-stopping smile. 'Sébastien Dumont. And I would be delighted to join you.'

Sébastien seats himself at the table while Amber signals to the waiter to bring another bottle of champagne. To our surprise, it arrives in record speed, along with more chocolate dipped fruit.

'You are enjoying your holiday so far?' Sébastien asks us.

'It's *wonderful*.' Cat has a dreamy look in her eye and I'm unsure what's at the root of this – the holiday or Sébastien himself. Or perhaps a bit of both.

'That is good to know. And you are here for how long?'

'Until next Thursday.'

'*Really?*' He raises an eyebrow. '*Moi aussi*. Well... I leave next Friday.'

'Are you here at the resort alone, Sébastien?' Amber eyes

him curiously and I give her a little kick, knowing fine well what she's up to.

'That is correct,' he replies. 'I am here mainly for business reasons, but also for some rest and relaxation.'

His eyes catch mine, sending a shiver of anticipation down my spine. I take a couple of swigs of champagne to distract my brain from complete sensory overload.

'What kind of business?' Amber continues her fishing.

'Hospitality,' he says. 'I buy resorts, and make them the most desirable places to be in the world.'

'Interesting. Resorts like this?'

'Resorts exactly like this.'

'Are you here to look at buying this one?'

'*Amber.*' I quickly interject. 'I'm sure Sébastien didn't agree to join us for a game of twenty questions.'

'It is fine, Emma.' Sébastien waves his hand a gesture of calm. 'I do not mind. No, I am not planning to buy this resort because I already own it.'

I almost spit out my champagne. 'You *own* this place? What? All of it?'

'*Oui.* Or at least my company does.'

'*Wowser.*' I'm thrown by this revelation. This guy is *rich*.

'It's such a great resort,' says Cat. 'The staff are all so happy and motivated.'

'That is because I ensure they are paid fairly and are treated well. As they should be,' says Sébastien. 'And where do you all work?'

'In boring offices.' Cat looks glum all of a sudden. 'Not amazing five-star resorts where the staff skip to work every day.'

Having been uncharacteristically quiet for a while, Amber sits forward, a worryingly mischievous look on her face. 'Hey Cat, we don't all work in boring offices. Not anymore.'

I shoot her a warning look not to disclose anything too

personal. Not that this man would care about my lottery win. He must be a multi-millionaire – at a minimum.

'Yeah, you're right,' says Cat. 'Emma's not tied down by the nine-to-five lifestyle right now.'

'You are not?' Sébastien regards me with interest. 'Why is this, Emma? What do you do?'

'Oh... well, I... uh...' I trip over myself as I try to think how to clarify my situation. 'I guess I'd have to say... I'm unemployed.'

This is the first time I've said these words out loud, even acknowledged my job status, and it doesn't feel good. Cringing at this, I direct my eyes to the ground to avoid Sébastien's reaction. There may be a good reason why I quit my job, but as Amber so kindly pointed out, I'm miles away from achieving my career dream right now – whatever that even is.

'I am sorry to hear this, Emma.' Sébastien seems a bit lost for words.

'Now, come on. That's not technically true, is it, Emma?' Amber gives me a just-go-along-with-it nudge with her foot.

'It's not?' I look up hopefully.

'Not at all. Sébastien, Emma's being modest. She's actually a highly sought after professional, and until recently, she held a strategic level role in a large blue-chip company.'

'Is that so?' He looks at me with a curious expression.

'It is,' says Amber, before I can say a word. 'She's been on a short career break to undertake some important charitable work – such a selfless person – and she's now deliberating her next career move: with a handful of unsolicited offers from big household names. Isn't that right, Emma?'

This time it's less of a nudge and more a foot wedged against my leg ready to boot me if I dare disagree.

'Eh... that's quite an image you've conjured up there, Amber,' I say through gritted teeth.

'She's being coy.' Amber's quick to smooth over my comment. 'Always does this when she gets a compliment.'

'*Alors*, Emma.' Sébastien lets out a low whistle. 'It sounds like you are an impressive young woman.'

'I... um...' I stammer. 'I'm not sure—'

'She is, believe me.' Amber talks over me and looks Sébastien straight in the eye. 'Honestly... so modest.'

'And she's not just super capable,' Cat joins in. 'She's an amazing friend too.'

'Oh, stop it, you two.' I have no choice but to play along, screwing my nose up bashfully at my two friends fake-bigging me up.

'So, Sébastien...' Amber sits forward. 'Surely a businessman like yourself is always on the lookout for talent like Emma. You must know that calibre of professional is *very* hard to find.'

Shit. I should have seen this coming. I dig the toe of my sandal hard into Amber's leg but she kicks me back, causing me to yelp in pain.

'Emma, *ça va?*' Sébastien looks alarmed. 'You have been bitten?'

'*No*.' I rub my leg. 'I'm fine. Just banged my knee.'

'Ah, OK. Do you need some ice?'

'No, thanks. I'll be fine.' I plaster on my most convincing everything's-just hunky-dory smile, despite the hot throbbing in my shin.

'As I was saying...' Amber draws Sébastien's attention back to her. 'Talent like Emma is *very* hard to come across.'

'I would agree.' Sébastien nods, while intermittently glancing at me to check I'm all right. 'Especially for the more senior roles. There are not many people who have the full package, as one might say: excellent problem solving and decision-making skills, the ability to deal with complexity and ambiguity, and think at a strategic level. All that as well as possessing the positive behaviours of a natural and credible leader. To find all of this in one person? *Trés difficile.*'

We nod along as if this is the most insightful piece of information we've ever heard.

'In fact, I am currently in the process of filling one of my senior roles,' he continues. 'It is a challenging process for this very reason. Sometimes I wish I could take the good qualities of a few individuals and put them together. That would create the perfect candidate but, of course, this is not possible. *C'est la vie.*'

'What about Emma for that job?' says Amber suddenly.

I freeze, unable to comprehend what's just come out of her mouth. Dropping hints is one thing, but this is quite another. I want to kill her for turning our rather enjoyable conversation with this French Adonis into a full-throttle career seeking mission.

Sébastien regards Amber thoughtfully. He's obviously trying to think of a way to let us down gently.

'I think... *peut-être* is too late to add Emma into the process. The interviews have already taken place. I am sorry, Emma.'

'Not at all,' I say, while burning with humiliation at being rejected for a job I didn't put myself forward for. 'Ignore Amber. She's not serious.'

'I'm *deadly* serious,' Amber unhelpfully adds.

'Well, as you said yourself, Amber...' I'm now speaking very deliberately to convey the message that she needs to shut the hell up. 'I have plenty of options, so I don't need you making my decision harder.'

'*Anyway*...' Cat leaps in to rescue the situation 'Perhaps it's time to call it a night.' She gives a huge fake yawn, earning herself a strange look from Sébastien.

'Yes, I think you're right.' I slither out my chair before

Amber can make the situation any worse. 'It's been a long day of... lying by the pool.'

Sébastien watches us, eyes filled with amusement as we haphazardly gather ourselves together and extricate a protesting, champagne-swigging Amber.

'Sébastien, it's been lovely to meet you,' I say. 'Please do excuse us. We're still a little jet-lagged. I'm sure we'll see you around the resort.'

'I hope so.' He gives us a warm smile. '*Bonsoir, mesdames*. It has been a pleasure.'

'Bye.' We give him an awkward wave and exit the terrace at high speed.

Chapter Six

'Thanks for that, Amber,' I bark over my shoulder as I march back along the path towards the main resort building, my two friends following closely behind.

'You're welcome,' she replies, in an infuriating tone.

'*No, seriously.*' I stop and spin around, hands on hips. 'I can't believe you did that. We were having a lovely time and you just had to take things too far. *As usual.*'

'Calm it, would you.' She scoffs, which only incenses me further. 'What if he'd said yes? What if you'd got an opportunity? You'd be thanking me now.'

'*Would I?* You sold him a load of bull. Since when am I the cream of the British corporate scene? Or being head hunted by multiple FTSE 100 companies? Or a bloody altruist?'

'OK, so I stretched the truth a bit—'

'*A bit?*'

'Well, you did have a good job before and you were churning out the work your boss was supposed to be doing. So, you are capable enough, you just never got the recognition. You also spent a good half an hour on the flight boring the shit out of us about the charity donations you were making with your lottery win, did you not?'

'That's not even nearly the same thing.'

'It still counts. You've also gifted money to your parents. And paid for me and Cat to be here with you on this freakin' awesome trip. I consider that pretty charitable. Why not bend the truth a little? People embellish their CVs all the time to make themselves sound better than they are.'

I can't help but smile. It feels good to imagine that there's the tiniest smidgen of truth in what Amber is saying. Giving a resigned sigh, I start walking again.

'OK, fair enough. It's still a load of bollocks but at least there's something of me hidden in there, however well concealed. I just wish you hadn't done that, because now I feel stupid for being rejected.'

Amber catches up with me and pokes me in the ribs. 'If you feel stupid then that's your problem. Lesson number one from the School of Amber: you need to put yourself out there if you want to get anywhere. Sometimes things will work out, and sometimes they won't. But a few setbacks along the way are totally worth it when you score something big. You'll see.'

Cat materialises at my other side, linking arms with me 'I have to say, honey, although that wasn't comfortable for you – and Amber didn't necessarily go about it in the right way – she does have a point. Successful people get where they are by being well networked and taking chances others might not. It doesn't come naturally to me either, but I've had to do a bit of that in my career and it has paid off.'

With Cat (partially) joining forces with Amber on this one, it becomes clear that I may have to back down.

'I suppose you're right. But he was *so* hot. I'd have happily spent the next week and a bit salivating over him – instead of fruitlessly trying my luck for a job, then having to avoid him for the rest of the trip.'

'I think you might be able to do both,' says Amber.

'I'm sorry... what?'

'It was obvious he wants in your knickers. That's why I mentioned the job thing. Hoped he was one of those men who thinks with their—'

'Thanks, I get the picture.' I frown at her. 'So, wait a minute, you think he likes me?'

'Totally,' Cat chips in. 'Kisses as a greeting, his concern for you when Amber kicked you in the leg... I'm assuming that's what happened anyway. He was also paying you much more attention than the two of us.'

'Well, in that case, maybe I *can* force myself to face him again.'

Cat and I giggle like schoolgirls, skipping back to our rooms, while Amber trails behind, pretending she doesn't know us.

∽

Back in my suite, after getting ready for bed, I punch in the code for the safe and retrieve my phone, which I had locked away to minimise my screen time during this trip. A true R&R experience does not involve endlessly scrolling through social media feeds. I'm also not expecting anything more than a few scam emails and a message from my mum checking I'm: a) not drinking the tap water; b) not spending too long in the sun; c) locking my valuables away; or more likely d) all of the above.

On illuminating the screen, I see that I'm right about my mum – this time it's a reminder of the increased risks of alcohol in hot weather – but there's also a new Messenger request: from a James McAdam. My heart leaps on seeing the familiar face staring back at me from the thumbnail photo beside the notification. A face I now know belongs to an amazing guy I'll be going on a second date with when I get home.

He's made contact. *Already*. And while *I'm* away. This is huge. I'm suddenly filled with springy adolescent excitement, which instantly morphs into guilt on remembering I've spent the latter portion of my night lusting after another man.

Banishing this unwelcome feeling, I hit accept and lay my phone on the bedside table. It's not likely I'll hear from him straight away given it's not even seven a.m. in the UK. He's probably still asleep. However, within minutes, my phone buzzes with a message from him. I snatch it up and read it.

Hi Emma, how's paradise? Hope it's living up to your expectations? Been thinking about where to go on our next date. x

My face breaks into a girlish grin, my stomach fluttering so much that it feels like there's an actual living, breathing butterfly in there. Ignoring the advice I've so readily dished out to Cat in the past about not being too available, I type out a response.

Hi, you're up early! We're having a fabulous time, thanks. Sun, sea and cocktails. What more can a girl want? So, you were thinking about our date, that's nice. Tell me more... x

His reply comes just as swiftly.

Woke up early so thought I'd use the time productively. Was thinking... as you're into extortionate plonk, how about wine tasting followed by dinner? x

40

I laugh out loud at his reference to our unfortunate first meeting – me fresh from a break up, unwittingly preparing to drown my sorrows with a two-thousand-pound bottle of wine pinched from my ex's wine cupboard. The cheeky sod.

My phone pings again.

Too soon? x

I giggle at his humour. Just over a week ago – through my veil of hypersensitivity – I considered his behaviour rude and arrogant, but now I see it as playful and endearing.

No, you're fine. Though I do have certain standards that you must meet – the wine must be drunk from the bottle, and only on a park bench. x

I spend the next hour squealing with delight and giggling like a teenager as the messages flit back and forth faster than a game of pro-tennis. By the time I finally settle down to sleep, I'm bursting with infatuated elation, all thoughts of Sébastien and his sexy 'Frenchness' having completely dissipated.

∽

The next morning, I get ready to join Cat and Amber for breakfast, and on leaving my suite, I come across a white envelope that has been pushed under my door. Assuming it's generic guest information from reception, I stuff it in my bag and make my way along the air-conditioned corridor to the breakfast buffet.

It's a huge, airy room with a panelled ceiling and lots of wooden beams zig-zagging above my head. While mainly enclosed, it has tall folding patio doors on either side of the main entrance, which are currently open, giving the feeling of being outdoors.

Cat and Amber are already seated, digging into plates piled high with delicious smelling cooked breakfast items, fruit and pastries.

'Good morning.' Cat smiles at me. 'Did you sleep in?'

'Yeah, didn't get to sleep till really late.' I pull out a chair and sit down.

'Why was that?' says Amber. 'Late night visit from a sexy Frenchman?'

'No. I was chatting to James.'

'Oh, amazing.' Cat claps her hands together in excitement. 'Who messaged who first?'

'He contacted me. On Messenger.'

'Even better. What were you chatting about? Tell me *everything*.'

I pour myself a cup of tea from the pot on the table and take a refreshing sip. 'We chatted about ideas for our date. I filled him in on how the holiday's going. Then... random chitchat. Just like you and Mike, really.'

'No nude pictures again then.' Amber assumes a dispirited expression.

'Correct. Sorry to disappoint you.'

I excuse myself and head for the breakfast buffet, where I wander round the endless spread of enticing breakfast options, unable to decide what to eat. Eventually, I load my plate with freshly cooked pancakes, strawberries and bacon, and add a dollop of syrup, promising myself I'll have an egg-white omelette the next morning.

Returning to the table, I dig into my food, then I remember the envelope and pull it out of my handbag.

'Did you get one of these under your door this morning too?' I ask Cat and Amber who shake their heads. 'Oh. Maybe it's something related to our booking then.'

I tear open the envelope and start reading, then clamp my hand over my mouth in astonishment.

Chapter Seven

'What is it, honey?' Cat asks. 'You haven't been hit with unexpected charges, have you? This place is supposed to be fully all-inclusive.'

'It's not that.' I look up at her, perplexed. 'It's from Sébastien. Asking me to have dinner with him this evening.'

'*Awesome!*' Amber whoops. 'Told you he wants in your knickers. I bet he's amazing in bed. Must be staying in the best suite in the resort too.'

In contrast to Amber's overinflated enthusiasm – which makes me wonder if she'd like to take my place – I have an unsettling feeling.

'You're conflicted, aren't you?' Cat has picked up on this.

'*Yeah*... I am.' I grimace. 'I mean, Sébastien is unbelievable. He's like the epitome of everything you'd want in a man... But it could never go anywhere, could it? It would be a holiday fling. And James, well... he's so lovely. He's all those amazing things too, just maybe in a slightly more real way. With him, there's also potential for something long-term.'

'So, have both.' Amber shrugs. 'What's the problem? Have

your holiday fling and then go home to your forever man. Sounds like the perfect scenario to me.'

'It's not that simple. James and I... we've only been on one date, but it feels like more than that, if you know what I mean?'

'I get that,' says Cat. 'I felt like that with Mike too.'

'There, so you know what I mean.' I flash her a grateful look. 'How can I have a passionate fling with another guy – no matter how hot – and be talking with James online? All the time getting closer to him, while I'm essentially sneaking around behind his back.'

'I bet that's why he got in touch,' says Amber. 'Clever bastard. Probably anticipated the potential for you having a holiday romance and decided to show his cards early. Respect to him because it worked.'

'Stop it, Amber.' I frown at her. 'You make him sound devious and calculating—'

'Oh, shut up. I just mean he likes you and he wants you to himself. What's wrong with that?'

I'm cheered by this thought. 'Nothing, I guess. But I'm also thinking, what if it doesn't work out with James, and then I've missed out on having a hot and steamy holiday romance? That would also suck.'

'That's where my head was at,' says Amber. 'No, actually, I was already licking Sébastien's abs and—'

'*All right.*' I shut her down. 'We don't need a graphic account of the dirt that goes through your mind. And I wasn't finished. Remember, James is about to go on his own holiday and he could hook up with some hot blonde or whatever himself. What if I'm reading this wrong and he's happy to get to know me while bedding another – or even multiple women while he's away?'

'Here's a suggestion,' says Cat. 'Why don't you go along tonight and see how it is? If you feel too guilty, you can cut it short. Then there's no harm done. And if it feels right with

Sébastien, you can cool off the contact with James until you get home and it's all over anyway. Remember, you're still officially free and single. You have nothing to feel bad about.'

'I guess that makes sense.' I feel better hearing Cat's logic. 'OK, I'll go. On that basis only.'

'Emma, you're a legend.' Amber high fives me. 'I can't wait to hear how big his—'

'*Stop!*' Cat and I cry in unison.

'What? I was going to say his suite – how big his suite is. I'm dying to know what the best ones in the resort are like. Ours are plush enough and we're just in the standard ones.'

I give her a pointed look. 'Right now, I have no intention of finding that out, so you can keep wondering.'

~

Cat and I spend the afternoon on the resort's pristine white beach: snoozing on our loungers and sipping deliciously refreshing mocktails served by the attentive hotel staff, while reading our books. Palm trees tower above us, swaying gently in the merciful sea breeze. Only when we get too hot or we feel like we want a slight change of scenery, do we wade into the cool crystal-clear water or take a short stroll along the sand. It's pure unadulterated bliss.

In contrast to our lazy day, Amber signs herself up for a raft of water sports: jet skiing, paragliding, windsurfing, and spends her time zipping back and forth across the seascape, hurling (affectionate) abuse at us for being 'such a bunch of wasters'.

'Does that even remotely bother you?' I ask Cat later in the day.

She props herself up on her elbows. 'What? Amber's circus of torment?'

'Good name for it.'

'Not at all. I find it quite funny. Makes me even more

content that I'm doing this and not that. The number of times she's come head first off that windsurfing board, I don't envy her for a second.'

'Same here.' I watch as, right on cue, Amber loses control of her sail and takes yet another nose dive into the sparkling water. 'How's Mike? Bet he's missing you.'

Cat suddenly looks bashful. 'He is. He video-called me this morning before I went to breakfast. Said he was missing my beautiful face and needed to see it.'

'That's so sweet.' I put a hand to my heart. 'Cat, you have no idea how happy I am for you. After all the bad dates and the wondering if you'd ever find the right man. Here he is. And he's totally obsessed with you. All the pain must feel worth it now.'

'It does. I just hope it lasts.'

'It will. I have a feeling about this one.'

'Speaking of feelings, what are yours about tonight now you've had time to digest things?'

'Um... not sure.' I take off my sunglasses and clean the lenses with my beach towel. 'Bit of nerves, bit of guilt. Bit of excitement.'

'That's all understandable,' says Cat. 'I'd be the same. I really like what I've seen of James so far, but as I said in the karaoke bar, you don't owe him anything – yet. Certainly not monogamy. Obviously, it would be great if things do work out with him, but no matter what, you're not being unfaithful or disrespectful. And this way, you'll have no regrets if it doesn't go anywhere with him.'

'Thanks, Cat. Your opinion means a lot to me as you know. I've also been thinking about how I put everything into my relationship with Dave and where that got me. I don't want to have similar regrets.'

'Makes perfect sense.' Cat smiles while tucking a flyaway section of hair behind her ear. 'On that note, shall we pack up so you can go get and glammed up for your date?'

'Sure, why not.' A nervous knot instantly forms in my stomach.

We gather our things, signal to Amber where we're going and wander up the beach towards our suites.

~

By the time I've showered and pulled on some comfy shorts and a T-shirt, the nervous knot has turned into a ginormous net of slippery, slithering fish. Wiping away the stress-induced sweat beads from my forehead, I grab a mineral water from the minibar and glug at it thirstily, hoping it will calm my nausea. Unfortunately, it has minimal effect.

'OK, breathe, Emma,' I say out loud to myself. 'There's nothing to get worked up about. It's just dinner with a very, *very* hot man. That's a good thing. Something to look forward to. And it's not at all cheating, because – *remember* – you and James have had one date. *One*. It's all hypothetical right now.'

I pace the room, taking big deep breaths and finally feel myself calming.

There we go. It's all fine. There's nothing to worry about. Nothing at all. *Oh hell, who am I kidding?* This is not fine. Sébastien is the hottest man on earth. I'm totally punching and even though getting it on with him would undoubtedly be as decadent as the finest champagne, it would mean that I'd have to be honest with James if he asked.

My eyes roam the room, seeking a non-existent solution. Then a thought pops into my mind: Lottie. She'll be home from hospital. Her wisdom is exactly what I need. I grab my phone and dial her on FaceTime, and she answers almost immediately.

'That was quick,' I say in place of a greeting.

'Hello, my love.' Lottie smiles at me in her kindly way. 'I was looking at some things on the internet as your call came through.'

'The internet? You don't use the internet.'

'It would appear I do now. James has been showing me how to go "on safari".'

'You don't go "on safari".' I chuckle. 'The internet app is *called* Safari.'

'I see.' Lottie's statement suggests understanding but her elderly face is one of bewilderment.

'I've been trying to persuade you to use the internet on your iPad for ages. How did James get you using it so quickly?'

'I'm not sure it was quick.' Lottie's eyes crinkle with amusement behind her spectacles. 'He spent nearly three hours talking me through it, showing me what to do, repeating it over and over. Such a patient young man. I kept getting into the most awful pickles.'

On hearing this, I feel ever so slightly envious that Lottie has spent this time with James. I want to spend hours alone with him – and I can think of better things we could do than a tech lesson.

'That's great, Lottie,' I say. 'That was really nice of him. Is that you out of hospital then?'

'Yes.' Her spectacle chain wobbles as she nods. 'My discharge papers were ready earlier than expected. James wheeled me along those corridors at some rate, I tell you. Wouldn't hear of letting a porter do it. He's just wonderful.'

'Sounds like it.'

I feel myself getting all gooey-eyed. James the good Samaritan. James the caring and the carer. My James. *Wait. No.* He's not 'my James'. He's just James. All we have right now is powerful chemistry and some witty banter on Messenger. And I have a date with another man. I must not get beyond myself.

'Emma, are you all right?' Lottie's voice cuts through my thoughts. 'You look like you have something on your mind.'

The slithering fish in my belly give an almighty nauseating flip. But instead of taking this opportunity to pour out my dilemma and lap up Lottie's wisdom, I hesitate. It may be my chance to get some solid advice, but I realise I can't go there. With Lottie spending so much time with James, I can't possibly put her in the position of knowing I'm dating (or thinking of dating) someone else – regardless of the situation. And what if he were to suddenly appear at hers and overhear me talking to her about it?

Plus – what the hell am I thinking? *My James?* I can't allow ridiculous notions like that to form in my mind. Good Samaritan he might be, but boyfriend he is not – not yet anyway. It's clear to me that, not only should I not implicate Lottie in my dilemma, it's already solved. I need to go on this date for a reality check, if nothing else.

'I'm fine, honestly,' I say. 'Probably still a bit jet-lagged.'

'OK.' She doesn't seem convinced. 'You know where I am if you need to chat.'

'I do. I'm so glad you're out of hospital and being looked after. I'll visit you loads when I get home to stop you getting bored.'

'That will be lovely.' Lottie gives me an appreciative smile. 'But, for now, may I request – once again – that you forget about me and enjoy your time away. It will be over too soon. Make the most of it.'

'I think I can do that.' I blow her a kiss. 'The enjoying myself bit. Not forgetting about you. Speak soon.'

'Goodbye, my love. Take good care of yourself.'

I end the call, toss my phone onto the bed and let out a faltering sigh. With my decision made, there's no point in putting things off. It's time to get ready for my date.

Chapter Eight

A while later, I find myself sitting on my balcony terrace, nursing a large medicinal gin and tonic from the minibar. I'm dressed in what I hope is an outfit sophisticated enough for a date with a multi-millionaire: a sleek printed wrap dress and pretty black high-heeled sandals, accessorised with a small clutch and some tasteful gold jewellery. Cat and Amber have joined me for a 'pre-date briefing session', which essentially involves Amber tossing innuendos at me from all angles, and Cat offering the more helpful, supportive advice.

'Where are you meeting him?' Cat asks.

'In the cocktail bar. Apparently, we'll head to dinner from there.' I stare into my drink apprehensively. 'He didn't even ask me to confirm. Guess he's willing to see if I turn up.'

'How exciting. I wonder which restaurant he'll choose. Maybe the fine-dining one. That seems his kind of thing.'

'Doesn't really matter, does it?' Amber snorts. 'He owns them all. Won't have to put his hand in his pocket.'

'Right, I'd better go.' I down the last of my drink, then we get up and make our way to the door. 'I'll see you girls later. Don't have too much fun without me.'

We go our separate ways, my heels click-clacking along the tiled floor, body jangling with nerves. *What the hell am I doing?* This man is perfect. So far out of my league it's not funny. He lives a life I – even with my lottery win of several-hundred-thousand-pounds – can only dream of. *Ugh.* I need to get hold of myself or I'll end up in a gibbering mess.

On reaching the terrace cocktail bar, I glance around anxiously for Sébastien. I'm on such high alert that I almost go into cardiac arrest when he suddenly appears behind me.

'Emma, *bonsoir*.'

I slowly turn to face him, my heart hammering in my chest. He looks devastatingly handsome: his hair damp from the shower, eyes crinkling in that appealing slightly-older-man kind of way. He's wearing an expensive looking suit, open at the collar, no tie, as well as the same heady fragrance from the evening before, which conjures up all sorts of desires within me.

'*Bonsoir*, Sébastien.' I murmur, as he kisses me on each cheek, setting them alight.

'So glad you could join me,' he says. 'You look *très jolie*. Now, we are not stopping here. The car is waiting.'

'The car?'

'*Mais, oui*. You did not think I was going to take you to a restaurant you have already paid for? No, we are going somewhere a little more special.'

'I think the resort's pretty special.'

'Of course.' He gives another sparkling smile. 'But tonight, you will have an authentic experience at the finest independent restaurant in the Bahamas.'

He leads me outside to a huge black Rolls Royce, opens the back door and ushers me inside. Then he gets in beside me and the chauffer drives off.

'I'll have you there in ten minutes, Monsieur Dumont,' the driver says to Sébastien, making eye contact with him through the rear-view mirror.

'*Merci bien*, Lyndon,' Sébastien replies and sits back, looking relaxed – the complete opposite to me.

We sit in silence while the car passes the resort security post, exits the grounds and joins the main road. With the light of the day quickly fading, I don't get as good a view of the palm tree-lined coast as I'd hoped, but as we pass more built-up areas, I am able to make out a curious mix of luxury accommodation interspersed with dilapidated buildings in desperate need of repair. I'm also surprised by the number of monstrous American-style trucks and pick-ups that pass us. It's certainly all very interesting to take in (and a good distraction from my nerves).

Sébastien seems to sense that I'm uneasy and engages me in light, easy conversation, mainly asking my thoughts on the Bahamas and the resort so far. As we talk, my nerves settle and I find myself enjoying the conversation, even occasionally stealing glances at him. He looks so sexy and masculine, the sharp contours of his face accentuated in the half-light, and I can't help imagining what it would be like to be kissed by him.

'You mentioned last night that you're mainly here for work,' I say. 'Is this a regular trip for you? To check everything's running as it should be?'

'Yes and no.' Sébastien shrugs in a non-committal way. 'I trust my team. But I do like to be present at times to offer my support and connect with our guests.'

'Makes sense. Great you can make a holiday of it too and get some down time.'

'*Absolument*, yes.' He smiles at me, and instead of the slithering feeling from the last few hours, my insides dance with excitement. 'Though in my line of business there is little opportunity for proper "down time", as you call it. I will have meetings every day, but I know I must also recharge to be able to give the best support my resort teams.'

I nod, impressed by Sébastien's work ethic and commitment to his people. This just makes him all the more appealing.

After a short drive, Lyndon pulls into a narrow road and stops in front of what looks like the entrance to a large estate. A few moments later, the gates open and we cruise inside and along a winding driveway to a small roundabout of sorts outside a tastefully-lit salmon pink building with a tiled roof. Lyndon pulls up outside the front of it and gets out of the driving seat to open my door for me, while Sébastien lets himself out of the other side. Sébastien then thanks Lyndon and he drives off.

'*S'il te plaît.*' Sébastien extends a hand, ushering me towards the main door of the building while following close behind. 'This is West Bay Estate, Emma. Do you enjoy seafood?'

'I do.' I try to hide the nervousness from my voice.

'*Bien.* Then we should have an enjoyable evening.'

'Good evening, Monsieur Dumont... ma'am,' the maître d' welcomes us as we enter a reception area just inside the door. 'It is good to see you again.'

'*Bonsoir*, Kavashti.' Sébastien greets the man. 'It has been too long.'

Kavashti shows us to our table in a large air-conditioned dining room with beautifully laid tables, and I find myself wondering how many women Sébastien has brought here. Am I the latest in a very long line of casual flings he has wined and dined? The staff never seeing the same beautifully made-up face twice?

Once we're seated, there's a flurry of activity. We're served water and chilled champagne, and the menus are explained to us. Sébastien laughs and jokes with each staff member as they come across to greet him, one after the next. It's clear that he's a VIP here – and a very popular one at that. Even the chef delivers some canapé-style snacks personally. I watch in awe as he charms every person he talks to, remembering personal details about them, giving them his undivided attention. It's easy to see why he's so successful in business. He's a natural born leader.

With my attraction to Sébastien growing, I will his adoring fans to leave us in peace so I can have him to myself, and eventually, my wish is granted. Our starter – a beautifully presented seafood platter – is served and the staff melt away, shifting their focus to their other clientele.

'*Alors*, Emma...' Sébastien's thick French accent makes my name sound way more exotic than it is. 'What do you think of this place?' His exquisite dark eyes meet mine.

'It's... great.' I feel myself redden. 'I'd love to see the gardens in the daylight. They look very well kept.'

'Ah, yes. The gardens. They are... *très romantique*.'

Heat creeps up my neck and I break eye contact, biting my lip coyly. It's an almost perfect moment with a seemingly perfect man.

So, why doesn't it feel right?

Frowning at this unwelcome thought, I try to push it aside. Of course it feels right. How could this *not* feel right? I'm a single woman – on holiday, enjoying the company of a very eligible bachelor. Sure, it'll be short-lived. We'll have our fun then go our separate ways, and Sébastien will no doubt return within weeks or months, with his next paradise island fling. But there's no harm in that if there are no expectations beyond this trip.

I re-focus my attention on Sébastien, attempting to fully immerse myself in our conversation, but I can't shake the feeling of discomfort that's plaguing me. Between courses, I excuse myself to the ladies.

'*What's wrong with you?*' I demand of my reflection in the mirror.

Maybe I'm still jet-lagged. Or maybe it's because I feel like I'm not worthy of a man so incredible. He is on another level with his money and charisma and superhuman hunkiness. The reality is that it's probably a bit of both, and I need to get myself in check.

Running the cold tap, I plunge my wrists under the flow of water in a bid to calm myself down: one of the few helpful nuggets of advice (among all the useless overbearing ones) I've received from my mother over the years. It works quicker than I expect, creating a soothing sensation through my body. This is fine. *Everything is fine*. I need to relax and enjoy myself.

'*Ça va*, Emma? Is everything all right?' Sébastien asks when I return to the table. 'You look a little... how do you say... *queasy*?'

I realise he's right. I may feel calmer but there's a clawing sick feeling in my gut.

'I'm OK... I think. Probably still jet-lagged or dehydrated or something. Not used to this climate.'

On hearing this, Sébastien tops up my water glass and signals for me to drink from it.

'Perhaps a break from eating would also help,' he suggests, once I've sunk a few mouthfuls. 'Lacherra, hold the main course, please. We will take a short walk in the gardens.'

'Yes, Monsieur Dumont.' Lacherra – our server – swoops across and accompanies us to a door that appears to exit the property at the rear.

I allow Sébastien to lead me outside onto a large terrace and along a path, which I can't help thinking could be made more of at night with some creative outdoor lighting. Despite having a brightly lit building full of people behind us, it feels very intimate.

As we weave our way around the gardens, I focus on breathing deeply, devouring the fresh air while enjoying what I can make out of the tropical trees and plants, which look almost eerie, but in a good way.

After a few minutes of continually checking that I'm not

going to pass out, and me eventually confirming that I'm feeling better, Sébastien stops me and points to the sky.

'*Regarde*, Emma.'

I look up and see hundreds of twinkling stars winking back at us. Under the cloak of darkness, interrupted only by the light from the restaurant's windows, it's a moment bursting with romance.

'*Wow*... that's so beautiful.' I glance up at him, jittering with nervous anticipation.

He must sense my eyes on him, because he turns his gorgeous face towards mine, our lips now just inches apart. 'It *is* very beautiful, though not quite as beautiful as—'

'*Stop!*' I suddenly blurt out. 'Don't say it.'

Chapter Nine

Having been shocked into a moment of comprehension, I now know why I feel ill: *I can't do this*. I can't find myself wrapped in Sébastien's arms, no matter how delicious an experience that could be – because of James. It may only have been one date and a slew of flirtatious messages, but it doesn't matter. We've connected in a way that I already know is special. I can't risk ruining that; especially not for a sizzling but ultimately meaningless holiday romp. Which makes this – whatever is developing between and Sébastien and I – impossible.

'*Pardon*, Emma.' Sébastien seems (quite understandably) perturbed by my reaction. 'What—'

'I'm sorry, Sébastien,' I cut him off to avoid this situation becoming any more awkward than it already is. 'I can't do this. I'm sorry, I shouldn't have led you on. You've been nothing but a gentleman... and probably every straight woman in the world would think I'm an idiot – of course they would...' I'm like a runaway train: I can hear myself, and I'm perfectly aware of how I sound, but I can't seem to apply the brakes. 'The thing is, I've met someone... not long before I arrived here. I didn't think it would matter to have a holiday fling with you, but it does. And I know I don't owe this other guy anything at this early stage, but I *want* to... not in a slutty way, to be clear... in a loyal I-want-to-have-a-shot-at-being-your-girlfriend kind of way. So, you see, this just can't happen...'

I continue to ramble almost incoherently, too terrified to stop and endure the humiliation of how we'll go our separate ways from here. And in doing this, I completely miss Sébastien's reaction.

'Emma. *Arrête.*' He laughs, putting a finger to my lips to silence me. 'Please.'

I stop and sort of hang there inelegantly, avoiding eye contact.

'Emma... why do you think I invited you here this evening?'

I trace a pattern on the path with my toe, unable to bring myself to converse with him.

'You think that I was trying to seduce you.' His words suggest quite the opposite.

I look up at him and wince. 'You mean you weren't?'

'No, Emma. That was not my intention.'

I puff out my cheeks as I digest this information, which on one hand is positive – I haven't hurt his pride by refusing his advances – but on the other, has now left me feeling stupid, embarrassed and undesirable, all rolled into one. *Why didn't he make this clear up front?* I already know the answer to that question. Because when we met in the wine bar, he was nothing but a perfect gentleman, and he didn't make anything resembling an advance. It was Amber and Cat who filled my head with silly ideas of him wanting in my knickers.

'OK... great.' I look around me, as if suddenly interested in every tiny detail of the gardens. 'So, if you weren't about to tell me I'm more beautiful than the stars in the sky and pull me into a super-hot movie-style embrace – not that I've been thinking about that at all – then... I think we're good.'

I flash him a forced, mortified smile, no longer caring that I just made things even worse for myself in front of a man who has now had the opportunity to reject me both romantically and professionally.

'Well, I am pleased that we have worked that out.' Sébastien chuckles, then looks at me seriously. 'Emma, I must make one thing clear. You are a beautiful woman. I already said you looked so when I greeted you this evening, *non?*'

I nod, eyes to the ground like a small child being brought round by an exasperated parent.

'*D'accord.* So now may I tell you why I asked you to dinner?'

In my discomfiture, I've overlooked the fact that, if Sébastien wasn't trying to seduce me, then there must indeed be another reason for his impromptu dinner invitation. I gesture for him to continue.

'The reason I wanted to meet with you, Emma, was one of a professional nature.' Sébastien makes a show of seeking out contact with me, leaving me with no choice but to meet his gaze. 'Last night, I was halted by my desire to be fair to the other candidates in the selection process for the job vacancy I have. However, what I need is the right person and it would appear that you have the skills and personal qualities I am seeking. After some thought, I have decided that, in this case, offering you an opportunity, it is the right thing to do.'

'*You're offering me the job?*' I'm completely gobsmacked, unable to believe that Amber's tactics, however questionable, have worked. 'Wow, Sébastien, this is—'

'*Excusez-moi,* Emma.' Sébastien stops me mid-sentence. 'I am sorry, I have not been clear. What I mean is that I would like to offer you the opportunity to go through the selection process for the role – bypassing the initial stages, of course.'

Fuck. I've just made a tit of myself – *again.*

'*I knew that.*' I wave my hand jovially. 'Sorry, I do that all the time. Us Brits and our humour.'

Oh my god, I need to shut the hell up. Like forever. And even that might not be long enough.

Sébastien's amused but lightly appraising look causes me to waver like a sunflower in the breeze. 'I enjoy your humour, Emma. You are likeable with an authentic quality that is very important in a leader – as long as you can be serious and take the tough decisions too.'

'That, I can.' I nod assertively, keen to redeem myself. 'Like second nature to me.'

'I am glad to hear this. So, does that mean you are interested in going through the process?'

'I'm certainly interested in hearing more. Some information about role would be helpful. Where is it based?'

'The location of the role is not important. We have people all over the world whom we bring together via technology. Home working is quite common within the "head office" arm of the company. There is also the requirement for international travel, and we have premises in Europe where our non-resort staff base comes together when necessary.'

I try to look calm and composed while my mind whirrs away at record speed. I'm struggling to process the shock, excitement, slight panic and embarrassment of this situation, all in one go.

'I have a job profile,' Sébastien continues. 'I will have a copy sent to your suite, and I can answer any questions you have this evening... if you are feeling well enough to finish our meal together?'

I look out across the gardens as a momentary self-check. I'm feeling many things, some of which aren't entirely pleasant, but queasy is no longer one of them.

'Yes, I am.' I smile at Sébastien. 'Let's go eat.'

'*Excellent.*' He pats my arm in a gesture that I interpret as think-no-more-about-the-misread-romantic-moment, which has the effect of making me think of nothing else, all the way back to our table.

~

A short time later, we've demolished our delicious main courses of fresh snapper, which was a fish I hadn't tried before, as well as a scrumptious dessert, and we're rounding off our meal with a rum liqueur. Despite Sébastien's offer to tell me more about the job, the conversation has been friendly and informal. I'm dying to know more, but I'm determined not to be the one to bring it up. With Amber having sold me as corporate personality of the year, and that being the driving factor for this whole professional encounter, I can't afford to drop that façade. Instead, I make a show of enjoying Sébastien's company and engaging in light-hearted, intelligent conversation to ensure that any doubts he might have after our unfortunate encounter in the gardens are washed away.

Eventually, when I'm starting to wonder if he has indeed changed his mind, he finally gets to the point.

'*Alors*, Emma...' His gaze lands on me in a manner that's just too sexy for its own good. 'Shall we bring this back to business?'

'Sure. Sounds good.' I mentally block out his magnetising effect and give a relaxed smile, hoping he's buying my laid-back act. 'I'm keen to hear more about the role.'

'Of course. It is a strategic level role to support the company's growth strategy. Essentially, it is about scoping out resorts with potential and overseeing the end-to-end acquisition process for the ones we buy up. They have to be integrated into the company financially, from a branding perspective, and also culturally. Does that make sense?'

'It does. I've worked on a few acquisitions in the past. It sounds like a very interesting and challenging job.'

Sébastien's done more than pique my interest. Until now, I

didn't even know this type of job existed. This is it. It's the dream career I've been seeking: in a totally different sector to my main professional experience, but I can tell from what Sébastien's saying, that it's a reasonably good match to my skills and experience. And as Amber said, if I don't put myself out there, how will I ever find the right opportunities?

'Can you tell me a bit about your experience, Emma?' says Sébastien. 'Perhaps a quick summary of your CV?'

'Erm... sure.'

Though I should have been prepared for this question, I find myself caught off guard – probably due to my brain being in holiday mode.

'Let's see... until recently I held a strategy and planning role within a FTSE 100 company...'

I give Sébastien a comprehensive run through of my professional experience, and I'm pleased to find that I don't have to embellish it at all. I just omit the fact that my ex-boss, Karla, had me do most of her work and stole all the credit. As I talk, I'm almost surprised by how articulate I sound and how much I'm enjoying talking shop. With my dreadful relationship with Karla having taken centre stage in my previous job, my confidence had taken a knock and any sense of achievement and self-fulfilment had evaporated. I knew I was good at what I did and I got a lot out of it. I just forgot.

'Well, Emma...' Sébastien, who has been listening intently, addresses me once I'm done. 'It sounds like you have quite an impressive skillset: in a different industry with different challenges, but the nuances of the hospitality industry can be learned.'

'I agree. I made the transition from retail to financial services several years ago – in a more junior capacity, of course, but the premise is the same. A change of industry is exactly what I'm looking for and just the challenge I need.'

'OK. Let me talk you through the selection process then.'

As Sébastien shares the interview and assessment approach, I sit forward, genuinely riveted by this experience. I can feel that familiar rumble of career hunger rising within me. Though I undoubtedly have moments where common sense evades me, I know I'm sharp and I've always done well in the roles I've held. In fact, until Karla got her claws into me, I was regarded as a serial high performer.

Well, watch out world... Professional Emma is back and it feels good. *Really good.*

'Emma? Is that all right with you?'

Shit, I wasn't listening. I've no idea what Sébastien has asked me. I should have saved my self-acclamation for after dinner. Scrutinising his face uncertainly, I decide it's probably best to agree rather than admit I wasn't focused on the conversation.

'Um... yes, of course. That's totally fine. I'm easy going with these things.' I give a little wave of my hand to accentuate this trait.

'*Super.*' Sébastien looks pleased with my answer. 'Your flexibility will certainly work in your favour, Emma. Not everyone would be willing to sacrifice their holiday for a job interview. Especially when they are already on it.'

Sacrifice my holiday? What the hell have I just committed to? I had (naively, I now realise) assumed all this would happen once I was home.

'Yes, well, that's me... always easy going.' I force as genuine as smile as possible. 'Um... the selection process you just shared with me, do you have a printed copy I can refer to as part of my preparation?'

'*Bien sûr*, Emma. I will have all the information you need delivered to your suite. Please also speak to Charnice at reception about getting access to any resources you need – including a laptop if you do not have one with you.'

'I don't. Thanks, that's great. And... when do you intend to make a decision by?' I mentally cross my fingers that he hasn't already told me this.

'Monday. The same day as your assessment. I committed to the other candidates that they would hear back by the end of that day, so it must be a quick turnaround.'

'Right.' I place my palms on the table in an effort to ground myself. 'So, I have three days to prepare.'

'Correct,' he confirms. 'I know that is tight, Emma, but you are clearly a focused and determined individual. I am sure that this will be another exciting challenge for you.'

Sébastien turns his attention to Lacherra to request the bill, while I struggle to take in what he's said. On Monday I have an interview for the biggest job of my life: a total game changer career-wise. I'm going to have to put in the hours if I want a shot at this, and I so badly do, which means my holiday is over – at least for now.

As I battle to keep myself from having a nervous breakdown on the spot, I feel the nausea from earlier returning – and settling in comfortably for the next four days.

Chapter Ten

Later in the evening, back at the resort, Cat, Amber and I gather on Cat's balcony for a late night debrief.

'So, he doesn't want to sleep with you?'

'It seems not, Amber.'

'*Huh.*' She looks genuinely perplexed.

'That's pretty much how I feel about it.' I push aside the irrational nagging feeling of being undesirable – something that's plagued me since my ex, Dave, suddenly ended our relationship. 'It's obviously an amazing opportunity Sébastien has offered me. I'm super excited about that. It's just... I'd have preferred to be appealing in *both* senses. I know that sounds ridiculous, especially as I didn't want anything to happen in the end – but I wanted *him* to want something to happen. If that makes any sense?'

Cat reaches across and squeezes my shoulder. 'It does, honey. You're still a bit bruised and vulnerable after your break up. It's only been a matter of weeks and Dave's "modus operandi" was cruel.'

'That's an understatement.'

'Maybe Sébastien does like you, but he sees it as unethical to pursue you romantically and professionally at the same time,' she says. 'He seems like a person with good morals.'

'That's true. Let's go with that theory.' I'm cheered by this thought.

'And now you have a dream job opportunity as well as a man – James – who seems to be very interested in you.'

'He does indeed.' I sit back with a coy smile, delicious memories of last night's Messenger chat with James flitting through my mind; a welcome distraction from the nausea that set in at the end of my dinner with Sébastien. 'Thanks, Cat. You always know how to put a positive spin on things.'

'It wasn't really that difficult.' She raises an appraising eyebrow. 'So, how do you feel about facing the biggest interview of your life in three days' time? Especially as you're on a luxury holiday – which was meant to be your chance to get away from it all? That must create some conflict for you.'

'You're not wrong there.' I place a hand on my churning stomach. 'I'm gutted about the timing. But if I don't go for it – just so I can lie in the sun doing nothing for a few days – I know I'll regret it. The job sounds incredible.'

'I think you're right there.'

'No idea how I can prepare for it in three days though. It's a bigger role than anything I've done before, which means I need to shine brighter than I ever have.'

Amber, who's been atypically quiet during this exchange, suddenly bursts to life. 'I know how you can be ready for it.'

'How's that?' I probably don't want to hear this, but I'm desperate.

'By enrolling in the "School of Amber". *Obviously*.'

I sigh. 'Any *helpful* suggestions, Amber?'

'I'm deadly serious. Remember how I said I'd help you sort your shit out? The other day, before we left for this trip?'

'Yeah... but—'

'But what?' She eyeballs me. 'You don't trust me with this?'

'No, that's not it—'

'Emma, do you want this freakin' job or not?'

'Yes, of course I want it. I so badly want a job that I love... that satisfies my ambition, and makes me feel like I'm doing more than slowly rotting behind a desk. Working for a luxury brand of resorts, leading a growth strategy, with international travel thrown in. It sounds *unbelievable*.'

'So, what's your alternative?' Amber cocks her head knowingly. 'How are you going to make sure you kick ass and outshine all the other candidates in that interview?'

I glance helplessly at Cat, who simply offers me an encouraging smile. 'Well, I guess I'll... um... read through the job description, prepare using the interview themes and the presentation brief—'

'*Blah, blah, yawn*.' Amber pulls a bored face. 'That's what everyone else will have done. What about how you're going to show your understanding of the company? You're here – right in it – so you need to use that competitive advantage and draw from the experience.'

'That's a good point, I never thought of that. Although I haven't had much time to think about anything yet.'

'And remember, he'll be zoning in on how you act in that interview as well, not just the answers you give.'

'Oh yeah, the behavioural side of things that he mentioned. I have to admit, I was finding it hard to focus on what he was saying so some of it passed me by.'

'Understandable. He is smokin' hot. But now you need to pull your head out your arse and focus.'

'*Shit*, you're so right.' I stand up absently and lean on the balcony railing. 'This will be one tough process, which means I'm going to need all the help I can get. OK, Amber, you're hired.'

'*Awesome*.' Amber high fives an unprepared Cat, who

narrowly avoids a smack in the face. 'Finally, you're my bitch. Emma, how do you feel?'

'Actually, I feel marginally less nauseous. That's got to be a good thing.'

'What about me?' says Cat. 'What's my role in this? I want to be involved.'

'Yeah, totally.' I nod enthusiastic agreement. 'Cat's done really well in her career, Amber. She can be your wing-woman.'

'Fine by me.' Amber shrugs. 'But remember that I'm in charge and that I get the final say. We'll pull a plan together tomorrow morning, once you have the info, then we can start putting you through your paces after lunch.'

'Oh, honey, this is so exciting for you,' says Cat. 'We'll be a great team. Bag you the job of your dreams.'

'Let's not get ahead of ourselves,' I warn her. 'But thank you so much, both of you. You have no idea how much I need your support.'

I grin at my two friends, and for the first time since Sébastien told me I have three days to prepare, I feel like I might have a chance at this.

∿

A while later, I'm getting ready for bed in my suite when my phone pings. Plucking it from my bedside table, I feel a similar adolescent rush of excitement to the previous night – because, of course, it's James.

Good night? Bet it was more exciting than mine. I hate packing. x

My feeling of elation is snu ed out in an instant when I realise that I can't tell him about my evening. Not the full technicolour version anyway. I think carefully for a moment, then tap out a response I consider to be honest, without giving away my original intentions for the evening.

Hi. Yes, really good night, thanks. Went for a meal on a fancy estate and took a moonlit walk in some beautiful gardens. You're up early again. Is it today you leave for your own trip? x

I'm keen to move the conversion away from me. James, however, is not.

That sounds romantic. Kind of hoping you and your friends have one of those weirdly close friendships... x

I give an uncomfortable chuckle, amused by his humour, but equally aware that he's sensed something, even within the limited information I've shared. *Bugger.* I don't want him to think I'm having a holiday fling, especially as I have no intention of doing that – not anymore anyway. Sticking with the light-hearted tone, I add a touch of reassurance, so he knows there's nothing to worry about.

We are strangely close, the three of us. Don't worry, I'm only looking for rest and relaxation here – no room for that sort of complication. Plus, I'm saving myself for a date with a hot man when I get home... x

I've intentionally left out the whole job interview thing because I'm already feeling the pressure and don't want to add to it. Also, I don't want James to think I'm a loser if I'm unsuccessful, and if by some miracle I do get the job, I'll have one hell of a talking point for our next date.

Ping. I lift my phone again.

I know I have no claim whatsoever, but I'm relieved that you just enjoy a slightly inappropriate level of intimacy with your girlfriends. Nothing wrong with that. In fact, I completely approve. x

I laugh out loud, rolling my eyes, and compose my equally predictable response – an essential part of the flirty banter.

You're such a typical bloke! There was me thinking you were different. Hey, you haven't answered my question yet. When do you leave for your own holiday? I don't even know where you're headed...? x

There's a pause and I'm wondering if he's going to reply, when his response appears on my phone.

Sorry, got distracted by mental images of your girly threesome. Actually, preceding blokey rhetoric aside, I think I am different. Like vintage wine – classy and worth the wait. Although maybe you won't appreciate that with the way you drink it... I do indeed leave today. Off to the east coast of the US with my mates. Ten days of beer and banter. Can't wait. x

I feign indignance at his wind up.

Cheeky! Just as well I'm easy going – these days. Sounds like an exciting trip. Is this something you do regularly with your friends or is it for a special occasion? x

Ping.

I kind of liked your oversensitive side. Made things interesting. It's sort of a joint birthday milestone thing. But our big 3-0s are quite far apart. Mine was already two years ago! x

Ping.

Hang on, mister. Only I'm allowed to bring up my flaws. Pleased to find out that you're older than me though. x

Ping.

How much older? x

Ping.

How old do you think I am? x

Ping.

I'm so not entering that minefield, lady... x

I laugh and gasp with fake outrage as we continue to flirt and chat, until I realise the time, and – with a day of interview prep looming tomorrow – reluctantly say goodnight.

Snuggling down in the bed, my mind is bursting with romantic scenarios for my second date with James. These pleasant thoughts push all worries about the job interview from my mind: the last one before I drift o being how nice it is that James already wants me to himself. And how much I want the same in reverse.

Chapter Eleven

On Friday morning, I'm greeted by another white envelope under my door, only this time I know what's inside. My cautious optimism from my conversation with Cat and Amber the previous night scarpers the second I lay eyes on it.

Resisting the temptation to go back to bed and pretend this whole job interview thing isn't happening, I pick it up, open the patio doors, and step out onto my balcony terrace in the hope that my amazing tropical surroundings will lessen the impact of whatever torturous process I'm about to find inside it. However, I'm so sick with nerves, I barely register the pleasant breeze, sparkling sea, and clear blue horizon. I want the job – more than anything – but I've never been one of those people who sails through interviews without breaking a sweat. I'm more of a kitchen roll wedged in my armpits while popping (homeopathic) anxiety pills like they're Smarties kind of girl.

After a few deep breaths, I plonk myself down at the table, rip open the envelope and extract the documents inside. There's not much there: just three printed sheets of paper, which I hope is a good sign.

Unfolding them, I start to read. The first page contains the job description. It's brief, but succinct. The job title – Head of Growth and Acquisition – simultaneously fills me with terror and fervour. It's a big step up and even just imagining having that title is petrifying. The thought that, if successful, I'd be exposed for the imposter that I might well be is wholly nauseating. But at the same time, another part of me is bubbling with determination, ambition and a feeling that this is something I've always been capable of achieving in the right workplace with a decent boss.

This inner conflict, as unpleasant as it is, further fuels my belief that I have to go for this. I need to push past the uncertainty and self-doubt and prove to myself that I am worthy.

I quickly read through the description of the role, heartened by the presence of familiar language. There's nothing particularly alien there. All I need to do is believe in myself and win a chance to put what's there into practice. Setting the job profile aside, I then scan the selection process details. The interview themes are based around the company values, which I'm pleased to note are an inspiring and energising read: making me want to grab a pen and get started, rather than reach for the TV remote. However, my optimism is short-lived, because on turning my attention to the third page, my eyes zoom in on a single – terrifying – word in the text: 'presentation'.

Fuck. Public speaking is an area I need to improve in, and I'd hoped to have some time to do so ahead of actively seeking my next job. Reading through the details, the words swim in front of my eyes.

The second part of the assessment is a twenty-minute presentation on your plan for your first ninety days in the role, followed by a question-and-answer session.

Beads of sweat appear on my forehead as I continue to read. Then comes the knockout punch.

People are the beating heart of our business and we like to include them in our decisions where possible. As such, we wi be inviting a carefu y selected group of resort staff and regular hotel guests with a keen interest in our company to attend your presentation and provide feedback on your performance.

Oh my god. A presentation to an interview panel is bad enough. But to a whole crowd, including the resort's most valued clientele? The pressure isn't just on, it's about to blow – and if I'm not careful I might just lose my head in the process.

Massaging my temples, I take some slow deep breaths to calm myself. I need to stay focused and take things one step at a time. The interview shouldn't be too bad, provided I'm well prepared and can keep a lid on my nerves. The presentation topic is also not too scary. I know my stuff and have worked with senior leaders and their plans. Plus, the internet is a job seeker's best friend.

But the other stuff – presenting, taking (probably very challenging) questions in front of an audience – fills me with dread. I literally have no words to describe the panic instilled by this request. The painful truth being: when it comes to public speaking, I'm a complete flake and about as engaging as an annual tax audit.

Realising I'm late for breakfast, I stuff the printed sheets back in the envelope, then go back inside and quickly throw on some clothes, before rushing to the breakfast buffet to join Cat and Amber.

'Where have you been?' Amber eyes my forehead suspiciously when I arrive and collapse into a seat, perspiring and panting, envelope in hand. 'No, strike that, *what* have you been doing? You look like a sack of shit.'

'Thanks.' I narrow my eyes at her. 'Good thing I don't have any deep-rooted appearance issues.'

Cat places a concerned hand on my forearm. 'You look stressed, honey. You haven't been up all night worrying about your interview, have you? It's a great opportunity but it's not worth making yourself ill over.'

'It's fine, Cat. I know I don't have to do it. I *want* to. At least I think I do. I actually slept really well. James and I were messaging until quite late so I was exhausted by the time I went to bed.'

'Ooh, that's exciting. Tell me—'

'*No. Don't.*' Amber cuts Cat off. 'Tell us why you're sweating like you've swallowed a Carolina Reaper.'

'A what?' says Cat.

'World's hottest chilli – or used to be anyway.'

'Ah. Yeah, you kind of do.' She turns to me with a grimace. 'Sorry, honey.'

I give a loaded sigh, and pour myself a cup of tea, taking a good slug before I fill them in.

'OK, this "sack of shit" is what happens when you combine hot humid weather with the news that, in a few days, I have to do a twenty-minute presentation. Not just to Sébastien, but also... *wait for it*... to an audience of resort staff and highly valued guests.'

'*Oh, my goodness.*' Cat's hand goes to her mouth. 'That's probably the worst thing they could have asked you to do.'

'Tell me about it.'

Even Amber seems thrown by this. '*Crap.* Seems we've got our work cut out for us. You'd have thought, after hearing you caterwauling at the karaoke that Sébastien would have more sense than to let you loose on his precious clientele.'

'Thanks, Amber. I was hoping for some words of support, perhaps even reassurance.'

'What? You want me to lie?'

I look to Cat, desperate for some sign that I'm worrying about nothing. She gently takes the envelope from me and scans the contents.

'OK, honey, let's think about this for a minute. You've done well in interviews in the past, haven't you?'

'Yeah. I get nervous, but I always seem to do a lot better than I think I've done. I'm not so worried about that bit. The presentation content shouldn't be a problem either. I do know my stuff.'

'Great.' She offers me an encouraging smile. 'And I'd say these company values are a good match to your own.'

'They are.' I nod. 'I was happy about that.'

'OK, that's also good... and Amber can help you prepare for the behavioural-based side of things. Although right now, I'm wondering if she's the best role model.'

Amber extends her middle finger at Cat and turns her attention to her heavily laden breakfast plate.

'Case and point.' Cat chuckles. 'So... that just leaves the delivery of the presentation and the Q&A. There are two things you need for that: the ability to confidently and coherently present to your audience in an engaging way; and the skills to manage some tough questions.'

My growing optimism suddenly deflates. 'Both of which I lack. What have I got myself into, Cat? I desperately want a shot at this, but right now, I can't see how I'll manage that.'

'You're panicking, that's all, and I get why. I also think our surroundings are making things worse for you. It's hard to think about something this serious and intimidating being where we are.' She takes my hand and gives it a squeeze. 'Amber and I will factor some presentation skills coaching into your plan. How about, for the next few hours, all you do is the prep you're confident with and after you can join us for lunch?'

'OK, sure.' I take a faltering breath, wiping a trickle of sweat from the side of my face. Then, on getting up to go to the breakfast buffet, a thought lightens my mood. 'Hey, Amber, I thought you were taking the lead on this. So far, Cat's doing a much better job than you.'

Amber's head jolts up from her food. '*Eh, no way, bitches*. I'm still in charge. And I'm top dog at this stuff, you'll see.'

Cat and I share a knowing look as I walk away. There's no surer way to get Amber to become useful, than to indicate that she's not.

Chapter Twelve

After breakfast, I return to my suite, while Cat and Amber head to the resort café to do some planning. Closing the door behind me, the bang seems louder and more echoing than I've noticed before, triggering a stark feeling of being alone. It's just me and a scary amount of interview preparation. As the feeling of overwhelm sets in, my first instinct is to FaceTime Lottie, which would serve the double purpose of procrastinating from the ominous task at hand, while providing me with the boost my self-belief badly needs right now.

I'm reaching for my phone when I have a moment of clarity. This – like my date with Sébastien that turned out not be a date – is not something to call upon her for. Because after all the drama of the last few weeks, Lottie was insistent that I should relax and enjoy myself, which means it's probably best I don't mention this job interview to her until I'm back home (and I've hopefully got the job). She'll only worry about me not taking time to rest and recover, and that won't help her own recovery. I don't want that on my conscience.

Deciding that a tidy room will help me focus, I clear away my clothes and accessories that are strewn around the furnishings, then I arrange my makeup and toiletries into neat clusters on the dressing table and re-jig the bits and pieces by my bedside. Once my suite looks better, I catch a glance of myself in the mirror and remember that I haven't yet had a shower today. Well, I'm obviously not going to have a fresh mind until I feel fresh all over.

Nearly an hour and a half later, I've cleaned every part of me that can be cleaned, shaved my legs, tidied my eyebrows and refreshed my nail polish. And just as I'm dithering over whether some makeup would help me get in the zone, I look at my phone and notice the time.

Shit. I'm due to meet Cat and Amber in less than an hour and I literally haven't done a bit of interview prep. They'll kill me if I turn up having not even started, while they've been devoting their precious holiday time to me and my future CV. Quite rightly too.

Feeling stifled being stuck inside when it's so beautiful and sunny outdoors, I grab the complimentary resort notebook and pen from my bedside table, and step outside onto my balcony terrace to do my thinking. Some fresh air should give my brain the shunt into action it needs. Unfortunately, however, my procrastinating mind is instantly alert to everything around me that I'm missing out on: the rhythmic crashing of the waves on the shore, the excited chatter and laughter of my fellow holidaymakers on the beach and by the pool, the enthusiastic chatter coming through the PA system from one of the resort's playmakers, whose job it is to help the resort guests have fun by running games and competitions. It's almost too much to bear knowing all that is out there and I'm not.

To reduce my FOMO, I opt for a relaxed approach by stretching out on one of the sun loungers instead of sitting at the patio table. I make myself comfortable and read through the information again, this time paying more attention to the detail.

Our company values are part of our DNA. We live and breathe them. They are the reason our customers return to us over and over. We therefore only employ people who live by these same values and who we know have something special to offer our family of resorts...

It's such an easy and inspiring read that I find myself wondering why I've spent nearly two hours avoiding it. The content excites me in a way I've never felt about anywhere I've worked before, perhaps in part because I've already experienced some of what Paradis Resorts has to offer and – rather than just being words on a page – it rings true (from a guest perspective anyway). The happy, energised employees also seem to point in the direction of it being a good company to work for.

Jotting down some initial thoughts, I can see that I'm a pretty good fit with what they're looking for in this role, and I'm just getting into a flow when I realise it's time to meet Cat and Amber. Oh well, at least I'm off the starting blocks. That's half the battle.

I hop off the lounger and quickly apply a coat of mascara and some lip gloss. Then I throw my pitiful-looking notes and pen into my handbag, sling it over my shoulder and head of out of my suite.

On reaching the resort café, which is situated between the bright white sands and the beach club pool (not to be confused with the main pool – this place has multiple pools, multiples of everything), I approach my two friends, who are sitting in cushioned wicker chairs at an outdoor table. I can see that Amber's telling Cat a story of some kind and I chuckle to myself at how animated she is: her arms gesticulating at rapid speed, like she's describing some kind of dive bomb off a cliff.

Cat's laughing, hands to her face, eyes wide with disbelief. Whatever it is, it must be a good story.

Ugh. This is the stuff we should be doing on this holiday, not mobilising as a team to try and get me through the toughest interview process I've ever faced.

'How are you getting on?' I greet them with a smile.

'Good,' says Cat, while I settle into one of the empty chairs and sigh contentedly as the heat from the sun hits my shoulders. 'Amber had a few off-the-wall ideas but I managed to reel her in on the most extreme ones.'

'Right...' This I'm not overly pleased to hear.

'Don't worry, everything in this plan has been approved by me. So please feel reassured that, even if it's uncomfortable for you, it's necessary and for the sole purpose of getting you that job.'

'OK, that makes me feel a *bit* better. Although I still can't say I'm relishing the thought of it.'

Amber surveys me disdainfully. 'Emma, the process itself – sitting in front of Sébastien and your whole bloody presentation audience – won't be *comfortable*, will it?'

I look to the ground. 'Well... no. I do get that.'

'So why are you expecting this to be?'

'I'm not. I'm just... you know... hoping you'll ease me in gently.'

'How is easing you in gently going to help you?' she demands. 'Especially when you have two and a half days to prepare. It's like preparing for a skydive by jumping off the bottom step of your stairs.'

'I think what Amber's trying to say,' says Cat. 'Is if you face some more challenging tasks in the run up to Monday – all aimed at strengthening the skills you feel less confident about – then the event itself might seem less of a shock. And you'll be ready for it.'

'That's *exactly* what I was saying.' Amber throws her hands up as if this was obvious.

'Maybe. Not quite so diplomatically though.' I see Cat give her a come-on-we've-already-discussed-this look.

Glancing from Cat to Amber, my mind is in overdrive, thinking of all the awful things they could have me doing over the next couple of days.

'It'll be OK, honey, I promise.' Cat puts a supportive hand on mine. 'We've also factored in some fun so it doesn't feel like such a chore. We'll be out and about around the resort, still enjoying the things you would have been doing if this hadn't come up. There's no point in the three of us being cooped up in your room like a group of teenage study-buddies, when we have all this at our disposal.' She waves her arm around to emphasise our luxurious surroundings.

'Oh, good.' I exhale with relief. 'I was getting cabin fever just spending the last couple of hours in my room.'

I decide not to mention that fact that I only managed about forty minutes of real work.

'Amber, how about you share our plan with Emma?' says Cat. 'Or do you want to tell us where you got to first, honey?'

'No need for that,' I say. 'I'm doing the boring stuff. Let's see what you've come up with.'

I mentally cross my fingers that they won't come back to my prep. Amber will see through me in an instant.

'OK, let's do this.' Amber turns over a piece of paper with what appears to be a well-structured and impressive-looking schedule on it.

'Wow, you did it by hand,' I say. 'I forgot to mention that Sébastien offered me use of one of the resort laptops. Though maybe that offer was just for me. Where did you get the stationery from?

'We asked Charnice at reception,' says Cat. 'She was so keen to help us, we had to stop her from giving us a truck load of supplies.'

'Aww... they're great here, aren't they? So cheery and—'

'*Anyway*.' Amber interrupts me. 'How about we look at this plan before the afternoon is gone and you've done no prep – *again*.'

'Hey, I've been prepping. I did at least...'

'Ten minutes?' Amber raises a smug eyebrow.

Dammit. She knows me too well.

'More like forty to fifty.'

'Not what you planned though, was it?'

'No.' I feel like a teenager getting a telling off from my parents for watching TV when I should be studying. 'But getting started is the hard part. Especially being here. It would be fine if I was back home in the crappy Scottish weather.'

'Well, as you don't have time to piss around, aren't you glad you have me and Cat to kick your backside for you?'

'I guess I am.' I give an apologetic grin.

'Good. Here you go then...' Amber turns the page around so I can follow as she talks me through it. 'This is your "School of Amber and Cat" interview prep plan. The days are broken down into sections – so, breakfast, morning, lunch, afternoon, dinner and evening. We've allocated a leisure activity to each non-meal slot – as Cat says, things we would have been enjoying had it not been for this coming up. And within each of those slots there's an activity that will help you prepare for Monday. Make sense?'

'Yeah, it does.' My eyes roam the page, taking in the detail of the plan.

'What do you think?' Cat asks, once I've had the chance to read through it.

'Do we rock or what?' says Amber.

I'm momentarily lost for words. 'It's... *incredible*. I mean, I don't know exactly what it entails, and I can see it's going to be full on... but, yeah... you seem to have everything covered. That as well as still making the most of our holiday.'

'Exactly what we were aiming for.' Cat looks pleased at my reaction. 'We don't want this to be a miserable, gruelling experience for any of us.'

'You've almost got me looking forward to it now,' I say. 'Still dreading the actual interview, but what better way to prep for it? I do have some questions though.'

'Shoot,' says Amber.

'OK, to start with, are we really having cocktails this afternoon? That doesn't sound like the most productive way to kick off a plan like this. Particularly when these surroundings are making me more prone to procrastination.'

'It's exactly the right way to kick it off. You need a motivational boost as well as a creative approach for your presentation to make sure you stand out. Some of the best ideas I've had have come to me after a couple of drinks. The usual boundaries go out the window.'

'Do you have any boundaries?' I give her a wink and turn to Cat. 'How did she get you to agree to that one?'

'I *was* a bit sceptical,' she admits. 'But it can't hurt to try it out.'

'OK, great.' I shrug. 'Why not? So then, what about the "company research" in the evenings? What's that? Other than you not wanting to give up your nights out.'

Amber cocks her head with a judgemental look. 'Actually, *dipshit*, that's about seeing what kind of guest experience is being created by the resort. I've said before, you need an in depth feel for what this place is all about—'

'I know, I was only kidding.'

'Good. Glad there's a brain in there somewhere. Even if it needs a bit of a kickstart.'

'*Hey, I object to that,*' I complain. 'Facing a scary interview while on the holiday of a lifetime would be a challenge for anyone. The heat and humidity doesn't help either. It gets to me.'

'And to your hair.'

'*Stop it.*' I self-consciously reach up and try to flatten it. 'My hair's a pain in the arse in this climate. You don't need to point it out.'

Amber sits back, her eyes twinkling mischievously.

'Amber, seriously...' Cat shakes her head in despair. 'Do you want to destroy Emma's confidence before you've even started working with her? All you'll do is give yourself an even bigger job.' She shifts her focus to me. 'Honey, your hair is fine. And I love that lip gloss on you.'

I cease trying to plaster my unfortunate barnet to my head as if that will somehow make it better.

'*Whatever.*' Amber rolls her eyes. 'That was your first test, Emma – which you failed. For this job, you need to be confident and not give a shit what others think of you. You also need to let things wash over you. There are nasty politics in every workplace, no matter how good it might appear from the outside looking in, and you need to be prepared for that. What will you do if one of the resort team takes a shot at you during the Q&A session? Not in an obvious way, but they could take a disliking to you for whatever reason and say something about your presentation that's engineered to make you look bad.'

'That's a fair point,' I say. 'The thought of that terrifies me. I'm not good at handling that kind of thing, especially under pressure.'

'Cat, what would you do?' Amber asks.

'Well...' Cat appears to think for a moment. 'I'd probably thank them for their input, acknowledge the comment and anything helpful within it, but not focus on it too much – it would likely be their own issues at the root of it, not mine. Then I'd politely counter their opinion, making sure I put my point across well.'

'And then?'

'I'd move on and forget about it.'

'*Text book answer*.' Amber slaps Cat on the back proudly. 'See, Emma. That's how it's done. Now we need to get you to the same point – by Monday.'

I give a nervous laugh. I really don't want to be the person who freezes during a takedown, or who lets others get to her. I want to be able to take on anyone and anything; to stand tall and come out confident and composed. The question is: can I really achieve that in two and a half days?

Chapter Thirteen

After a leisurely lunch at the cafe, during which Amber, Cat and I chatted some more about my interview prep plan, we make a pit stop at Cat's suite to pick up her iPad, before heading to the cocktail bar to start 'work'. Once settled at a table in the shade overlooking the mammoth-sized swimming pool, we order some cocktails and Amber disappears to the ladies, while Cat gets connected to the Wi-Fi.

I pass the time with some people watching and a thought strikes me: will any of these fellow holidaymakers be at my presentation on Monday?

Before I know it, I'm assessing their potential for giving me a hard time. There's a small group of middle-aged women deep in conversation, with positive, affectionate body language. I can imagine them smiling encouragingly, trying to put me at ease. Yes, I'd be happy enough for them to be there. Then there are two mature couples sitting together quietly. The men – both wearing cowboy hats – seem to have nodded off, while their other halves converse in almost a whisper, most likely to avoid disturbing their dozing spouses. They can definitely come too.

My ears then tune into raucous laughter, and my gaze

lands on what appears to be a large family gathering: eight adults, a handful of excitable children, and a couple of awkward-looking teenagers engrossed in their phones. One of the men in the group – clearly the alpha from the way he's behaving – catches my attention. It's nothing more than an instinct, but straight away there's something that makes me uneasy about him. He's telling a story, his companions transfixed, and he's so loud that it's impossible not to pick up what he's saying.

'And that's when I'd *had it*,' he all but bellows. 'Who does she think she is? She's a bloody *maid*, she's there to serve *me*.'

Shocked by this pompous, superior air, I study the man more carefully. He's greying, probably early to mid-sixties, with an American accent and an unhealthy redness to his face: more the product of years of overindulgence, than being light-handed with the factor thirty.

'I called for the duty manager,' he continues. 'She'd better deal with it properly so that girl remembers her place in the pecking order. Makes me wonder who they're hiring here.'

My shock turns to indignation. This man isn't just pompous, he's vile. What's worse is that the other adults of the group are nodding along, making similar derogatory comments. *Who the hell do they think they are?* I imagine myself striding up to the man and putting him firmly in his place.

While lost in this vengeful daydream, I forget that I'm still watching him.

'Can I help you, ma'am?' He suddenly interrupts my thoughts, voice dripping with arrogance.

'Um... no, sorry...' I stutter. 'I was... miles away.'

Flustered, I bang my knee painfully against the table, and it takes every ounce of my willpower not to cry out in agony. Then I hear the man mocking me.

'Nosey one, she is. If it's not the staff then it's the other darn guests. We should think about going somewhere else next time.'

Flinching at the viciousness of his words, I feel a sting I know I shouldn't allow from a total stranger.

'You OK, honey?' Cat gives me a little nudge.

'Yeah, fine.' I re-focus my attention on her. 'Is that you on the Wi-Fi?'

'I am, yes. It wasn't working at first but I'm connected now.'

Amber returns just as our drinks arrive, and within moments, my unfortunate encounter is forgotten.

'Cheers, ladies.' I clink my glass against theirs. 'To what will probably be a very productive, enlightening – and slightly terrifying – few days.'

'And to hopefully bagging the job of your dreams.' Cat rebounds with another clink.

I grin at my friends and take a long refreshing sip of my Rum Punch.

'I've got one.' Amber thrusts her Bahama Mama into the air, nearly soaking Cat in the process. 'To Emma being rejected by the sexiest man on earth.'

Cat and I put our cocktails down and look at Amber in bemusement.

'*How is that something to toast?*' I say. 'I was trying to forget it ever happened.'

'Look at it this way: if the two of you *had* got it on, you wouldn't now have the best career opportunity of your life. You'd also be a complete pain in the arse, agonising over whether you'd ruined your chance with James – *again*. I consider that a win for all of us.'

'OK, thanks for that, Amber.' I furrow my brow, feeling slightly wounded. 'Guess if you strip everything back then that's the bare-faced truth.'

'You're welcome.' She looks undeservedly smug.

'So, I guess we should get going with this then?' I say.

'Can we start in five minutes?' Cat pleads. 'I'm *dying* to hear about your Messenger chat with James last night.'

'Does my schedule allow for that?' I ask Amber with an angelic face.

'Go on then.' She nods. 'There had better be something interesting in there though. And when I say interesting, I mean *dirty*.'

'I know exactly what you mean. And I'm afraid, like every other time, you'll be sorely disappointed.'

She pulls a bored face, sits back and angles her face at the sun.

'There's not that much to tell...' I lean in towards Cat, who pushes her iPad aside. 'Though he does seem to be hoping I won't have a holiday fling.'

'Ooh, that's interesting,' she says.

'He's also leaving for his own holiday today, and generally we just seem to click – in a way I've never experienced with another guy. Certainly not with Dave. I mean, we talk about nothing, but it's so enthralling. I'm like a giggly teenager. He teases me... in an affectionate way. And he's really funny. I haven't laughed so much in ages.'

'That's so great. There's obviously a strong connection between the two of you.'

'I told you that weeks ago,' Amber grumbles.

'I know you did.' I playfully ruffle her hair and she bats my hand away. 'You were right. I just wasn't ready to hear it then.'

'So, where's he off to on holiday?' Cat asks me.

'All he said was he's going to the east coast of the US with some friends. So maybe Boston, New York... Philadelphia? I must admit, I'm a little apprehensive about what a group of single guys will get up to when surrounded by hot American women. But he has every right to "shop around" – as I almost did myself. I want to believe that he won't, especially with him being open in his concern about me doing it, but once he's there...' I screw up my face as an unwanted image of James chatting up a gaggle of beautiful, slim, flirty women pops into my head.

'Whatever goes on, chances are you'll never know about it,' says Amber. 'So, no point in giving it much thought.'

'That doesn't help.'

'Wasn't meant to. It's called realism.'

'What do you think, Cat?' I ask. 'Do you think he'll hook up with other women on his trip?'

She grimaces at the weight of this question. 'Honestly, honey? I don't know. He doesn't seem like a player and he's obviously keen on you, but what someone intends to do and what happens in the moment can be two different things. I know that's not what you want to hear, sorry.'

'Don't apologise. I'd rather you were honest with me.' My heart sinks a little.

'But I do think Amber's advice is good,' she adds. 'I'd put it out of your mind, because it's out of your control. You'll find out in time if he's the right guy for you. And right now, all the signs are positive.'

'They are, aren't they?'

'Yes. They are. Just keep reminding yourself that he's not Dave. He's a totally different person. Seems much more respectful.'

'Thanks, Cat. That makes me feel a bit better. And Mike? He's still missing you like crazy?'

'Yes.' She sips at her drink with a bashful smile. 'Sends messages to that effect every couple of hours.'

'Aww... that's so sweet.'

'Aww... *that's so barf*.' Amber rolls her eyes. 'Right, I'm calling time on this. Not the slightest bit of action in any of that, so let's get to work.'

Cat and I share a look of she's-just-jealous and reluctantly shift our focus to my prep.

~

Two hours later, we're mildly sozzled and I've planned out the (high level) content of my presentation, which is looking pretty good if I may so myself. And that's not the drink talking.

'OK, that's enough of that side of things,' says Amber. 'You've got a solid foundation there.'

'And in case you haven't noticed, you've come up with all of it yourself,' says Cat. 'Amber and I have just been a sounding board. That must surely give you some confidence that you can be ready for this by Monday.'

'Yeah, maybe,' I say, scrolling back through my notes on Cat's iPad. 'But that wasn't the hard part. It's about how I come across on the day.'

'I know, but from what I've seen here, I'd hire you. Wouldn't you as well, Amber?'

'Only if Emma agreed to G&T Thursdays – every week,' she says. 'Failure to attend would result in immediate disciplinary action, and likely dismissal.'

'That's a yes.' Cat laughs. 'High praise from all involved. Now, let's get onto the fun bit. What can you do to give your presentation that extra *je ne sais quoi*?'

'I see what you did there.' I give her a toothy smile before considering her question. 'I'm drawn to the idea of taking things from a fresh angle.'

'That sounds good. What do you have in mind?'

'That's the problem. I have no idea. I've been chewing on it since this morning, but I can't seem to come up with anything.'

'What about a theme of some sort?' says Cat. 'Though I'm not sure what.'

'How about a Caribbean twist of some sort, or... I know.... beach party,' says Amber. 'You could present in your swimwear to keep with the holiday vibe. Might earn you some extra points with Sébastien the sex god too.' She gives me a sly wink.

I stare at her in disbelief. 'I don't even know where to start with that. I thought you were meant to be useful.'

'I'm trying to help you think creatively. Nothing should be off limits at this point – it's the process that's important. Consider even the most far-out ideas and you might have a moment of genius.'

'Fair enough,' I concede. 'But I do not want to stand in front of a sea of strangers essentially in my underwear. That's the stuff of nightmares – like when I dream I'm at work and I've forgotten to put my trousers on.'

'I've had that one.' Cat wrinkles her nose. 'It's horrible. Only with me it happens on a date.'

'That's surely related to our insecurities: mine being work and yours being men. Anyway, now we've done bikinis and missing trousers, what else could... hang on... *that's it!* I've got it. I know what angle I'm going to take. Amber, you're a genius.' I get up and pull her into a bear hug.

'*Oi! Get off,*' she complains, trying to escape me.

I quickly fill them in on my thinking and then we kick back to enjoy some well-deserved down time.

'So, a successful first outing for the "School of Amber and Cat" then.' Amber looks mighty pleased with herself as she slugs at her drink. 'Sexy Sébastien's not going to know what's hit him.'

Chapter Fourteen

We're enjoying our final wind down drink over some light-hearted chat, when I spot Sébastien entering the bar terrace.

'*Oh shit. Hide.*' I instinctively duck down under the table.

'Honey, what are you doing?' Cat looks at me in bewilderment.

'It's Sébastien. He can't see me sitting here drinking. He'll think I'm not taking this seriously.'

'What? No, he won't. He probably won't even notice us. The bar's quite... *oh... no...* he's spotted us. He's coming over.'

'*Shit. Shit. Shit.* Do something. Stop him.'

'Emma, don't be ridiculous,' says Amber. 'The man won't expect you to take a vow of abstinence from fun because you have an interview on Monday.'

'*Amber, please,*' I plead with her. 'I'm begging you.'

'All right.' She gets up from her seat and I peer over the table top as she sweeps towards Sébastien like a heat seeking missile.

Moments later, when I've ducked down out of sight again, I hear her greet him.

'*Sébastien*, how nice to see you again. How are you today? Having some time to yourself, I hope.'

'*Salut*, Amber,' he says. 'My day is busy, but good. You are still enjoying your stay?'

'Absolutely. It's exquisite here,' she simpers, in a very un-Amber-like way.

'*Bien*. I am very pleased to hear this. Though I see Emma is not with you this afternoon.'

Sébastien may be making a statement, but it's very much a question. I cower lower under the table, praying he won't spot me.

'No, she's not,' says Amber. 'She's in her suite working on her presentation. Wouldn't hear of coming to the bar. She has some work ethic – though sometimes I wish she'd chill out and enjoy life a bit more.'

I purse my lips in irritation. This is a pointed comment aimed at me – not just Amber playing out her role as diverter in chief.

'Emma is staying in her room to work?' Sébastien sounds perplexed. '*Mais, pourquoi?* Why, when there is all this sunshine and these beautiful surroundings?'

'That's what I said to her. But would she listen? *No*.'

I awkwardly shift position, while filing a mental note to give Amber a proper briefing next time I ask her for a bailout. I'm willing her to wrap things up and send Sébastien on his way, when the conversation takes a turn in an alarming direction.

'If Emma will not listen to you, then perhaps she will listen to me,' says Sébastien. 'I will go to her suite now and tell her she must still enjoy her holiday.'

Oh, for god's sake. Amber had better pull off an Oscar winning performance now.

'I don't think that's necessary,' I hear her say. 'Cat and I will talk to her later. Get her to see sense.'

I hold my breath, waiting for Sébastien's reply.

'No, Amber. I will follow up with Emma. She needs to hear this from me. Please excuse me while I go and speak with her.'

'Really, there's no need,' Amber tries again, but there's no reply, indicating that Sébastien has already left.

I cock my head above the table in time to see him striding through the door to the main resort building. Amber shoots across to our table.

'*Amber, what the hell?*' I say. 'He's gone to my room? You were meant to deal with it.'

'I did deal with it, dumbass. He didn't see you here, did he? How was I meant to know he'd go for a personal visit? Ooh, maybe he's got more than—'

'*Enough*. Now's not the time. What do I do?'

'There's a short cut to our suites from here,' says Cat. 'Through the gardens, past the tennis courts. I used it yesterday. If you run, you'll beat him. Go, honey, *quick*.'

I look at Cat, then Amber, who simply offers a shrug of 'go for it', and I don't need any further encouragement. I dart across the bar terrace, canter down the wide stone steps to the poolside and take off across the resort gardens at a speed I didn't know I had in me. Sprinting past the meandering holidaymakers, I attract more than a handful of odd looks, but I don't care. Only one thing matters: *I must make it to my suite before Sébastien.*

On reaching the accommodation block where my room is located, I creep through the door from the garden into the corridor and sneak up the stairs to make sure that Sébastien isn't already there.

He's not. I've made it.

I slip inside my suite, panting heavily from the unexpected exertion, and empty the contents of my handbag onto my bed to find some chewing gum to mask the smell of the alcohol. I'm chewing furiously, while simultaneously fanning myself with a magazine, when the bell to my suite rings.

After a leisurely count to ten, to appear like someone so 'in the zone', I didn't even register the interruption at first, I wander across to the door and open it.

'Sébastien, what a surprise. What can I do for you?'

'*Salut*, Emma.' He greets me with a twinklingly sexy smile that almost sends my overheated body into meltdown. 'I was wondering if I might speak with you?'

'Eh... yes, of course.' I look at him expectantly and we stand awkwardly for a moment, before I realise that he's waiting to be invited inside. 'Come on in.'

He gives an appreciative nod as he walks past me and I close the door.

'Take a seat.' I gesture to the sofa. 'Would you like a drink from the minibar? Some water, maybe?'

'*Non, merci*. I will not take up your time. But I thought it important to speak with you.'

'Oh? Why's that?' I sit a safe distance from him, hoping I'm giving off the air of someone not in the know. 'You're not cancelling the interview, are you?'

'Ah, no, not at all. My apologies, Emma, I did not mean to cause you concern.' Sébastien fixes his intense gaze on mine and suddenly my temperature is rising again, this time because we're alone, with a bed no more than five metres away. He may have made it clear he has no romantic intentions towards me, but unless my radar is completely off, this moment is turbo-charged with sexual chemistry.

'Maybe we should sit outside,' I announce, jumping up from my seated position. 'I could do with some fresh air.'

Before Sébastien has a chance to say anything, the patio doors are open and I've stepped outside, leaving him with no option but to follow. Then, halfway through the doorway, he stops, steps back inside and looks around.

'Everything OK?' I ask.

'*Eh... oui*.' He joins me on the balcony terrace and we take a seat at the table. 'I was... thinking about your preparation. I do not see any notebook, laptop, pen.'

Because they're all at the bar. *Bugger.* What's my excuse?

'Oh, right.' I chuckle, stalling for time. 'They're... um... in the bathroom.'

What the hell? Why did I say that? Now he'll be imagining me sitting on the pan swotting up on the hotel's vision and values.

'I see.' Sébastien is too polite to question this further, but there's a trace of amusement in his eyes. 'Amber tells me that you will not take time to enjoy your surroundings, while preparing for your interview, and I find this concerning.'

'You do?'

'*Bien sûr.*' He fixes his gaze on mine once more, but this time the earlier sexual chemistry I sensed is distinctly absent; perhaps due to my unfortunate bathroom admission. 'Emma, as the owner of this resort, I know you have paid a lot of money to be here. I am also assuming that you do not take voyages like this often, yes?'

'Well, yes, but it's no big deal. My career is more important than any '

'*Emma, s'il te plait.*' Sébastien holds up a hand to silence me. 'I do not agree. Rest is as important as a career. Without rest, we cannot do our best at work or in life. I understand that – as your interviewer – I must not interfere with how much preparation you do, but I can make some suggestion towards how you do it. I propose that you make the most of your surroundings: do your thinking while swimming in the pool, practise your presentation in the bar, have your friends test your interview skills on the beach. Please do not stay in this suite and miss the opportunity for some relaxation and enjoyment while you prepare for your interview. And perhaps also some inspiration.'

Sébastien's words are like a beautiful symphony to my ears. He's suggesting more or less exactly what Cat and Amber have planned for me. Now I have full licence to go ahead with our plan without him thinking I'm not taking this seriously.

'You know what...' I make a show of thinking this through. 'You're absolutely right. That's what I need to do. Thank you, Sébastien.'

'*De rien*. You are welcome.' Sébastien gives a satisfied nod. 'I will leave you alone now.'

I see him to the door, cringing as I pass the bathroom, and an instinctive urge to fix my earlier faux pas takes over me.

'Thanks for coming round, Sébastien. I appreciate your concern. Guess I'll need to transfer my stickies to Cat's iPad then, if I'm going to be out and about.'

'Your "stickies"? What is this?' He looks at me quizzically.

'Sticky notes. I use them for my preparation. Didn't want to risk marking the paintwork in here.' There, that'll do it.

Sébastien's face flickers in recognition. '*Ah, oui*, sticky notes on the bathroom tiles. Very creative, Emma. Though please know you may use our other resources as well as stationery. A laptop might offer better functionality for developing your presentation.'

'Thanks, I'll definitely do that. The stickies method I just find useful for my early thinking when I'm working on something big.' This is actually true, despite me not using them right now – and having never used them in a loo.

Giving him a bright smile, I quickly usher him out of my suite before this conversation can go any further or he asks to see my creativity in practice.

Chapter Fifteen

A couple of minutes after Sébastien leaves my suite, my doorbell chimes again. I fling open the door and my inebriated, giggling friends practically fall inside my suite.

'Did you pull it off?' Amber hops onto my bed and stretches out.

'It took some Olympic-style sprinting, some chewing gum and some on-the-spot thinking – but yes, I did. And now I'm totally sober from the ordeal.' I lie down next to her and Cat does the same on the other side.

'*Attagirl.*' Amber high fives me awkwardly from her horizontal position. 'So, fill us in.'

The three of us stare at the ceiling, watching the relentless circuits of the revolving fan while I play back Sébastien's visit – minus the bit where I gave him an unwanted image of me on the loo.

'It's great because now I can follow through with your plan, without worrying what he might think of me,' I say as a finisher.

'You didn't need to worry in the first place, ya dafty. You made a big deal out of nothing.' Amber affectionately knocks on my head with her fist. 'Tell me, what was it like having sexy Sébastien in your room? Were you tempted to jump his bones? I would have been.'

I raise my eyebrows at her. 'You mean you would if you didn't have a doting husband back home?'

'*Obviously*. So?'

'Well, leaving aside him having made it clear he's not interested in me that way, it certainly felt like there *was* some level of sexual tension between us – at first, then it dissipated.' I cringe at the memory. 'Maybe I'm wrong though. My radar could be off.'

Unable to verify or nullify this statement, Amber and Cat say nothing in response. It's another peaceful, companionable moment, where we could just be three friends chilling on the holiday of a lifetime with zero obligations. Unfortunately, that's not the holiday we're on.

'Right, shall we get showered and ready for the evening ahead?' says Cat.

'Defo,' says Amber. 'We've got interview prep to do over dinner, and I've scoped out two different entertainment acts for us as company research afterwards.'

'Let's do it.' I jump up and see them to the door. 'Shall we do the seafood restaurant tonight?' After my fish and seafood experience the evening before with Sébastien, I'm keen to try more of what this wonderful island has to offer.

'Perfect, see you then.' Cat gives me a wave as she and Amber disappear down the corridor, and I head for the shower.

～

A couple of hours later, we're seated in Tide, the resort's signature seafood restaurant, which is situated above the waves on a pier-like structure. It's a mesmerising experience, especially having watched the incredible sunset from here, and now with the swell of sea in semi-darkness, framed by a midnight blue, moonlit horizon.

'I'm not sure I can ever go home.' I stare out across the water dreamily. 'Do you think if I get the job, Sébastien would allow me to base myself here?'

'Ooh, yeah. *Do it*,' says Amber. 'I fancy a holiday home here.'

'So, *me* living here means *you* have a holiday home?'

'Eh, *yeah*.'

'Ah, fair enough, I'd probably see it the same way.' I chuckle. 'You do know I'm not serious though, right? I'd miss you guys too much. And Lottie. Even my parents, much as they can be a pain in the backside. Anyway, we're getting ahead of ourselves. I probably won't even get the job.'

'Wrong attitude.' Amber points a disapproving finger at me.

'I've got to be realistic, Amber. This interview is going to be tough, and if I get my hopes up too much, it'll be harder to take the knock if I'm unsuccessful.'

'You need to visualise getting it, without becoming emotionally invested.'

'OK... sure.' I have no clue what she means, but I don't want to get into it right now.

'How are you doing with your menu choices?' A buoyant waiter has appeared at our table, standing tall, arms behind his back.

'Have we decided?' I look to my friends who nod. 'OK, I'll go first. The conch fritters followed by the lobster hollandaise, please.'

'Yes, ma'am. Excellent choice.' He turns to Amber and Cat, who then relay their own orders.

'So, interview prep...' says Amber, the moment the waiter is out of earshot.

'You don't waste any time, do you?' I gaze longingly at the other diners who are chatting and laughing together, feeling the stark contrast between the kind of evening this should be, and the kind of evening it's going to be.

'Sooner we start, the sooner we're done.'

'That is true.' I pull the interview brief from my clutch and unfold it.

'OK, read out the company values,' she instructs me. 'That will help us decide what angle to take.'

'Good plan.' I scan the page and read aloud. 'Here goes... "*Passion* – we love what we do and we provide an unmatched experience to our customers; *Empowerment* – we trust our people to wow our customers in the way that they know best; *Creativity* – we thrive on fresh and exciting ideas; *Responsibility* – we love our planet, we use biodegradable and sustainable produce and processes wherever possible".'

We allow these words to wash over us, while sipping at our drinks.

'You'll need to demonstrate that your own values align with those.' says Amber. 'What stands out most for you on that list?'

I purse my lips, reading them once again. 'Probably the first two. I'm passionate about my career and I always go above and beyond – even worked my backside off on stuff I knew I'd never get any credit for.'

'And you'd be able to give solid examples of this?'

'Yeah, I can think of loads where I did the hard graft, I just never got to present to the board and no one knew it was my work.'

'Great, well use them. Structure your answers so they showcase your contribution without lying about any part you didn't get to play. How important is it really that you weren't the one doing the schmoozing with the big wigs? You made these things happen.'

'I did. OK, let me chew that over...' I take the iPad Cat's offering me and tap my finger against the side of it while my mind whirs through my options. 'I think... Yes, I know what I can use for this one. I can also talk enthusiastically about not wanting to work for a glory stealing, micromanaging boss who sucks the life out of me. Though I wouldn't put it quite like that.' I type some notes on the screen.

'You're at your best when given the freedom to decide how to do your job might be a way of putting it, which aligns well with their Empowerment value,' says Cat and I give her a thumbs up as I continue tapping away.

'OK good, what about the *Creativity* one?' says Amber. 'That's a bit more difficult. People like to say they're creative, but it's a tough one to demonstrate. What have you got?'

'I've got loads of examples of continuous improvement projects.'

'*Yawn.*' She rolls her eyes at my predictability.

'So, what then? I haven't done anything huge because I've never had a *huge* job – unlike the picture you unhelpfully painted to Sébastien.'

'*You really want to go there?*'

'No. I'm just saying this is harder because—'

The waiter arrives with our starters and I stop short, temporarily distracted from my frustration.

'This looks delicious, thank you.' I give him an appreciative smile, and he seems pleased with this feedback.

'Enjoy yourselves, ladies.'

We tuck into our dishes, my interview preparation temporarily forgotten as we 'ooh' and 'aah' over the food. I savour my delicious fritters while enjoying the warm, briny sea breeze on my face. It's a simple but wonderful moment – an escape from the pressure I'm feeling.

'Can I say something before we continue?' Cat eventually breaks the silence – and my zen.

'Sure,' I say. 'What's up?'

'I think you're trying too hard to be the person Amber sold to Sébastien. You need to be *you*. These values aren't alien to you, honey. You're a passionate person who wants to take the initiative, right?'

'Yes. Definitely.'

'You care about the environment too?'

'Of course. I hate the damage we're doing to our planet, though I realise that's a bit hypocritical, given we've flown all this way. But I did pay extra to offset the carbon emissions and I do try to play my part at home – I can give examples of that. Also, Paradis Resorts is a company that promotes world travel, so perhaps it's about keeping it in context. It's certainly important to me that they're operating in a sustainable way as far as possible and that they're doing proactive stuff to support local communities affected by climate change.'

'There you go.' Cat waves a fork-wielding hand to punctuate her point. 'And the creativity... that might not jump out so much, but you have more creative flare than you give yourself credit for. You showed that when you came up with your presentation theme, and it will come across on the day. Ultimately, Sébastien wants to know if you're the right fit for the job and I think you are, as long as you let them see *Emma*.'

I consider what Cat's just said. 'You're right, I need to be *me*.'

'Shall we start again then?' she suggests. 'With you being you?'

'That's a great plan.' I grin at her.

'And exactly what I was trying to get you to do in the first place,' Amber complains through a mouthful of shrimp kabob.

'Well, if you weren't so preoccupied with points scoring, it might have been a more successful strategy,' says Cat, giving me sneaky wink, and I stifle a giggle as the founder of the 'School of Amber and Cat' is silenced by her own partner.

Chapter Sixteen

After dinner, we wander along the beach, sandals off, feet in the water, enjoying the rhythmic breaking of the waves, the sound of which seems amplified by the quiet of the evening.

'What's on the "schedule" for tonight then?' I ask, still not entirely convinced that the 'company research' part of my prep plan isn't more about Amber wanting her nights out than getting me interview ready.

'There's a dance group at the beach,' says Amber. 'We'll do a pit stop there and then head to The Cave where there's live music on.'

'OK, sure.'

We trace the bend of the resort's private beach until the beach bar comes into view, lively music and intermittent cheers floating across the sea breeze towards us.

'Sounds like it's already started.' says Cat.

We increase our pace, and as we get closer, I can make out a female dance group performing on the beach in front of the feet-in-sand bar tables. They're dressed in carnival style outfits in a kaleidoscope of bright colours, with elaborate plumes sprouting out of their headdresses: the clear intention being to enhance the visual experience of their act. They're moving in perfect sequence to lively Caribbean-style music, the resort guests in the bar enthusiastically clapping along to the beat.

On reaching a free table we sit down and are immediately sucked into the experience.

'This is *amazing*,' Cat calls across to us over the loud music.

'It really is.' I call back, already shifting to the beat.

We watch in awe as the women energetically perform dance after dance, none of them appearing to even break a sweat. They're obviously used to the climate, but I still can't help wondering how they do it. The evening is warm and balmy: it's a bit like doing a workout in a greenhouse.

After about twenty minutes, the performers wrap up their act to loud, appreciative applause.

'That was brilliant!' I declare through my enthusiastic clapping. 'They definitely do things a level above at this resort.'

'Useful insight for sure,' Amber agrees. 'Right, let's get moving.'

We vacate our table and head for The Cave, which isn't far away.

'Ladies, good evening.' The same hostess from our last visit greets us when we arrive. 'Are you here for the live music?'

'Yes, please. It's just the three of us,' says Cat.

The hostess gives a nod of acknowledgement and leads us to a table in the indoor part of the bar, where there's a band set up but the live music doesn't seem to have started yet. We're then handed drinks menus by another member of staff.

'I'm going to stay off the booze tonight and just have a club soda and lime.' I cast mine aside, looking around at the décor which matches that of the terrace outside, giving the place a very cave-like feel.

'Me too.' Cat lays her own drinks list on the table. 'This afternoon was enough.'

'I'm with you.' Amber does the same, triggering Cat and I to share a surprised but relieved look as the waiter returns.

'Have you heard anything more from James since last night?' Cat asks me, once our order is in.

'No, and I'm not sure how much he'll be in touch now he's away on his own trip. Guess it'll depend on his Wi-Fi access and...' I trail off with a grimace.

'And what?'

'Whether he becomes "otherwise occupied".'

'I told you not to think about that,' says Amber.

'I haven't been... until now.'

'I bet he can't stop thinking about you.' Cat gives my hand a reassuring squeeze.

'That's not what you said before.'

'Well, I've changed my mind. I think he'll be so focused on you, he won't even notice the other women around him.'

'Oh, OK.' I'm cheered by this, despite there being no rational reason for this. Sometimes blind faith is all we need to get us through.

Our drinks arrive and we sip at them quietly, lost in our thoughts, until the attractive and elegantly dressed lead singer introduces herself, and she and the band and kick off their set with Eric Clapton's *Wonderful Tonight*.

'Wish I could sing like that.' I lean on the table, gazing dreamily at the singer, whose voice is smooth and melty as butter.

'Bet the punters in the karaoke bar the other night wished that too.' Amber quips, and I jovially flick her with a napkin.

'It got me noticed by Sébastien, didn't it?'

'Yeah, though I'm not sure anyone within a one-mile radius would have missed that yowling.'

'And you were so much better? Hurling yourself around like you were possessed.'

We continue our sibling-like bickering until we're interrupted by Cat.

'*Children*... You might want to pipe down. Look who's just arrived.'

We follow Cat's gaze and our eyes land on Sébastien – who's looking heart-stoppingly handsome in an open collar linen shirt and causal dinner jacket. He's at the bar talking to two staff members – one male, the other female. They're laughing and smiling. It's obvious they have a lot of respect for him, but there's something more to their behaviour. It's like they're fawning over him, in the way people do when they're drawn to someone – and not necessarily sexually. It seems Sébastien's magnetism can pull in anyone and everyone.

The male waiter pours him a glass of white wine and Sébastien appears to thank him, before turning and toasting the singer – who offers him a flirtatious smile in return. He then scans the room and I'm caught between wanting him to notice us and hoping he won't. But before I can register what's happening, Amber's caught his eye and beckoned him over to join us. Returning her invitation with a broad grin, he sets off in our direction.

'What did you do that for?' I say. 'He's like my potential boss-to-be. I can't relax if he's sitting with us.'

'This is a bonus research opportunity.' Amber waggles her eyebrows at me. 'Let's see what "intel" we can glean from him to help with your prep. Plus, he's great eye candy... *Sébastien*, how are you? Please come and join us. Can't have you sitting by yourself again.'

'*Mesdames, bonsoir*...' Sébastien makes his way around each of us, this time offering double cheek kisses to all and an oxytocin-inducing waft of his aftershave. 'You are all looking radiant. Emma, it is good to see that you have taken my advice.'

'I have indeed.' I beam back at him, automatically switching into best behaviour mode. 'And *such* good advice it was too.'

I sense Amber prickling from Sébastien getting the credit when she and Cat had already put the plan he suggested in place. And I can't help but enjoy it a little.

'I was glad to be of assistance.' He takes off his jacket and hangs it over the back of his chair, before sitting down to join us. 'How is your evening? Where did you dine?'

'At Tide. It was *magical*,' says Cat.

At first, I wonder if she's remembering the experience accurately – it was lovely, but I wouldn't call it 'magical' – until I realise, she too has fallen under Sébastien's spell.

'It's a lovely setting being over the water like that,' I pitch in. '*C'est une experience nue.*'

On saying this, I tune into the singer, who's now crooning an impressive rendition of Shakira's *Underneath Your Clothes*, and it dawns on me that *'dans la nature'* was the term I was looking for – which means I've just mixed up my rusty French and... *oh no*... did I just talk about eating dinner naked?

I glug at my mineral water to cover up my embarrassment, however Sébastien either misses my faux pas, or he's too polite to let on that he heard it.

'*D'accord.*' He nods thoughtfully. 'It is a pleasant experience, dining with the water around you. You speak a little French, Emma?'

'I... erm... *un petit peu?*'

'Very good. We all must start somewhere.'

I'm at a loss for what to say next, my cheeks still burning from my error, so I shoot Amber a silent SOS, which she acts upon immediately.

'Sébastien, I noticed from the brochure in my suite that you have several resorts in the Caribbean. Seems to be a hotspot for your company. Which is your favourite?'

He rubs his chiselled jaw with us following his movements like hypnotised serpents.

'I think my favourite is this resort,' he says. 'For two

reasons. It was the first I purchased in this part of the world, so it is... I think you might say... close to my heart. But also, I have put some of myself and my roots into it. *Par exemple*... this very bar was inspired by the area where I grew up which has many caves that one can visit. They are spectacular... feats?'

'Feats, yes.' Amber confirms correct use of the term.

'*Bien*. They are spectacular feats of nature.'

'Yes, they are.' I finally come back to life. 'I remember visiting one on a school trip years ago. *La Grotte de la Salamandre*... I think that's what it was called anyway.'

'Ah, yes, I know this one.' Sébastien looks wistful for a moment. 'It is very impressive.'

'The singer is really good, Sébastien,' says Cat. 'Is she a regular entertainment act here?'

'That is Lola.' Sébastien glances across at her, catching her eye, as if she was waiting for him to notice her. 'She has been with us for the last seven years.'

We simply nod by way of a response and focus our attention on Lola, who is continuing to do justice to her ballad. A handful of couples are up dancing, making the most of the romantic ambience, and I feel a pang for how amazing it would be to enjoy this experience with a significant other. Maybe James? Or Sébastien, my mind offers me unexpectedly. I quickly shake the thought away.

'It's lovely seeing those people up there, all so in love.' Cat props her chin up with her hand and it's obvious she's engaged in a similar romantic fantasy about Mike.

'Do you like to dance, Sébastien?' Amber asks.

'I do.' He nods. 'It is something I have always enjoyed. But not something I manage often, working as I do.'

'That's sad,' says Cat. 'There must be lots of women – or men – here who would be willing to dance with you.'

Sébastien seems amused by Cat's added inclusivity clause. 'I prefer to dance with women, but that is just personal taste.'

'I'm sure Emma would be happy to dance with you,' says Amber.

My eyes widen at this statement and I give her my laser beam stare, urging her to retract her statement. Unsurprisingly, she doesn't.

'You are fond of dancing also, Emma?' Sébastien asks me.

'I'm... eh... not sure I'd say that.' I give an awkward chuckle. 'My dancing isn't much better than my karaoke.' I'm hoping this is enough to put him off, but it seems it's not.

'I can teach you if you would like?'

Before I can answer, Amber hijacks our interaction with a gleam in her eye. 'What a lovely offer, Sébastien. Isn't it, Emma? Off you go then.'

Chapter Seventeen

Sébastien looks at me expectantly, gesturing towards the other dancing couples, and before I can properly register what's happening, I'm getting to my feet. With the current song coming to an end, I'm hoping the next one will be a bit more upbeat, but instead the band transition seamlessly into *Let's Stay Together* by Al Green.

Oh god. It had to be one of the most romantic songs ever written.

Lola warbles the lyrics, eyes closed, face all mushed up in that soppy kind of way, and I can't help wondering if she's picturing Sébastien. Sébastien, meantime, has slipped one arm around my waist, clasped my right hand with the other, and is sweeping me round the makeshift dancefloor with skills to rival the contestants from *Strictly Come Dancing*.

It turns out that I had nothing to worry about regarding my dancing abilities. I'm basically his puppet, and he has total control over my movements. The whole experience is quite overwhelming. The lyrics make me blush, especially when we make eye contact. Then there's the feeling of Sébastien's muscular back through his shirt, him being so close that I can feel his breath on my neck and the wafts of his heady fragrance mixed with his natural masculine scent. I feel like I might spontaneously combust. It's too much doing this with the man who will be putting me through my professional paces on Monday.

Then Lola opens her eyes, and my discomfort reaches a whole new level. She shoots me one of the filthiest looks I've ever seen; a stark contrast to the romantic soulful melody she's projecting to the room. Now I *know* she was fantasising about Sébastien – and is probably thinking about how she'd like to kill me with her guitar.

Sébastien continues to shimmy me around the floor, while I attempt to block out Lola's murderous looks and Amber's smug face across at our table.

'*Ça va*, Emma?' Sébastien seems to tune into my discomfort. 'You are OK?' I can feel his smouldering eyes on me.

'Yeah... I'm fine.'

'I am sensing that you are not at ease with the dancing.'

'Oh, no. It's nothing like that.' I attempt a wave of my hand and he course corrects me, keeping us in time with the music. 'It's just... you're going to be interviewing me in a few days' time. Whatever way that goes, it kind of makes me feel like I'm dancing with my boss.'

'And it would be a problem for you to dance with your boss?'

'Us Brits are awkward about this stuff. You know, "stiff upper lip", that kind of stereotypical nonsense that has some truth behind it.'

Sébastien chuckles. 'It is good then that I am not British, and I can spin you around this dance floor with no qualms whatsoever.'

'I suppose, but also... us being seen dancing like this, and then you assessing me quite publicly for the job. People could make assumptions.' I regret this comment the second it's out of my mouth.

'Ah, OK. You are concerned that my staff and guests will think that I am favouring you for the role, and if you are successful this will be the reason for it.'

'Well, yes.' This didn't actually dawn on me until I said it but it's quickly becoming my main concern.

Sébastien chuckles again, and performs a slick dance move that involves twirling me away, and pulling me back into him in one smooth snapping action. He then draws me even closer.

'I will share a secret with you, Emma,' he says. 'I do not care what anyone thinks. The decisions I make are for the right reasons, and I do not need to justify them.'

His breath tickles my ear, which on top of the proximity of our bodies, sends my pulse racing, and I briefly wonder if he might kiss me. Feeling ever more self-conscious, my eyes scan the room as Sébastien continues to sweep me round in circles. I can see Cat and Amber's delighted faces, the bar staff giggling and whispering to each other as they watch us, Lola shooting cruise missiles in my direction, and James looking shocked and horrified by the entrance to the bar.

Wait... what? James? I try to glance back towards the entrance, but Sébastien (unknowingly) thwarts this attempt by performing another of his fancy dance tricks. The movement and the confusion make me feel dizzy and I stumble, prompting Sébastien to bring us to a halt.

'Emma, you are looking off colour.' He takes my face in his hands.

'I'm... um, yes... I think maybe I'm dehydrated again.' My eyes dart to the entrance but there's no one there.

I *must* be dehydrated if I'm now hallucinating. James isn't here. *Of course he's not.* He's in the US with his mates, probably celebrating his first night of holiday freedom by drinking too much – a move he'll likely regret in the morning. I make this assumption because that's exactly what I did.

Sébastien signals to the waiting staff to bring some water and leads me back to our table.

'What's wrong?' Cat gets up to help me into my seat. 'You're really pale, honey.'

'I'm OK, don't worry.'

The water arrives and Sébastien practically force feeds it to me. '*Pardon*, Emma. I apologise if the dancing was too much.'

'I think it's *you* that's too much for her,' Amber mutters under her breath and winks at me.

'It's fine, Sébastien,' I say between gulps. 'The dancing was lovely. And thanks for the water. I probably just need some sleep.'

'I think that is a good idea,' he says. 'I will call the concierge to drive you back to your suite.'

'There's no need for that. I'm fine to walk.'

'*Non*, Emma. You must not walk if you are feeling faint. Allow me.' He disappears across to the bar to arrange the transport.

'How are you feeling now?' Cat places her hand against my forehead.

'I'm OK, but...' I shake my head to clear the jumbled thoughts. 'I was dancing and it was weird... I saw James... He didn't look happy, like he assumed that Sébastien and I were "together".'

'Sorry... you saw who?'

'*James*. I saw him over by the entrance. At least I thought I did, but... that can't be right, can it?'

I catch Cat and Amber sharing a concerned look.

'Let's get some more water down you and pack you off to bed.' Cat rubs my back soothingly. 'You might have a touch of sunstroke or something.'

'Um... I feel a bit better,' I say. 'Can we go for a walk around the resort? I want to check if it was him.'

'Emma, it couldn't have been him,' says Amber. 'He's in the US. You told us that yourself.'

'I know, but—'

'Emma, you *imagined* it.' Amber's tone is caring but firm. 'Your mind is playing tricks on you. You must have seen someone who looked like James and your brain filled in the rest. It's probably a mix of stress, dehydration and the guilt you've been feeling about liking Sébastien. It's created the perfect tropical storm.'

'I guess.' I sigh, only half-convinced. 'It seemed so real though.'

'*Mesdames*, your chariot awaits.' Sébastien has already returned with a colleague. 'Ricardo will see you to your suites. I wish you a goodnight and, Emma, I will check on you tomorrow.'

Before we can say anything else, he shoos us out of the bar and onto the waiting golf buggy.

Back in my suite, once Cat and Amber have tucked me up in bed, made me promise to go straight to sleep and left for their own rooms, I get straight back out of bed and retrieve my phone from my clutch. Disappointment washes over me as I see I have no messages. Nothing from James, which means he's either too busy having a great time to message me, or he really was in that doorway – and now he hates me. Neither of these options are particularly appealing, but it's not like I can message him to ask which it is, because the far higher probability is that my brain *was* playing tricks on me. He'd think I've lost the plot.

Climbing back into bed, I place my phone on my bedside table and settle down for an inevitably restless night, as I repeatedly check for a non-existent message.

~

I wake up early the next morning, and despite my broken sleep and there still being no word from James, I feel quite good – a blessing considering the amount of interview prep I'll have to pack into my day.

After doing some more work on my presentation content, I have a quick FaceTime call with Lottie, who I'm pleased to see is still recovering well, then I get showered and changed and wander along the corridor to breakfast.

On approaching the entrance to the restaurant, Sébastien materialises by my side.

'Emma, *ça va?* I was hoping I would see you. How are you this morning?' He greets me with his signature double kisses, to which my body responds with a flush of awkwardness and involuntary desire.

'Morning, Sébastien. I'm good. And well hydrated.'

'I am glad to hear this. I was concerned for you, especially after you were also feeling unwell the evening we went to dinner. I can arrange for you to see a doctor if this would be helpful?'

My flush deepens at this suggestion. Obviously, I don't want to lie to Sébastien but I can hardly tell him that the cause of my "sickness" is a guilty conscience.

'Thank you, that's very kind, but there's no need. I'm feeling much better.'

'*D'accord...* if you are certain.' He doesn't seem satisfied with my decision but it's clear that he respects it. 'If you change your mind, please ask reception to contact me.'

'I will. Have you had breakfast?' I inwardly curse myself for asking this in case he takes it as an invitation. I can barely stomach the effect he has on me, so he's hardly a good pairing with a buffet breakfast.

'I have eaten, yes,' he says, to my relief. 'I am what I think you British call "an early bird". I wish you a pleasant one, Emma.'

We part company, and despite being delayed by our unexpected interaction, I'm first to arrive. I grab a table near the breakfast buffet and order jugs of tea and coffee, which arrive at the same time as Cat and Amber.

'How are you feeling this morning, honey?' Cat slides into a seat and pours herself a cup of tea. 'I was worried about you last night.'

'Believe it not, I'm fine.' I give her a bright, reassuring smile. 'Raring to go. Must make sure I drink lots of water while I'm here because that seems to be a real energiser.'

'That's good. Glad you're feeling better.'

'I assume James didn't appear at the end of your bed in the night?' Amber's tone is mildly sarcastic.

'*Very funny.*' I fix her with my best get-lost face. 'I haven't heard a thing from him. Now he's got the entire staff of Hooters to play with, he doesn't need me anymore.' I'm aware of how this sounds, but I can't help feeling a bit hurt that James hasn't bothered to check in since going on his own holiday.

'*Oh, boo hoo!*' Amber mocks me. 'Like you haven't spent every minute of the day fantasising about Sébastien throwing you around your suite naked.'

'*What?* I haven't.'

'You keep telling yourself that.'

'Well, can you blame me if I have?' I throw my hands up in frustration. 'Sébastien is undoubtedly the hottest man I've ever—'

'Hotter than James?' Cat interrupts me.

I frown in contemplation. 'Well, yeah. If you put it on physical attributes alone.'

'He oozes sex appeal too.' Amber reaches for the coffee jug. 'Only needs to look at a woman and she's dropping her knickers.'

'*Amber!*' Cat and I reprimand her for being so crass.

'What? Is it not true?'

'That's not the point,' I tut at her. 'You sound like a misogynistic male.'

'So, sue me. Anyway, you were saying. Sébastien is hotter than James...' She prompts me to continue.

'That's not what I was saying at all. What I was trying to say is that Sébastien *appears* hotter than James. He would win the "sex god" category – no contest. But James has this way about him that makes him equally appealing. He's cheeky and quick witted. That's such an attractive quality.'

'Which means he'd win the "funny guy" category. *Ouch*.' Amber pulls a face while Cat stifles a giggle.

'I know what you're doing, Amber, and it's not going to work today.'

We get up from our seats and head for the breakfast buffet, where I'm determined to exercise more restraint than the previous mornings. I need to keep a clear head today – healthy food for a healthy mind and all that. After two laps of the extensive offerings, I opt for a two-egg omelette with herbs and pile another plate high with fresh fruit. That should do it.

I return to our table, where Cat and Amber are already tucking into their own breakfasts. We eat in silence, sipping at our drinks, until Cat pipes up.

'According to the interview prep schedule, we're meant to be reviewing your progress from yesterday, honey.'

'Yup,' says Amber through a mouthful of croissant. 'Let's do it. How do you think things went?'

I slurp at my tea thoughtfully. 'Well... I feel good about my presentation content. I spent some more time on it this morning, so it's nearly ready, but I obviously still need to work on my "creative" element. Last night's "company research" also gave me a sense of the level of finesse here, which was helpful. I'd say my approach – if I can pull it off in the way I hope – will match the tone here quite well.'

'I agree,' says Amber. 'It'll be spot on if you pitch it right.'

'Thanks, I appreciate that vote of confidence. I've also had some interview examples swimming round my head, so I've been adding them to my notepad app and I'll keep doing that as they come to me.' I lift my phone out of my bag and pop it on the table as if to evidence this, having reluctantly abandoned my R&R policy of locking it away.

'This is all great,' says Cat. 'See, you're making progress, honey.'

'I am. It's encouraging. What else is on the plan for today?'

Amber plucks it from her bag and unfolds it. 'After breakfast, you'll be working on your company knowledge, then over lunch we'll do some interview practice. The afternoon is personal development by the pool.'

'Sounds great. What will the personal development involve?'

'You'll see. Just stay focused on each part as it comes up.' She looks at the sheet of paper again. 'Then there's presentation practice over dinner and more company research after. I've got two more entertainment acts earmarked for tonight.'

'Perfect.' I grin at my friends, while spearing a chunk of pineapple. 'Am I just swotting up on the company in my room after breakfast then?'

'*Uh-uh.*' Amber shakes her head. 'Our approach will be way more effective than that.'

'And your approach is...'

'Wait and see. Patient one, aren't you?'

A creeping discomfort works its way through me. Amber's being intentionally evasive, which means I'm probably not going to like what's about to come next.

'Why don't you tell us a bit more about your interview

examples, honey?' Cat suggests. 'Maybe we can give you some feedback so you're ready to practise over lunch.'

'OK, sure.'

I bring up my notes on my phone and share my thinking with my friends. But despite their interest and encouragement, it's hard to concentrate. I just can't shake off the feeling that I'm about to be hurled so far out of my comfort zone that I might end up on a different island.

Chapter Eighteen

After breakfast, Cat nips to her room to get a plaster for a blister that's bothering her, while Amber and I make a quick pit stop at the resort 'Business hub' to test out the AV equipment.

'That went well,' I say to her, as we make our way along to the atrium by reception to meet Cat. 'I'm relieved it was so easy to use.'

'Always good to test it out just in case,' she says, and then gives me a sideways glance. 'You do know all I want is for you to succeed, don't you, Emma?'

I ponder this unexpected question. 'Yeah... I do. Sometimes the way you rib me, it feels a bit counterproductive, but I guess that's banter between friends.'

'It is. And you're able to give it back – some of the time. I know you think I do it for my own entertainment – and I admit there's some truth in that – but I'm also trying to toughen you up, so you can cope with anything and anyone that comes at you. There is a lot worse than me out there, Emma. You deserve to be happy and successful, and as your friend, I want to help you get there.'

This is one of Amber's rare moments of benevolence, which I don't take lightly.

'Thanks for sharing that.' I smile at her. 'And thanks for having my back. It's appreciated.'

'No problem.' She gives me an (almost) affectionate nudge. 'But if you tell anyone, I'll deny all knowledge. Can't have people thinking I'm getting soft.'

I chuckle. 'Don't think there's much chance of that. But my lips are sealed, I promise.'

We reach the open, airy atrium and sit on one of the plush cream sofas while we wait for Cat. She joins us a few minutes later after briefly diverting to speak to Charnice at reception.

'Better?' I ask her.

'Much.' Her face is etched with relief. 'Those damn sandals. They look so comfortable, and they are, as long as I don't move in them.'

'It's always the way. So, what are we here for?'

'Is Charnice ready for us?' Amber says to Cat.

'Yes.' She throws a shifty sideways glance at me, and my earlier feeling of unease instantly returns.

'What's going on, you two?'

'Come and find out,' says Amber.

She and Cat get up and make their way across to reception, and I have no choice but to follow.

'Good morning, ladies,' Charnice greets us in her sing-song voice, her dark ponytail of braids swinging from side to side as she does. 'Emma, hello. Are you looking forward to this?'

'Looking forward to what?' I raise my eyebrows questioningly at my friends.

'We haven't told her yet,' says Amber. 'We wanted it to be a surprise.'

'What's the surprise?' My teeth are now gritted. *What the hell have my two so-called best friends cooked up?*

Charnice, who doesn't appear to have picked up on my

reaction, gives me a wide smile. 'This morning, Emma, you're joining me here at reception to look after our guests. I have your uniform ready.'

I'm what? Panic gushes through me as Charnice bends down and re-emerges clutching the exact same blouse and skirt that she herself is wearing. She hands them to me, and I accept them out of nothing other than politeness.

'Erm... can I speak to you guys quickly?' I say to Amber and Cat.

They share a look and we shuffle off in the direction of the sofas so we're out of earshot.

'*What the hell are you playing at?*' I eyeball the two of them. 'I'm not going to work behind reception. This is *ridiculous*.'

'Why is it ridiculous?' Amber challenges me.

'Because... I don't know the first thing about being a receptionist. And... *it's embarrassing*.'

'Why? Who's going to see you? We're the only people that know you here.'

'Sébastien might see me.'

'I knew you still wanted to bed him.'

'It's not about that, Amber,' I growl, ensuring I keep my voice low. 'I want to come across as a credible candidate for this job. How ridiculous am I going to look if he stumbles upon me at reception, grinning like an idiot, wearing the hotel uniform. He'll think I've lost it.'

'Actually, when you paint it like that, it *is* pretty funny.' Amber snickers and Cat elbows her to get her back on track. She neutralises her expression. 'That's one way of looking at it, yes. But there's a more realistic angle – which is that Sébastien sees you and is super-impressed at the lengths you'll go to for the job. It's just as important to learn about the frontline operation as it is to know the strategic stuff.'

'*Huh*. I guess that is another way of looking at it.' I can't fault her logic but I'm still not happy at all about this.

'It's also a great way to see more of who stays here,' Cat chips in. 'You'll hear firsthand what's important to guests. What's working for them, what they're dissatisfied about, what questions they have. We're offering you a window into Paradis Resorts' highly valued clientele. Why would you not want that understanding ahead of your interview?'

My overriding reaction is still one of mortification and wanting to flee to the safety of my suite, the beach, poolside – anywhere but here. But I can see the sense – and the opportunity – in what my friends are telling me.

'OK, I'll do it,' I say after a long pause, during which I beg the universe to intervene and it fails to answer my plea.

'Good girl.' Amber pats me on the shoulder, while Cat slips a supportive arm around my waist and gives me a squeeze.

We shuffle back across to Charnice, who springs to attention, still smiling broadly.

'All right, Emma? Are you ready to join me?'

'As I'll ever be.' I plaster a smile on my face. 'Where can I change?'

'The ladies powder room is across the atrium. Or you can use your suite if that would be more comfortable for you?'

'The powder room will be fine, thank you.' I turn and walk away, muttering under my breath. 'If I go to my suite for this, you'll never get me back out again.'

'You'll be OK,' says Cat, who is walking beside me. 'It's only for a few hours, then we can enjoy a nice lunch together.'

'I suspect it's going to be the longest "few hours" of my life. And since that's the case, the last thing I need is you two peering at me from the sofas. Go on, *disappear*.'

'Aww, come on,' says Amber. 'You've got to let us see you in action.'

'Not a chance. You disappear or the deal is off. And can you take this for me for safekeeping?' I hand Cat my handbag, which has my phone in it.

'I think that's our cue to go,' says Cat to a still protesting Amber. 'If it were me, I'd feel the same.'

'*Fine.*' She gives in. 'We'll see you at lunch.'

'Sure... if I don't die of embarrassment before then.' I give a last hopeless shake of my head and push open the door to the ladies loos.

Chapter Nineteen

F ive minutes later, I've changed and I'm standing in front of the full-length mirror in the toilets (a.k.a. the ladies powder room).

'*Oh man*,' I groan out loud.

The bottom half is inoffensive: a knee length black pencil skirt which almost fits me, but the blouse is hideous – on me anyway. It's like someone knocked over a bunch of tins of paint and this was the result. I suppose some people pay hundreds of thousands of pounds for this kind of design when it's on canvas, but when the canvas is a fair-skinned Scottish woman, whatever appeal there is becomes quickly lost. It's also about three sizes too big for me, causing it to billow around my waist like a poorly erected tent.

Swallowing thickly, I drag my horrified expression away from the mirror and pick my way across the atrium with my legs feeling like they're no longer attached to my body. I can't bear to make eye contact with anyone around me.

'Ah, there you are. This way, Emma.' Charnice, who looks a million times better than I do in the uniform, gestures for me to walk through a door to the left of the solid wood reception desk.

I pull it open, make my way through the small office and back out again into the space behind reception.

'Are you OK?' She asks me. 'You look a little... unhappy.'

'I'm fine,' I reassure her, fully aware that this isn't her fault and also not wanting to disrespect the important role she plays in the effective running of the resort. This is definitely *not* about that.

'Shall I tell you a bit about the resort and what I do while we have some quiet time?'

'Sure, sounds good.'

'This is where all of the guest reservations and information is held.' Charnice gestures to one of three computers in a row. 'We have an active record of everyone staying with us, as well as information on upcoming and past bookings. Normally there is at least two of us here, but my colleagues are in a meeting just now.'

I peer at the screen with growing interest. 'You'll have an active record for me then.'

'Yes. Let us look you up as an example so I can show you.' She taps my surname into the search field.

'*Wow*, you remember my surname? That's impressive. I suppose it's your job to know who everyone is.'

Charnice looks at me and smiles. 'Shall I share a secret with you?'

'Go on.' I lean in, thinking she's about to pass on some amazing memory trick that I can use in the future.

'When your friends asked if you could come and work with me this morning, I looked up your details and memorised them.'

'*Aha*. And there was me thinking you had a photographic memory or something.'

'Sadly, no. I would love to be able to address every guest by name, but we have around four hundred checked in today alone.'

'That's a lot of people.'

'It is,' she says. 'I do know the names of some guests: those who return to us regularly, but that is all.'

She clicks out of my information, then gives me a demonstration of the room allocation system, along with an overview of the resort from an operational perspective. After a few minutes, an older couple, perhaps in their sixties, approaches the desk. Their clothing and the hand luggage they're carrying make it obvious that their stay has come to an end.

'Good morning, sir, ma'am,' Charnice greets them. 'You are checking out?'

'Unfortunately.' The man, who has a southern English accent, gives a despondent sigh. His wife looks equally flat.

'Have you enjoyed your stay with us?'

'It's been wonderful. Will be a shock returning to normal life, won't it, Betty?'

His wife nods.

'And where is normal life for you, sir?' Charnice takes the room key card from the man and expertly taps at the keyboard, while remaining fully engaged in the conversation.

'Dorset, in the UK. We gather it's about fifteen degrees cooler with stormy weather rolling in every couple of days.'

Betty visibly shivers at the thought.

'Maybe you can focus on your nice memories to distract you from the rain?' says Charnice. 'If it makes you feel better, it will be hurricane season here. We'll have a lot of rain here too.'

'*Gosh, yes*. Perhaps better to have our British storms. Right, Betty?'

'It does make home sound more appealing.' Betty perks up all of a sudden.

'I'm glad.' Charnice plucks a sheet of paper from the printer and places it on the desk. 'You are checked out, Mr and Mrs Jeffries. Here is a copy of your invoice. I wish you a good journey home and I hope you will come and visit us again soon.'

'We hope so too,' says Mr Jeffries. 'Perhaps for our golden wedding anniversary in a few years' time.'

'I hope to see you then. Neville here will show you to your transfer to the airport.' Charnice turns to me once Neville has seamlessly taken over care of Mr and Mrs Jeffries. 'There you are, Emma. That is how you check the guests out.'

'That was really impressive, Charnice,' I say.

'What was impressive?'

'You didn't just check them out. You made them feel good about going home. They were so disappointed to be leaving, then one comment about hurricane season and they practically skipped off to their transfer.'

'My job is to make people happy.' Charnice shrugs as if her actions aren't worth mentioning. 'It's easy to do this when they arrive and they're excited to get their first taste of the resort. But they should leave happy too.'

'I love that. Is it really that bad here during hurricane season?' My eyes widen in anticipation of her answer.

'No. Unless a very big one comes, and that's not often on this island, thankfully. But people are afraid of hurricanes, especially those who have never experienced them. It's a way of helping them appreciate what they have, though I use it sparingly. We still want people to visit all year round.'

'Well, I think it was genius. Perfectly pitched for those two guests.'

'Thank you, Emma. I'm glad to impress you.'

I observe Charnice in action for around an hour, giving outstanding personal service to every guest who approaches the desk: processing their check outs, giving them information about sightseeing excursions, answering their questions about the resort. She's a complete pro and I can see that she's the epitome of everything the company wants to showcase.

'Would you like to manage the next check out, Emma?' she asks, when we find ourselves with another lull in activity. 'I will manage the computer while you speak to the guests?'

'*Really?*' I cringe. 'Are you sure you want to let me loose on your customers?'

'Why not? I think you will be very natural at this.'

'OK, sure. Let's give it a try.'

I step forward, fixing a friendly smile on my face while I await my first customer. Suddenly, I see a man storming across the atrium towards us – and he doesn't look happy at all. It's the man I overheard in the bar the other day: the one who was talking about a housekeeping staff member in a derogatory way.

'Emma, this is not a check out,' says Charnice. 'I will handle this.'

I step back, relieved.

'Good morning, Mr Miller. How may I help you today?'

He ignores Charnice's greeting, instead choosing to bark at her. 'I want to speak with the hotel manager. *Now.*'

Charnice doesn't even waver, her smile remaining as genuine as it was with the previous (nicer) guests. 'The duty manager is dealing with another matter currently, Mr Miller. Rather than you waiting, may I help you?'

Mr Miller looks like he's about to explode, his face even redder than it was that afternoon in the bar. '*Did I not make it clear before that I wanted that maid dealt with?*'

'I remember, sir. She is no longer cleaning you or any of your family's suites as I recall.'

'That may be the case. But she's still here – at the resort. I've just seen her cleaning rooms on another wing of this place. How is that *dealing* with her? She needs to be *fired*.'

'Mr Miller, I'm afraid I cannot comment on this issue

specifically, however, I will ask the duty manager to contact you as soon as she is available.'

'This is *horseshit*. I am *not* waiting around in my room all day for a call. Use my cell number.' He thrusts what looks like a business card at Charnice, and to her credit, she doesn't even flinch.

'Of course, sir. Is there anything else I can help you with?'

'Can you wave a magic wand and get this place running like it used to?'

'I understand you are frustrated. I will ensure that the Duty Manager contacts you as quickly as possible.'

'*You'd better*. Otherwise, I'll be taking my money elsewhere in future.' He glances across at me and his eyes narrow. 'You're that nosey girl from the bar.'

I instinctively recoil from his accusing stare.

'Sorry, sir? Is there something else you would like to discuss?' It's clear that Charnice is keen to shift his focus away from me.

'You can add *her* to the list as well.' He flicks an angry finger in my direction. 'This one was blatantly eavesdropping on my *private* conversation with my family in the bar. What was she doing drinking in there anyway when she's staff?'

'Mr Miller, I'm not—' I try to explain that I'm not an employee, but he cuts me off.

'Do *not* talk back to me. You'll be lucky if you still have a job by the end of the day.' He looks me up and down in disgust. 'Is it so hard to get an outfit that fits you? You look like a deflated beach ball.'

My face burns with humiliation as he stalks off in the direction of the pool.

'Emma, are you OK?' Charnice turns to me with an apologetic face. 'I'm sorry for the way Mr Miller spoke to you.'

'You have *nothing* to apologise for,' I say, my cheeks still hot from the altercation. I lower my voice. '*He's* the one with the problem. Where does he get off behaving like that? I've never seen such snobbery and entitlement.'

'He has his ways, but he is also a regular guest with a lot of money.'

'That shouldn't give him the right to tear into people like that.'

'No, it should not, and I have not seen him quite like this before. Between you and me, he recently struck a big business deal. It was in the news that he is expected to become a billionaire within five years. Perhaps this has had an effect.'

I frown and shake my head. 'Future billionaire or not, it's *never* OK to behave in that way.'

'He's not the only one, I'm afraid. It comes with the job in a resort like this. And it's something you will need to know about if you end up working with us.'

I feel a deep pang of empathy for Charnice. 'That's really sad. I'm sorry you have to deal with that kind of stuff.'

'Thank you, Emma. I learned a long time ago not to take it personally.' She shrugs and smiles her bright smile once again. 'Look, here comes another check out. Are you ready?'

'Yes, I can do this.' I attempt to smooth down my billowing blouse and shake off the raging self-consciousness that's now hovering around me like an unrelenting mosquito.

This time, it's a group of women who are checking out. I smile sweetly at them as they approach the desk, wheeling their cabin bags along behind them.

'Good morning, ladies. Are you checking out?'

'We are,' says the woman who's taken the lead. 'Here are our key cards.'

'I'll take these.' Charnice takes them from her and taps the information into the computer.

'Have you all enjoyed your stay?' I ask.

'*It's been wonderful!*' another one of the group calls from further away.

'Really wonderful,' the woman who passed over the key cards says. 'This place is paradise. The service was excellent too. So good that we would like to leave this for the staff as a tip.' She hands me a bulky envelope, which evidently contains a pile of bank notes.

'That's extremely kind of you.' I turn to Charnice to check it's all right to accept it. She gives a subtle nod without removing her eyes from the screen. 'Thank you so much. It's great for our employees to know they have served you well and that they have been appreciated. How long is your journey home?'

The woman launches into a detailed description of their return itinerary, which I listen to attentively. That is, until a familiar voice floats across the atrium, pricking my attention. Confused, I glance over the woman's shoulder in time to catch sight of three blokes sauntering across the atrium dressed in swim shorts, T-shirts and flip flops, and my breath catches in my throat. I blink a couple of times to make sure I'm not seeing things – but this time I'm definitely not hallucinating. One of the three men is James. His face, his voice, his sexy smile.

Chapter Twenty

'Emma? Are you OK?'

Charnice's voice filters through to my consciousness and I tune back into my surroundings. The group of women we were checking out are wheeling their cases away, led by another member of the concierge.

'Sorry... *oh, gosh*, I do apologise. I just saw someone—'

The door James walked out of suddenly re-opens, and he strides back into the atrium alone, heading in the direction he first came from.

Fuck. My immediate instinct is to hide but I'm not fast enough. He looks across in our direction and stops dead.

'*Emma?*'

'*Hi.*' I give a mortified wave, all too aware how weird this must look without the context of my job interview.

James approaches the reception desk and Charnice politely excuses herself, no doubt to give me some privacy. He's looking hot: all trendy summer beach gear, shades perched in his thick dark hair and gorgeous white teeth. A stark contrast to my current predicament.

'What are you doing behind reception?' he asks. 'And why are you wearing the hotel uniform?'

I glance down at my outfit and my humiliation deepens. With my 'holiday hair' and my 'deflated beach ball' blouse, he couldn't have seen me looking much worse.

'I'm... learning how this place works... because I have an interview for a job with Paradis Resorts on Monday.'

'You have an interview?' He looks understandably baffled. 'How did that come about?'

'How do you think?'

'Amber?'

'Got it in one. We got chatting to the owner of the company in one of the bars, he happened to mention he was recruiting and Amber put on the hard sell.'

'Sébastien Dumont,' says James, and I see a flicker of something I can't quite identify pass across his face. 'Right. So, you're going for a job... on reception?'

'No. It's a role in resort acquisition, supporting the company's growth strategy.'

There's another unreadable expression. 'Great. Well, good luck with that, Emma. Enjoy your stint on reception. I'll see you around.'

He gives me a curt nod and walks off in the direction he was originally heading. Stunned by his reaction, it's only once he's out of sight that my brain kicks back into gear – with a lot of questions. I was so appalled by him seeing me in this abominable outfit that I didn't think to ask what he's doing here on this resort when he's meant to be in the US. As well as how he knows Sébastien (although it's probably because he works in the travel industry himself), and also, what the hell is wrong with him? Where's the charming, flirtatious guy that was so into me before?

Then realisation catches up. Last night was no hallucination or case of mistaken identity. It *was* James –

which means he *did* see me dancing with Sébastien, and now I've told him I've got an interview with Sébastien's company too. So, basically, he thinks I've hooked up with the rich guy, and I'm planning to run off with him to hell knows where. *Shit*. No wonder he was cold with me. I need to find him and explain.

'Uh... Charnice?'

'Yes, Emma.' She turns to me and I pull an apologetic face.

'I'm really sorry, but I need to go and deal with something urgently.'

'Of course.' She appears unfazed by me bailing on her. 'Is everything all right? Can I help at all?'

'Thank you, but no. I'm fine. I'll get it sorted. I'll also drop this uniform back to you later if that's OK?'

'That's fine.' She gives me a sympathetic smile that indicates she overheard at least some of my conversation with James. 'Good luck.'

Grabbing my clothes, I take off after James, but as I rush down one corridor of suite doors after the next, it becomes clear that I'm never going to find him. I let out a frustrated wail before catching a glimpse of myself in one of the resorts decorative mirrors. *Oh my god, I really have to change.*

I high-tail it back to my suite where I quickly throw on my original clothes, apply some mascara and lip gloss, and attempt to tame my humidity ravaged hair. Once I'm happy that I look more presentable, I send a WhatsApp message to Amber asking where they are, and she replies almost instantly with their location – on the beach.

'Why are you not on reception?' she asks when I approach them several minutes later.

'I had to finish up early.'

'Because?'

'Because James is here. I spoke to him.'

'*James is here?*' Cat's voice rises an octave. 'I thought he—'

'Hold on.' Amber cuts her off. 'That was a reason to duck out of your interview prep because...?'

'Amber, did you not hear what I said?' I'm incredulous at her reaction.

She tips up her sunglasses and surveys me with irritation. 'I heard you. But it doesn't sound like a reason to skive off and make a bad impression. You do remember that some resort employees will be at your presentation and feeding back to Sébastien. And that will probably include Charnice.'

'It's fine. I told her I had to see to something urgently – and it *is* urgent. Even she could see that.' I'm now dancing around with impatience, willing Amber to move beyond the fact that I left my posting early.

'And that something urgent is getting in James's undies?'

'*No.* Will you let me explain?'

'What is it, honey?' Cat sits up and pats the space next to her on her lounger. 'Come and tell me everything.'

'Thank you, Cat.' I perch myself beside her. 'What's *urgent* is that James was so shocked to see me behind reception that the focus was all on that. So, now he thinks I've hooked up with Sébastien and I'm about to move half-way across the world to work for him. Plus, I don't even know what James is doing here, and—'

'*Whoa*, back up a bit, will you?' Amber sits up as well, finally interested. 'How do you know he thinks that, and why didn't you *ask* him what he's doing here?'

'He thinks I'm with Sébastien because it obviously *was* him in the doorway last night. He saw us up close and personal – James knows who Sébastien is. And I told him about the role because he quite understandably wanted to know why I was "playing hotel" when I'm not five years old. He caught me off guard so I didn't get a chance to say that I wasn't *with* Sébastien, or that the job location is flexible. Now he thinks I'm a terrible person.'

'Did he say that to you?' asks Cat.

'No. But he was weird and formal and kind of cold with me. He said "he'd see me around". I know exactly what that means.'

'Hmm, OK.' She grimaces. 'Makes sense based on what you've told us.'

'Yeah – for once,' says Amber.

'Do you have my bag with you so I can message him?' I ask Cat.

'No, sorry,' she says. 'I left it in my room. Your phone is locked in my safe.'

'I'll message him,' says Amber. 'See where he is and then you can go sort it out.'

'OK, sure.' I chew my lip anxiously. 'Hopefully he has his phone with him. And hopefully he replies.'

'We'll find out soon enough.' She taps out a message and sets her phone down beside her. 'So, as much as that's a bit of a cock up, I'm still not convinced you should have done a runner half-way through your slot on reception.'

'Sorry, I panicked. I already nearly messed things up with James before. Don't want to risk doing that again. He'll only give me so many chances, Amber.'

'Fair enough. What did you learn on reception?'

With nothing else to do but wait, I angle my face to the sun and consider her question. 'I learnt a lot about how the resort is run. And that Charnice is a superstar. She really connects with the guests and she *oozes* the company values. She's also so calm and unflappable. Didn't even flinch when this horrible man who's a regular guest was ripping into us.'

'That sounds awful.' Cat's eyes widen.

'It was. I saw the same man the other day. He's rich and entitled. Treats the staff like shit.'

'The resort shouldn't stand for that.'

'No, they shouldn't. But apparently, he wasn't as bad before.' I fill them in on what Charnice told me.

'You realise there's a good chance this guy's going to be at your presentation on Monday,' says Amber. 'If he's got that much power and influence.'

'That thought has already crossed my mind.' My hand goes to my stomach, which is churning unpleasantly. 'I take it James hasn't replied yet?'

'No, not yet.'

With these two issues weighing heavily on me, I feel quite deflated. It must show because Cat puts her arms around me and gives me a big hug, which I lean into.

'Don't let this stuff throw you off track, honey,' she says. 'By Monday we'll have you ready for anything – even that nasty man. The issue with James will be resolved too. It's just a misunderstanding.'

'I hope you're right.' I sigh, closing my eyes.

'What's more interesting is why he's here in the first place,' says Amber.

'It's odd, isn't it?' I say.

'It sure is...' says Cat, who purses her lips as if she's trying to work it all out, then seems to quickly give up. 'Why don't you grab a lounger and lie here for a bit? Give that poor brain of yours a rest. There's nothing on your schedule till lunch now anyway.'

'Good idea.' I get up and commandeer the empty lounger next to her. 'Can I borrow some lotion? Didn't come prepared for sunbathing.'

Cat tosses the bottle across to me, and I apply the sunscreen while gazing out across the turquoise water, where a couple of windsurfers are balancing precariously on their boards. It's windier today than the previous days, making the water choppier and the waves taller – creating a bigger challenge for them.

Once I've lotioned-up, I pass the bottle back to Cat, and settle back on my lounger.

'*Ahh*... that's better. Think I need this downtime.'

I close my eyes and focus on nothing but the feeling of the warm rays on my skin. It feels good, and to my surprise, I'm able to park my personal dilemmas for now. In fact, I'm on the verge of nodding off when a high-pitched screech breaks through the quiet of the beach. Lifting my head, I see a huge muscular man holding a woman in a fireman's lift. He's cantering towards the water, with her pounding his back, shouting at him to put her down – much to the amusement of their holiday companions and other onlookers. It's all very good natured, but I can't help feeling embarrassed on the woman's behalf as she hangs there inelegantly with her backside on display.

Once the show is over, I'm settling back into my sunbathing, when I spot three bare chested men walking along the beach in our direction, chatting and laughing together. Squinting across at them, I do a sharp intake of breath and reach across to prod Cat on the shoulder.

'Is that him?'

She stares in the direction I'm pointing in. 'I think so...'

Amber sits up. 'That's him all right. Nice body. He's no Sébastien, but I doubt there are many men who'd rival his physique.' She turns to me. 'Well, what are you waiting for? Get over there.'

I puff out my cheeks, suddenly feeling immensely insecure. 'He's with his friends. What if he tells me to bugger off?'

'Then you can sleep with any other single man on this resort with a clear conscience.'

'Helpful, thanks.'

'Shut up and move your arse.'

'OK, wish me luck...' I get up from my lounger and straighten my beach dress.

'Good luck!' Cat calls after me.

I pick my way across the fine white sand towards James and his friends, who are closer to the shoreline.

'*James, hi,*' I call across to him when I'm close enough to do so.

He and his friends' look over and he appears to excuse himself, while they continue to walk on and come to a stop at enough of a distance to give us our privacy.

'Hi, Emma,' he says when we reach each other. 'Were you looking for me for something?'

He's still being overly polite and formal, which causes my confidence to waver. What if there's more to this than I'm aware of? What if something's changed in the last day and a bit and he's just not interested anymore? But then that would make no sense. *None* of this makes sense. *Why is he even here?*

'Can we talk?' I say. 'I need to explain something to you.'

'You don't owe me any explanations.' His demeanour remains cold and distant. 'My friends are also waiting for me. Can we do this later?'

It's perfectly clear to me that in this context, 'later' means 'never'. He wants me gone.

'Um... OK... I'll leave you in peace then,' I mumble. 'Sorry to have bothered you.'

'No problem. Have a good one.' He gives me the same curt nod he did at reception and walks away towards his waiting friends, leaving me standing alone and completely gutted.

Chapter Twenty-One

While watching James go, I glance across at Amber and Cat, who are making questioning gestures at me and indicating that I should go after him. I respond by throwing my hands up in my own gesture of 'what can I do?', then I let out the same frustrated cry from earlier – though at a much lower volume.

'*James, why are you here?*' I suddenly yell after him.

He stops and turns. 'This was always where I was coming on holiday. I wanted to surprise you – though I realise now that was a pretty stupid idea.'

'Why was it stupid?'

'Are you really asking that? Is it not obvious?'

I take a few tentative steps towards him. 'Because you saw me dancing with Sébastien last night? It was just a dance. Nothing more.'

'That's not how it looked from where I was standing. And I was *fifteen* feet away.'

He's not wrong. In fact, he appears to be confirming what I've been thinking myself. That there is chemistry between me and Sébastien, but that's all it is: a raw biological connection. It's no match to what I've felt with James and he needs to know that.

'Look, James, Sébastien's a great-looking charismatic man. I'm not sure there's a straight woman in the world who'd—'

'You don't need to offer a defence.' His face is now betraying the hurt he's clearly feeling. 'I get it. He's hot. You couldn't resist. I was supposed to be hundreds of miles away, and I have no claim to you anyway.'

'Nothing has happened, James. *Nothing.*' I take another couple of steps towards him. 'Sébastien did ask me to dinner, and I went, but only because I wound myself up worrying that you'd hook up with some hot blonde on your own holiday. When I thought he was making moves on me, I put a stop to it, because I didn't want to ruin things with you. Then it turned out he only wanted to talk about the job... I actually made a bit of a tit of myself.'

James studies me, and I remove my sunglasses so he can look me in the eye and (hopefully) trust that I'm telling the truth.

'Not like you to do that.' He keeps his expression neutral, but I know I've won him over. I can see a hint of the lovely man I enjoyed a date and a knee-trembling kiss with at the airport sneaking through.

'Very funny.' I playfully wrinkle my nose, before slipping my sunglasses back on and turning serious again. 'Please tell me you believe me.'

'Shall we take a walk?' he says and I nod.

James calls to his friends to say he'll catch them up in a bit, and I signal a similar message to Cat and Amber. They respond with four enthusiastic thumbs up. Amber then punctuates her message by jumping up and making thrusting gestures, which I sincerely hope James does not see.

We make our way down the beach, and I take off my flip-flops so I can enjoy the feel of the gentle sweeping tide chasing my feet while we wander along the shoreline.

'So, this job thing?' James prompts me.

'Yeah, as I said, that was Amber doing her usual.' I roll my eyes and he laughs. 'Sébastien wasn't going to consider me for it, because he was already well through the selection process. But then he had a change of heart and offered me a chance – as long as I do the interview while I'm here.'

'*Wow*. That's quite something. And a bit weird having to do it here – on your holiday.'

'Tell me about it. I'm sacrificing nearly half my time here to do it. But I think it's worth it. Amber and Cat are helping me prepare, and I'm still able to make the most of the resort, so it's not that bad.'

'Fair enough. And this job, if you get it. Is it based out here in the Caribbean?'

'No. That's the great thing. It doesn't matter where it's based. The company is geographically dispersed and the Head Office staff tend to work remotely. I'd have to travel, but I can be based back home.'

'Right.' James removes his own flip-flops and joins me in the water. 'That's good news. And there's really nothing going on with Sébastien?'

I put a hand to my chest. 'Promise there's not. Believe me, I've been as confused as you about his intentions towards me. But after my initial wobble over what you were going to get up to when you were away, I was resolute that there would be no holiday romance, no matter what.'

'And now?'

'I mean it, James. Honestly.'

'And *I* mean... what about a holiday romance with me?' He stops and locks eyes with me, the corners of his mouth twitching.

Despite my sunglasses providing something of a barrier

between us, I feel myself redden from the intensity of his gaze. 'Well... for you I could make an exception.'

'I was hoping you'd say that.' James's face breaks into a satisfied grin and my breathing becomes shallow as he takes my hands in his, gently pulling me towards him. Then he leans in and kisses me, his sexy days old stubble tickling my face, while fireworks go off inside me. I melt into him, and within seconds, we're devouring each other hungrily. A cheer and a wolf-whistle comes from the distance, which I suspect is Amber.

Eventually, we break apart and continue to wander along the beach hand in hand, stealing delighted – and slightly bashful – glances at each other.

'Hey, you've got some explaining to do too,' I say. 'You told me you were going to the east coast of the US.'

He shrugs. 'This the east coast of the US – sort of. Just off it anyway.'

'*Come on.*'

'OK, a few hundred miles off it and a completely different country, but it's not *that much* of a stretch.'

I shake my head to signal that he's not getting away with such a poor excuse.

'Suppose I'd better 'fess up then.' His expression turns sheepish. 'I might have influenced you and your friends a little when it came to choosing your holiday destination. But in my defence, I fancied the pants off you, and I figured if you wouldn't give me the time of day back home, this tropical paradise might lower your barriers a bit.'

'*What are you like?* Could you not be sacked for that?'

'Only if it didn't work out and you reported me – which for about twelve hours there, I thought could be a distinct possibility.'

'Aww, no. I'd never do that. I think it was sweet.' I squeeze his hand, my heart melting at this admission.

'Do me a favour and don't be using descriptions like that in front of my friends – or yours for that matter. You'll ruin my rep.'

'*Ha*, OK. Your rep is safe. So, was any of it true? About it being a thirtieth birthday celebration for you and your friends – who I'm assuming currently think I'm a horrible person.'

'Don't worry, I'll fix that.' James nudges me guiltily.

'Which means they do.'

'They're my bros, they always have my back. But they'll see how great you are. And yes, the part about the birthday celebration is true. I get a discount through my job, so we decided we'd go all out for this one. Vegas isn't really our style, and we fancied a beach holiday, so here we are.'

'*Nice*. And you know Sébastien because...?'

'I don't know him as such. I know *of* him. We sell holidays to all his resorts, so it's my job to know who he is.'

'That's what I figured. I can introduce you to him properly when we next see him.'

'Are you sure you want to risk that?' James raises his eyebrows questioningly.

'Why? I already told you there was nothing going on.'

'I mean in case *I* fall for his charms. Who's to say he won't turn *me?*'

'Oh, stop it.' I give him an affectionate push, and he takes the opportunity to sweep me into another delicious kiss. 'Wait...' I pull away from him suddenly. 'Did Lottie know you were coming here?'

He looks cagey. 'I might have told her... and swore her to secrecy.'

'Eh, since when does Lottie's loyalty to you take precedence over hers to me?'

'Since she realised that I'm the right man for you?'

'Or...?'

'Since I got down on my knees and begged?'

'That sounds more plausible.' I laugh.

Looking along the beach towards Cat and Amber, I can see that they're getting their stuff together. Amber spots me and signals towards a non-existent watch on her wrist, and I give her a wave of acknowledgement in return.

'That's my cue to go,' I say to James. 'I've got interview practice over lunch.'

'Sounds fun. Where are you eating?'

'I'm not telling you that. Last thing I need is you and your buddies turning up to watch me get grilled harder than my lunch.'

'That obvious, was it?' He gives a sly smile.

'I may not know you well yet, but I've already got a sense of how that mind ticks. Anyway, I'd better get going.' I squeeze his hand again, before detaching myself from it. 'See you later on? We'll be at the pool in the afternoon – apparently with me doing some "personal development".'

'What does that involve?'

'No idea. I've been told to leave it to the experts.'

'Sure. We have no plans this afternoon, so we'll swing by and you can meet the lads.'

He plants a delicious goodbye kiss on my lips, and I head off in the direction of my friends, my stomach swishing and swirling with all sorts of giddy gooey feelings, which is a nice change to the nausea that's taken over recently. *He's here.* He's *really* here. And I haven't cocked things up. Interview aside, this is an *amazing* holiday.

By the time I reach Cat and Amber, I'm already lost in a daydream about James and I dancing to one of Lola's songs, with Lola happily serenading us because I'm lost in James's eyes, and not Sébastien's.

'That seemed to work out well.' Cat interrupts my little fantasy, her face brimming with excitement.

'Yes, it did.' I waggle my eyebrows in response. 'I'll fill you in over lunch.'

'*After* your interview practice,' says Amber.

'*OK, Mum.*' I duck out the way as she flicks her towel at me.

We set off up the beach, and as I'm disappearing back into the same delectable daydream, a thought strikes me. Was it such a good idea inviting James and his buddies to the pool later? With this morning's prep turning out to be what it was, who knows what hell on earth Amber has in store for me this afternoon. Or whether I'll come out of it with my dignity intact.

∾

We decide to eat lunch in the buffet restaurant (the same place where we have breakfast) so that we can focus on my interview practice without being continually interrupted.

As soon as our bums hit our seats, my grilling starts. Amber and Cat fire question after question at me, pausing only to order drinks and fill our plates. When I say it's both of them, it's mainly Amber. They're not so much 'good cop, bad cop' as 'good cop, nail-your-ass-to-the-wall cop'. This goes on right through our first two courses, until I almost can't take any more.

'Are we done yet?' I wipe away the rivers of sweat trickling down my forehead and push my plate aside. 'Your questioning style is making me dangerously dehydrated, Amber.'

She shrugs. 'I'm giving it to you tough so you can cope under pressure on the day.'

'I get that, but we've been at it for an hour. Surely that's enough for now.'

'You're doing really well, honey. You should feel pleased about that.' Cat offers me some much-needed praise. 'Amber, how about we stop there? Emma still needs to complete the rest of her prep today. Let's not exhaust her in one sitting.'

'Fine,' she says. 'We'll leave it at that.'

'Thank you.' I glug at my water like a parched gun dog.

'And you *are* doing well. You're not flapping like you normally do.'

'*Eh*... thanks... I think.'

'That was a *compliment*.' Amber's eyes go to the ceiling. 'Surely you can recognise that.'

'Yeah, but only because you had such a low opinion of me in the first place.'

'No, I didn't. But I do know what your weaknesses are. Plus, you've already indicated yourself that being put under pressure is an area where you struggle.'

'That's true.'

'I'm saying you're on the road to success here. Pay attention to *that* part, all right?'

'All right.' I allow a small swell of pride to push through. 'Can we celebrate by me telling you about what happened with James earlier?'

'*Yes, please*,' says Cat. 'I'm dying to hear this.'

Finally able to relax, I sit back in my seat and fill them in on every little detail. Cat is riveted from beginning to end: her reactions priceless as she emits shock, disappointment and hope at all the right moments. It's as if she's watching the climax of a romcom unfold right in front of her. She even squeals with delight over and over when I get to our kiss and all that happened after that.

Amber seems a bit bored by the detail, but when I'm finished, she sums up the situation as 'boss'. Though she's not one for the mushy stuff, I know she's a fan of James. She wanted us to get together from the moment she clapped eyes on him, which was well before I would even credit him as a decent human being. How wrong I was.

'I still can't believe he's here.' I beam at my friends.

'Neither can I,' says Cat. 'Makes me kind of wish that Mike was here too. Do you wish your hubby was here, Amber?'

She scoffs. 'Not even slightly. That's the difference between you two and me. You're all gooey-eyed and loved-up because you haven't yet had to pick up their stinking socks or clean their skid marks off the toilet.'

Cat and I make repulsed faces.

'I can't imagine Rich doing those things,' says Cat.

'Oh, he doesn't,' she says with a self-satisfied smile. 'He's always had better standards than that. But how many women do you know whose live-in partners' or husbands' home habits aren't a major talking point?'

'What a way to spoil the romance, Amber.' I glower at her.

'All I'm saying is that your blokes are on their best behaviour right now and real life is a far cry from that. That's why I'm happy to have a husband-free holiday.'

'Well, anyway...' says Cat, 'As Emma and I *are* in that blokes-on-their-best-behaviour-hormones-flying-all-over-the-place phase, we shall make the most of it.'

'Yes, we shall!' I whoop. 'Although... does it bother you, James having turned up? I was so busy getting excited about it, I overlooked that it's yet another thing hijacking our girls holiday together.'

'Not at all,' Cat reassures me. 'James being here isn't going to ruin things. He's here with his friends too, so he'll need to spend time with them. Maybe we can all hang out together a bit. Might be fun.'

'Provided his friends aren't dickheads,' Amber throws in.

'Which I'm sure they won't be if James is anything to go by,' says Cat.

'OK, great.' I'm relieved by Cat and Amber's easy-going nature. 'They're coming by the pool when we're there later, so we'll meet them then.'

I watch my friends carefully for any sign that I should be concerned about my next interview prep task, but there isn't a hint of anything unnerving. Perhaps it will be OK after all and my time on reception was the worst of it.

Chapter Twenty-Two

After lunch, Cat and Amber go straight to the pool, while I divert to my suite to get changed into my swimwear and pick up my stuff. I quickly apply some extra make up – mascara, eyeliner and lip gloss, to ensure I'm looking ultra kissable – then I throw my sun cream, makeup for any additional touch-ups and a book into my beach bag and head out again.

Joining the girls by the vast, glistening lagoon-style swimming pool, I strip down to my bikini, perch myself on the edge of lounger they've saved for me and begin the laborious process of applying my sun cream.

'I'm so ready for this,' I say. 'Can I maybe have half an hour of downtime before we start whatever this afternoon's task involves?'

'Sure, why not,' says Amber from her face-down horizontal position. 'Better to have you fresh and ready for it.'

'Exactly what I was thinking. You two could probably do with a bit of a break from the prep too.' I smile at Cat, who looks super relaxed and simply nods in agreement.

Returning to my lotion application, I'm rubbing it into my

legs when two young children run past me with water guns, spraying them at each other, and soaking me in the process.

'*Argh... that's freezing.*' I jump up and leap out of the way while they continuing their boisterous play battle along the poolside, seemingly oblivious to what they've done. 'Surely a resort like this doesn't allow water fights round the pool.'

'What they gonna do?' says Amber.

'Um... tell them off?'

I dry myself down and resume applying my sun cream, but within moments, the same children are back, acting out an imaginary duel on the bridge that crosses the narrowest point of the pool – and which unfortunately is right across from me.

I retreat behind my lounger, hoping they'll move on again. However, they seem to enjoy the added excitement the bridge brings to their game, and after a minute or so, I decide that, as long as they stay there, it's probably safe to return to my spot.

'Want me to do your back, honey?' Cat offers.

'Yes, please.' I scooch to the end of my lounger to make things easier for her, and as I hand her the bottle, a powerful jet of water hits me square in the face.

'*Arghhh! What the hell?*'

Snatching up my towel, I frustratedly wipe the water from my face just in time to see the two children giggling and pointing in my direction, then darting across the bridge to the other side of the pool.

'*You'd better run!*' I shout after them.

'Oh gosh, honey, are you OK?' says Cat. 'That was... unfortunate.'

'*The wee bastards.* Did you see them laughing there? If they do that one more time, I'll—'

'You'll what?' Amber tips up her sunglasses long enough to shoot me a sceptical look, and I'm about to back chat her when Cat intervenes.

'Let's get some sun cream on you before you burn.' She squeezes lotion onto my back and rubs it in.

'Thank you. At least someone around here is helpful. Is my mascara running?' I turn so she can inspect my face and she grimaces.

'It is, yeah. That was quite a soaking you got. I have a compact mirror in my bag if you want to use it?'

'Nah, it's fine. I'll nip to the ladies once you're done. Thanks anyway.'

'No probs. Do you know what time James and his friends are joining us?'

I shake my head. 'He didn't say.'

'Well, that's your sun cream done, so off you go.'

'Thanks, Cat.'

Grabbing my beach bag, I hurry along the poolside, watching out for James as I go. I *do not* want to bump into him and his mates while looking like I lost an argument with a garden hose.

When I reach the mirror in the ladies toilets, I gasp on seeing that Cat was being kind. It wouldn't take too much imagination to think I'd secured the starring role in a new film called *Zombie Vacation*. Using a wet paper towel, I wipe away the heavy black track marks under my eyes, reapply eye makeup and pull my partially soaked hair into a (purposefully) messy ponytail.

Once I'm happy that I'm presentable again, I head back to rejoin my friends, and as my lounger comes into view, it looks like someone is on it. Confused, I stop and double check my bearings, but I'm looking at the right spot. I can see Cat and Amber stretched out on their own loungers, but there's a woman lying face down on mine. And on closer inspection, I can also see that my resort-branded towel and clothes have been discarded on the ground. *How rude!*

Unsure of what to do, I hover above the woman, hoping

she'll notice me and voluntarily move out of guilt or embarrassment, but she doesn't even twitch – meaning I have no choice but to move on or speak up.

'Um... excuse me?' I keep my tone as polite as possible. 'I think you're on my lounger.'

She doesn't look up. Doesn't even seem to notice me.

'*Hello*... excuse me, please?'

The woman finally twigs that I'm talking to her and cranes her neck so she can see me. 'Yes?'

It's clear from her expression that she's irritated by the disturbance.

'I'm afraid you're on my lounger,' I say. 'That's my stuff on the ground. I only nipped to the toilets.'

The woman turns over and looks me up and down. 'It was free when I got here. Not my fault you forgot to put your stuff on it.'

'No, but that's the thing... my stuff *was* on it. You must have removed it.'

'*Excuse me?* I didn't touch anything. As I said, the lounger was free.'

I hesitate, the discomfort of this interaction making me want to give up and walk away. Almost but not quite. She's clearly stolen my lounger and I want to be next to my friends.

'It *wasn't* free though,' I try again. 'My towel and clothes were on it.'

'Are you calling me a liar?'

'No, of course not.' I feel my cheeks start to burn. 'But my stuff was there before I left, so... *someone* must have moved it.'

The woman scowls, making it abundantly clear that I'm pissing her off. 'Well, if *someone* moved your stuff, then I suggest you go and have a word with that *someone*, and leave me in peace.'

Exasperation and a sense of injustice rears within me. She has *obviously* seen that there are no other loungers available and taken mine for herself, rudely discarding my things in the process. I glance across at Cat and Amber, hoping for some support, but they're both lying face down, either asleep or unaware of the scene playing out beside them.

'*I'd appreciate it if you'd get out of my sun.*' The woman takes another verbal swipe at me at me, this time in an even more hostile tone.

Cowed by her aggression, I give in and go in search of another lounger. Luckily, a young couple are packing up not too far along the poolside, so I wait until they leave and then set myself up in their spot. I'm annoyed that I'm now separated from my friends, especially because we're meant to be doing my interview prep shortly. But as there's little I can do about it, I might as well enjoy what free time I have left.

Once I'm settled again, I take my book out of my beach bag and attempt to lose myself in it, but I find it difficult to relax. Not surprising really, given what has gone down in the last twenty or so minutes.

Discarding my book, I opt for some people watching instead and it's a good choice. In no time at all, I'm feeling more relaxed from simply drinking in the 'summery' scene around me: couples, friends and families frolicking merrily in the pool; people strolling past sipping rainbow-coloured frozen drinks against the luscious backdrop of the azure blue sky, palm trees and other tropical shrubbery. The chill beats floating across the omnipresent sea breeze from the speakers of the outdoor entertainment system also enhance the holiday ambience. It's a mood lifter all right. An infectious atmosphere of happiness and contentment. In fact, I become so lost in the loveliness of it all that I almost miss the empty lounger next to me being commandeered by a new occupier: a woman around my age with long blonde hair wearing an ankle-length blue beach dress.

I nod politely at her and resume my people watching.

However, after a minute or two, I become aware of a sniffing noise coming from her direction. Assuming she's got allergies or something, I pay her little attention, until she makes a noise that sounds like a hippopotamus choking on its lunch. I glance across and see her lifting her sunglasses and wiping her eyes, which are unmistakably red and puffy. She's crying.

'Hey, are you OK?' I ask, without thinking.

'Oh... yes... I'm fine. Sorry.'

She seems embarrassed that I've clocked her emotional state, and this appears to upset her even more. Her body shudders as she tries and fails to quell her distress.

'*Goodness*, you're not OK at all.' I sit up and give her my full attention.

'I'm... s... sorry,' she stutters, between sobs. 'This isn't... me. I'm... being stupid.'

Taking her willingness to engage with me as a positive sign, I decide that it's safe to offer her some support.

'I know we've never met, but do you want to talk about it? You can tell me to get lost if you want – I won't be offended at all – but I get the feeling you could do with a friendly ear.'

She stops sobbing momentarily and looks at me. 'You're Scottish.'

'Yes, I am. And you are too.' I smile kindly at her, understanding the statement: one of relief at having found a 'kindred spirit' during her moment of need.

'I'm from... Aberdeen.'

'I live in Edinburgh. My name's Emma. What's yours?'

'Fiona.'

'It's nice to meet you, Fiona. Though I wish it had been under better circumstances.'

'Me... too.' She lets out a heavy, faltering sigh.

Sensing that she'll be OK with some physical contact, I move myself onto her lounger to sit beside her and put my arm around her while she silently works through her turmoil. Her almost hopeless demeanour reminds me of how I felt after my break up with my ex, Dave, a few weeks back. It's a heartbroken cry – no question.

'This is my honeymoon,' Fiona says eventually. 'It was meant to be the holiday of a lifetime. Us starting a new adventure together. I was so excited to become Mrs Lawson... and now... now I find out he never wanted to get married. Says I pressured him into it... that *everyone* pressured him into it.' She looks at me with devastated eyes. 'But I didn't. I would never do that. It was all in his head. He wound *himself* up.'

I keep quiet, giving her the space to vent as much as she needs, only speaking when it's clear that she's looking for input or emotional support from me.

'Could it be a touch of post-wedding anxiety?' I ask and she frowns.

'I don't think so. There were signs before the wedding. I just didn't want to see them. I also think he might be cheating on me.'

I've been there, I think to myself, but I don't verbalise this. Being cheated on by your boyfriend of four years is one thing, but by your new husband is quite another.

'What makes you think he's cheating?' I ask instead.

'He's secretive with his phone. I'm not like that because I have nothing to hide. He knows my passcode, my email password, everything.'

'But he won't share his with you.'

'No. I mean, I haven't asked him to. I'd never ask that. It's more that he doesn't volunteer it and he always has his phone with him. He's also stayed out all night a few times in recent months. Tells me he's slept on his mate's couch, but why would he choose to do that? We live ten minutes further down the road.'

'I'm really sorry you're feeling like this on your honeymoon.'

I give her a sympathetic squeeze. 'Have you tried talking to him?'

'Yes.' She blows her nose on a tissue she's found in her beach bag. 'But every time it turns into an argument. It's like he resents me for everything.'

'Well, I'm sorry to say it, but it doesn't sound like he's behaving like a grown up – and certainly not a husband.'

'Maybe it *is* all my fault.' Fiona hangs her head miserably. 'Maybe I did unintentionally push him into this, and that drove him to—'

'Hey, let's not have any of that,' I say. 'You haven't forced him into anything. Or driven him to anything. He's a big boy who's perfectly capable of making his own decisions. If he's playing the victim and he's allowed himself to get married without wanting to, then I'm afraid that's on him. You're not responsible for his decisions or his behaviour. And you certainly don't deserve to be treated like this.'

'You sound like you're talking from experience.'

'I am. Sort of. I was living with an arrogant pig until recently. He dumped me in a very cruel way and then it turned out he was cheating. I blamed myself – as you're doing right now – but ultimately, I realised that I'm better off without him.'

'Good for you.' She gives a weak smile. 'I wish I was that strong.'

'You're stronger than you know,' I assure her. 'But you won't find that out until you're really tested. Could you perhaps find a way to work it through with your husband in a safe environment – maybe somewhere public? So you can ask the questions you want answers to without him blowing up at you.'

'You know, I never thought of that.' Fiona lifts her head and looks at me, the faintest glimmer of hope in her eye. 'I'm going to tell Neil I want to talk over a drink in the bar. He'll never make a scene there. Thank you, Emma. You've been so kind letting me vent like this.'

'Not at all. We ladies have to stick together, eh? Whichever way this goes, remember it'll all work out in the long run. You deserve to be with a man who adores you, and if that man isn't your new husband, then it will be someone else.'

'You're right, again. I *do* deserve more. Thank you for helping me see that. I'm going to do it now. Wish me luck.'

'Good luck. You've got this.'

I feel sad for Fiona as I watch her gather her things and leave the poolside, but at least she's looking more together than when she arrived. It must be awful being in her position – especially having it happen while away from home.

While contemplating this, I become aware of some activity behind me. I turn to see what's going on, and before I have time to register anything, I'm hit square in the face by two powerful jets of water – and this time there's no question that the two little shits have done it on purpose.

'*Arghh! Are you kidding me? Right, that's it...*' I quickly wipe my face with my towel and take off across the poolside after them.

Chapter Twenty-Three

'*Come here, you wee monkeys!*'

I'm barefoot, tearing across the grass in hot pursuit of my miniature assailants, when I hear someone shout my name. Fuelled by the unwillingness to allow the little monkeys to escape, I ignore whoever is calling me. That is, until I hear my name a second time and come to my senses. Halting suddenly, I slowly turn in the direction of the voice and my heart sinks.

'James, hi.'

I flush heavily from being caught in this compromising position, while probably once again modelling the look of the undead. I swipe at my under eyes and hope for the best.

'What's going on?' He regards me with a quizzical expression. 'You looked like you were ready to throttle those kids.'

'No... I wasn't... I was... *Oh, what the hell.*' I let out a peep of frustration. 'Not sure you can judge me any more than you already are. *They're wee buggers!* Soaked me three times with their water pistols – and the third time was definitely deliberate. They took aim and fired like they were a professional hit squad.'

'I see. That's not acceptable. But... what exactly were you planning to do to them if you caught them?'

'I... erm... don't know. Is it not OK to grab them by the scruff of their necks and march them to their parents anymore?' I decide that humour is the only way out of this one.

'Pretty sure that would land you in a cell for the night.' James's mouth twitches with amusement.

'Right, well maybe I'll leave them be then.'

'Probably for the best. Want to meet my mates?'

He jerks a thumb towards two blokes standing about twenty feet away, who seem to be watching our exchange with interest. I want to die on the spot. It's bad enough that James witnessed me in this compromising situation, never mind them too – and especially after their first impression of me wasn't the best. James is at least familiar with my unfortunate habit of embarrassing myself in public.

'*Shit*. I can't believe they saw that.' I self-consciously swipe at my under eyes again.

'They won't judge you. Not too much anyway,' he adds with a chuckle.

'That really doesn't help. Let me go clean myself up and I'll see you by the pool.'

'Good plan. Now can I trust you not to take off after those children again the minute my back is turned?'

'*Too soon, James.*' I shoot him faux daggers – while stifling a giggle at my own expense – and stalk off towards the pool, my face burning with humiliation.

Once I've cleaned myself up for a second time, I make my way back across to Amber and Cat, noting with irritation that the woman who took my lounger has already vacated it. They sit up as I approach.

'Where have *you* been?' says Amber.

'Are you OK, honey?' Cat appears to spot my less than cheerful demeanour.

'No. I'm having a crap afternoon.' I plonk myself down on the empty lounger. 'After those little brats soaked me here, some nasty woman dumped my stuff on the ground and stole my lounger. Then after I moved, the wee bastards soaked me again – on purpose – and I went after them, only to be caught doing so by James.'

Amber snorts with laughter. 'You went after them? What were you planning to do?'

'That's exactly what James asked me.' I huff.

'And?'

'I don't know. Talk to their parents, maybe? Anyway, the point is... I'm not managing to relax at all, so shall we do my interview prep?'

Amber shoots Cat a look I can't decipher and Cat seems to subtly shake her head.

'What's going on?' I glance from one to the other. '*Tell me*.'

Amber appears to weigh up what Cat was communicating to her before seemingly disregarding it. 'Emma, I've got something to tell you that's not going to improve your mood.'

'Oh god, what now?'

'I went by reception to ask about excursions for our remaining days after your interview and Charnice told me there's been an error with our reservation. Apparently, she had been looking for you to talk to you about it.'

'What kind of error?'

'It turns out they've only got us booked in until tomorrow and the resort is full. They're not sure how it happened, but it makes no difference because they're moving us to another one.'

'*They're what?*' I'm so shocked I can hardly take this in. 'They can't do that. We've paid for those suites. I have the paperwork to prove it. They should re-locate the other guests who are arriving, not throw us out.'

'That's what I said.' Amber holds her hands up in apparent frustration. 'But apparently, they can't. Or they won't. They are arranging a car to ferry you back and forth on the day of your interview though, and we're getting a refund for the days they're not putting us up – so that's something, at least.'

'I don't believe this.' I clamp my hands against my head. 'I don't want a refund. I want to while away my days on *this* resort, drinking champagne in The Cave, enjoying the amazing food and the surroundings, and... it means we'll be on a different resort to James. Maybe we should speak to Sébastien.'

'Do you think that's a good idea?' says Amber. 'Because I don't.'

'Probably not. *Ugh*, this sucks.' My miserable gaze lands on Cat who looks as pained as I feel.

'*Ladies*, how are you all?'

I look up and see that a grinning James has approached without us realising.

'What's with the glum faces?' he asks.

'It's nothing.' Amber waves his question away. 'We're good. How are you? *Hi, guys!*' she calls to James's friends who are hovering behind him.

James beckons for them to join the conversation. 'Lads... meet Emma, Amber and Cat. Ladies, this is Rob, and this is Tyler.' He points out which friend is which, and they give a friendly nod and a 'hi' in return.

Rob is skyscraper tall and just as lean, with bright blue eyes and strawberry blonde hair. He looks like he'd be successful as a basketball player or a high jumper. Tyler is closer to average height like James, with dark afro hair and gorgeous espresso-coloured eyes. They both seem up for some chat, which is unfortunate, given how disappointed I'm currently feeling from Amber's revelation.

'Good to meet you all.' I attempt a welcoming smile, but it falls flat.

'What's up, Emma?' James sits on the lounger beside me. 'Are you still upset about those kids? Want me to buy a bigger water gun and get revenge?'

I chuckle hopelessly at his joke. 'No, it's not that. We've just found out there's been an error with our booking and we have to move to a different resort tomorrow.'

'*Huh?* You're kidding, right?'

'I'm not. Charnice from reception spoke to Amber about it. They have our departure date wrong in their system.'

'Mistakes happen, but throwing you out is *bang* out of order and not at all in the spirit of my employer's relationship with Paradis Resorts. I'll go and speak to—'

'There's no need for that, James,' Cat jumps in. 'Emma won't want to make a fuss.'

'She's right, I don't.' I put a calming hand on his arm to emphasise this. 'Not when I have my interview coming up.'

James sits thoughtfully for a moment, then shakes his head determinedly and gets up. 'No, I'm sorry, I've got to sort this out. I booked this trip for you, and I'm not having this on my conscience.'

He strides off across the grass towards reception and I look to Amber and Cat to gauge their reactions, which are quite different to what I expected. Instead of Amber cheering James on and Cat looking deeply uncomfortable on my behalf, they seem to be caught in a bickering match.

'Amber, this has gone *too* far.' Cat sounds uncharacteristically furious with her. 'You need to stop it *right now*.'

'Stop what?' My eyes narrow at Amber. 'What have you done?'

'All right, all right. Keep your knickers on, both of you.' Amber rolls her eyes in exasperation. 'Be right back.'

To my surprise, she hops off her lounger and takes off after

James, only to return with him a few minutes later. He's laughing and joking with her, which confuses me even more.

'What on earth is going on, Amber?' I demand as they rejoin us, then I remember James's friends. 'Rob, Tyler, please grab a perch on Cat and Amber's loungers – or feel free to give us a wide berth if you don't want to get involved with whatever *this* is.'

They grin at each other and shake their heads.

'I only wish we had popcorn,' says Tyler.

'Your friends seem well-matched to you,' I say to James, who simply shrugs in agreement. 'OK, Amber, fess up. If the real reason we're getting banished from this resort is because of your ridiculous antics, I want to know now.'

'What? You think *I've* got us thrown out?' she says. 'That's hilarious.'

'But not altogether unrealistic, given your track record.'

James and his friends share a collective smirk, which I take as a point for me.

'*Tell her,*' Cat commands.

'OK.' Amber sighs as if we've pressured her into spending the rest of the holiday teetotal. 'We're not being relocated tomorrow. I made it up.'

'*You made it up?*' I'm flabbergasted at this admission. 'Why would you fabricate a story like that?'

'It was part of your interview prep.'

'How is telling me a big fat lie, and making my already crappy afternoon worse, part of helping me prepare for my interview?'

'It was for you personal development slot. I set up a few scenarios so I could observe you in action and then give you feedback.'

'You were *assessing* me?' I glance at James, who I can tell is trying his best to look appalled, but is clearly finding this all very amusing. 'Amber, I was gutted at the thought of us having to move resorts. Especially after the crappy afternoon I've had already. You didn't think that maybe I'd been tested enough?'

'*Ahem*...' Cat clears her throat in a blatant signal to Amber, who this time seems to accept defeat.

'I set it all up,' she says. 'The whole afternoon.'

My mouth drops open in shock, while James, Rob and Tyler look like they've been told a new national holiday has been announced to celebrate beer and football.

'You mean the soakings from those kids? The woman who stole my lounger? Fiona? *Wow*... Fiona was one hell of an actress.' I become momentarily distracted.

'Who's Fiona?' Amber appears confused.

'The woman who thought her husband was cheating.'

'Ah, her. No, that was what I'd call a bonus roll. When I clocked you chatting with her, I sneaked across and eavesdropped on your conversation.'

She looks so proud of herself that I feel the urge to wipe the smug look off her face.

'So, basically you ruined my day for your own entertainment?'

Her expression becomes defiant. '*No, that's not it*. As I already said, it was a live experiment to assess you in action. It was very carefully put together, and I got a lot of insight from it – insight that'll help you prepare for your interview.'

I'm about to hurl back another biting retort, when I remember my delighted audience. No matter how misguided Amber's actions were, I don't want to come across to James and his friends as ungrateful and unable to take a joke. Instead, I take a deep breath, and aim for the moral high ground.

'Fine. If you think it'll help then I look forward to your feedback – which I'll receive when?'

'Attagirl.' Amber smiles sweetly at me, making me want to throw her tiny arse in the pool. 'We'll do it over dinner.'

'How about we go for a swim?' suggests Cat, in a blatant attempt to move us into calmer waters
almost literally .

'Good idea.' James jumps up and pulls off his T-shirt.

My eyes land on his muscular chest and toned arms, and it's exactly what I need to bring me out of my funk. There's nothing I want more right now than to be cavorting in the pool with him like all the other couples I was watching earlier. Amber has crossed a line all right – but I'll deal with her later.

Chapter Twenty-Four

Half an hour later, all is (temporarily) forgotten, and I'm in pure bliss as the cool, topaz blue pool water laps gently around my shoulders. James and I have broken away from our group for coconut mojitos and a little private time by the swim-up bar, leaving Cat, Amber, Tyler and Rob to get to know each other better at the other end of the pool.

The flirty banter is flowing, but we haven't yet made physical contact, and to say I'm craving it is a massive understatement. James looks so sexy, his hair wet and sort of slicked back, water droplets glistening on his muscular shoulders. My brain is practically screaming at him to take my hand, put his arms around me, kiss me – *anything*.

'So, what's the story with you and Lottie?' He casually sips at his cocktail while leaning against the edge of the pool. 'I didn't realise you weren't related until something she said the other day made me twig.'

'Did your mum and dad not say?' I cock my head in surprise. 'She was my next-door neighbour when I was a kid. I used to sneak into her garden and read in her shed to get peace from my parents.'

'You were hiding from them? Why was that?'

'Because they were horribly overbearing. Still are – they treat me like I'm eight years old and incapable of making my own decisions. They're not bad people or anything,' I quickly add to stop him drawing the wrong conclusions. 'They're just too much. Think it's partly because I'm an only child.'

'Sounds plausible.'

'Anyway, Lottie was a recluse. She'd lost her granddaughter and daughter in a short space of time: cancer then suicide.'

'*Oof.*' James winces. 'I'm so sorry to hear that. It would be enough to make anyone lose faith in the world.'

'Totally. And she did. She had shut herself away and was resistant to the idea of having anything to do with me at first, but I wore her down.'

'Like *I* wore *you* down?' He waggles his eyebrows humorously.

'Ha, yeah, maybe.' I laugh. 'You were much more respectful though. You knew when to back off. I kind of forced my way into Lottie's life, with no thought for how she felt.'

'You were a kid. You didn't know any better. And it was probably the best thing that could have happened to her.'

'It was. And now she has your parents as friends too.'

'And me.'

'Yes, and you. She seems fond of you already. Don't you go breaking her heart, or I'll have to deal with you.'

'Are we still talking about Lottie now? Or you?' James grins, running a hand through his hair while my eyes follow this movement.

'Maybe a bit of both.' I nibble my bottom lip, uneasy with showing my vulnerability.

He reaches for my hand and pulls me towards him, the movement made smoother by the water. Once I'm close enough, he slips his arms around my waist and pulls me into him, kissing me gently at first, then more passionately as I relax into him. The water and the feeling of my bare flesh against his heightens my senses, making every touch more intense until I'm fizzing with arousal – and ready to drag him back to my suite for some proper action.

Eventually, we pull apart – slightly breathless – and smile shyly at each other, which makes me wonder if he's had the exact same thought as me.

'Shall we rejoin the others?' I suggest, not really wanting to but feeling like we should.

'In a bit. I want to hear more about your job interview. It sounds like a great opportunity.'

'It is. It's like it's the job I've been dreaming of that I never knew existed – if that makes any sense at all?'

'I get what you mean.' James nods.

I fill him in on how the opportunity came about, how my professional experience to date aligns with the role to a certain extent, how Amber oversold me and what's been requested of me for the interview.

'How are you feeling about the presentation?' he asks. 'That's always the toughest part.'

'Tell me about it.' I grit my teeth. 'I'm dreading that part most. I think I've got a good angle for it though, which I'm hoping I can pull off.'

'Great stuff. Talk me through it then.'

I hesitate. I wasn't expecting this request and I'm not sure I want to get into it with him.

'Um... would you mind if I didn't? It might sound odd after the stunt Amber pulled, but I'd rather stick to my prep with her and Cat so I stay as focused as possible and don't get sidetracked by differing opinions. They've put a lot into doing this for me.' I search James's face to gauge his reaction. The last thing I want is to start off on a bad footing.

'Hey, it's no problem.' He tickles me under my chin affectionately. 'You do what you need to do. From what you tell me, it sounds like you've a good chance at the job. I wouldn't want to get in the way of that. You might be punching a bit, as you say, but we all need to take a step into the unknown if we want to realise our potential.'

'You sound like you're quoting from a self-help book.'

'Is it not true?'

'It is.' I straighten my face and clear my throat. 'You're right. That's how I've been feeling for ages – like I need a proper chance to prove myself.'

'Well, hopefully this is it.' He smiles at me. 'I know you've got a solid team in Amber and Cat, but I'm happy to help out in any way I can too. I went through my fair share of interviews before I happily waved the corporate world goodbye, and started my Masters course.'

'In Astrophysics, you said?'

'That's the one.'

'So, what will you do when you graduate?'

'I'm not sure yet.' James rubs his jaw and I can tell that he's put a lot of thought into this exact question. 'I'm tempted to go on and do a PHD. That would likely lead to becoming a research fellow at a University, but I'll see what the job opportunities are like. I'm also interested in climatology. Or I could aim for something like a role in data science.'

'I have no idea about any of those jobs.' I shrug. 'But they all sound impressive.'

There's a comfortable silence between us, during which we sip at our drinks and James looks thoughtful.

'Hey, Emma, after our drink at the airport, you messaged me and asked if I had planned to give you my number the first night we met in the shop. You said you'd fill me in on our next date – does this count? I've been curious about why you would ask that.'

'Oh, um...' I shift awkwardly.

I'd forgotten about that message and now I'm caught off

guard. James obviously has no idea what it relates to – or that he's inadvertently asked a very personal question. Am I ready to tell him about my lottery win? I still barely know him, but I did indicate (without thinking it through, I now realise) that I'd fill him in, and I don't want to lie to him.

'You OK?' He gives me a little nudge. 'Kind of lost you there.'

'Sorry... I was... erm...'

What do I do? Should I put my trust in him? I mean, I've already met his parents, who are basically saints, and he was interested in me without knowing about the money, so it's not like I need to second guess his intentions. *Not right now anyway*, a voice in my head unhelpfully chips in.

'OK...' I pull myself up out of the water to sit on the poolside and pat the ground beside me, signalling for James to join me. He obliges, his arm muscles flexing sexily as he practically springs out of the pool and makes himself comfortable next to me. 'The reason I asked about your phone number was because something happened that night. Something big.'

'Bigger than tanking a two-grand bottle of vintage red from your ex's wine collection after he broke up with you?'

'Yes. And I need you to promise me that this stays between us.' I take his hand in mine in a gesture of seriousness.

'One hundred per cent, Emma. I know we haven't known each other long, but you can trust me.'

'I sense that, which is why I'm telling you.'

'Did something bad happen?' James suddenly looks concerned. 'Please tell me it wasn't in The Meadows. I *knew* I should have come with you, regardless of the fact you didn't want me to.'

'It's nothing like that, don't worry,' I reassure him. 'And the way I was that night, you were better off well clear of me.'

I cringe at the memory of me sobbing on the park bench

after Dave dumped me in such a vicious way – it seems incomprehensible now that I could cry over him, knowing what a selfish arsehole he is.

'So, what is it then?' he asks. 'You're really making me wait for this.'

'Sorry. I'll get to the point, which is... that night, the shopkeeper talked me into buying a lottery ticket and two weeks later I discovered I'd had a sizeable win – of over seven-hundred-and-fifty grand.'

'*Wow*.' James lets out an impressed whistle. 'That's massive. Bet you're glad that dickhead dumped you now.'

'I sure am. But there's more.'

'How can there be more? Did you then win the jackpot the following week?'

'No, silly.' I giggle. 'Are you not wondering where my message asking if you were going to give me your phone number comes in?'

I can almost see James's brain ticking over. 'I am now, but I'm coming up empty handed.'

'Not surprising really. Did you know that when you ripped up your number that night, you dropped part of it on the floor?'

'Nope. Wasn't paying that much attention... wait, are you about to tell me that you used my phone number to pick your lottery numbers?'

My mouth spreads into a smile. 'Spot on. You saw the state I was in that night. I was incapable of any logical thought – including choosing my own lottery numbers. So, I looked around for inspiration and spotted the scrunched-up piece of paper on the floor.'

James shakes his head as he struggles to comprehend all this. 'You're telling me that *my* phone number won you three quarters of a million pounds?'

'Exactly that. Well, part of your phone number did. The

first couple of numbers were obviously missing from it being torn in two.'

'Bloody hell. That's incredible... and... I call dibs.'

'Sorry, what?'

'I call dibs. You used my number. Surely that means I should get a cut.'

I blanch as it dawns on me that I may have prematurely put my trust in James.

'Oh... right. I guess I can see how you might '

'Emma, I'm kidding. *One hundred per cent kidding.*' He looks mildly horrified that I've taken him seriously. 'That really is incredible. I'm so pleased for you.'

Relief floods through me and the smile returns to my face. 'I'm kind of pleased for me too. Still can't quite believe it. Though for a bit there, I thought it was a curse.'

'How so?'

I fill James in on all the drama I went through after winning the money.

'That's partly why I couldn't see you for the great guy that you are back then,' I explain. 'I was all over the place.'

James puts his arm around my waist, pulling me close, and I nestle into him, enjoying the intimacy as well as the heat from the sun on my back.

'I think that's understandable, given what you've told me,' he says. 'Being unexpectedly dumped by a long-term partner is enough of a head wrecker without a substantial lottery win in the mix. People have lost their way because of far less.'

'Thanks for understanding.' I look up at him and he plants a kiss on my lips.

'Of course. And to be clear, I'm not interested in your money. I left a high paying job in the corporate sector to pursue a career in science, where the financial rewards are nowhere near the same. I hope that will reassure you.'

'I don't need reassuring. The way you've been with Lottie –

and so patient with me – I can tell I've found a good one.'

'Took you long enough,' he jokes, and I playfully splash him with water. 'So... I guess my phone number is your lucky number of sorts, which means that – by proxy – I'm your lucky charm. You might want to keep me around.'

'Oh, I'm planning to.'

This time it's me pulling James into a scrumptious – and rather handsy – snog. He tastes like chlorine and sun cream, and I couldn't be happier.

'How about the six of us have dinner together this evening?' says James, when we eventually disentangle ourselves, his arm now casually draped across my shoulders.

'Sure. Provided the others are getting on all right. Amber can be an acquired taste.'

He squints across at our friends, who have obtained a beach ball from somewhere and are batting it across the pool to each other, laughing and joking as they do.

'Looks like they're getting on fine.'

'Excellent... *oh, um...*' I hesitate on remembering what's planned for dinner.

'Ah yeah. Your personal development feedback. You don't want me there for that.'

'I don't want *me* there for that. It's going to be torturous.'

'I could give you moral support?' he suggests.

I consider this for a second, then my libido makes the decision for me. '*Ah, sod it.* I've made an arse of myself in front of you plenty of times already. Seems there's no putting you off.'

'That's the spirit.' He kisses the top of my head. 'Plus, my friends have already seen you chasing little kids around. How much worse can it get?'

'Don't remind me.'

'So, we're on?'

'Yeah, we're on.' I gulp as I say this. 'Let's give your buddies the full uncensored initiation experience.'

Chapter Twenty-Five

By seven p.m., Cat, Amber and I are sizzling in our evening outfits and we're on our way to meet the guys for dinner at Barcoa, the resort's barbeque and grill restaurant, which promises southern-style American soul food with a Bahamian twist. We wind our way along the path, between the tropical vegetation and open grassy stretches, the balmy heat of the day still lingering. The relaxed surroundings, as well as the delicious memories of my earlier stint in the pool with James, almost cause me to forget that I have a serious bone to pick with Amber. *Almost.*

'That stunt you pulled earlier was well out of order, Amber,' I say with the most authoritative tone I can muster.

'You'll thank me later.' Her reply is so casual that it has the instant effect of winding me up.

'I think you owe me an apology. You ruined my afternoon.'

'Yeah, it looked awful, you snogging James's face off in the pool. I'll pray for you.'

'I'm not referring to that part.'

'So, I *didn't* ruin your afternoon then. Only part of it.'

'Well, yes.' I frown. 'But that's not the point. It stressed me out, all those things going wrong like that.'

Amber stops and turns to me. 'Emma, that there – what you just said, is the *real* point. Why don't you wait for your feedback over dinner before you make a judgement about my actions?'

I look to Cat for support and she steps up.

'Amber, I think what Emma's trying to say is that you took things a bit far. And I agree with her.'

'Thank you, Cat.' I fix Amber with a pointed look.

'All you told me was that you had some pre-planned scenarios,' Cat continues. 'If I'd known they were going to antagonise Emma that much, I would have told you to tone things down.'

'Which is exactly why I didn't tell you what they were.' Amber shrugs as if this is obvious. 'The scenarios had to put her under pressure, otherwise the whole exercise would have been pointless.'

'Well, you certainly achieved that.' I fold my arms while I walk, still waiting for an apology that evidently isn't going to come.

'Look, if you want to do this on your own terms, Emma, feel free.' She holds up her hands in a clear threat of absolving herself from the responsibility. 'You wanted my help and I'm giving it to you – the best way I know how.'

'I know, and I'm grateful for that – for the most part. It's just that... at times it feels like I'm part of some messed up boot camp.'

'I told you the School of Amber would be tough. But it's effective. What's your alternative?'

'Oh, I don't know.' I kick a small stone on the path in frustration. 'I still want your help, but I also want to retain a sense of calm and dignity along the way. Is that too much to ask?'

'*Yes.*' Amber looks me square in the eye. 'This needs to be hard to prepare you for that interview and the job beyond it. And it's going to be even tougher to keep your eye on the prize now lover boy has turned up, so suck it up.'

Cat and I share a hopeless look and follow Amber along the path to the restaurant.

A few minutes later, we arrive at a large barn-like structure with what appears to be a retractable roof that's currently open to the elements. We're greeted by the maître'd, who leads us to our table (which is more like a luxury picnic bench), where James, Rob and Tyler are already seated.

'Evening all.' Amber is the first to greet them. 'Not got the shots in yet? Poor show.'

'Didn't know that was a requirement. We'll need to up our game.' Tyler grins at her and she seems delighted by this response.

'He's quick to adapt,' she says to me. 'You could learn something from that.'

'Whatever. Sorry about her.' I offer the guys an apologetic look as I sit down at the table. 'What Amber means is it's lovely to see you, and she's looking forward to spending the evening with you.'

'What is this? *Made in Chelsea?*' she hoots.

'It's called manners, Amber. You should try acquiring some.'

'Good one, coming from the woman who threatened to beat up a couple of eight-year-olds.'

There's a collective stifled snigger from around the table causing my cheeks to flame hotter than the restaurant grill.

'I wasn't going to beat them... *oh, you're insufferable.*'

I realise that I need to pipe down. I should have known better than to poke the bear – which tells me that, as much as this feedback session is going to be super painful and humiliating, perhaps she's right that I badly need it.

'How are you?' James murmurs in my ear, subtly slipping his arm around my waist.

'I've been better.' I give a resigned smile, to which he responds with a reassuring hug.

'Don't worry, no one's thinking badly of you. Your little spats with Amber are quite endearing.'

'I'm glad they work for someone.'

We're interrupted by a waiter who comes to take our order, and several minutes later our table is laden with beer, wine and starter platters piled high with mouth-watering barbecued shrimp, squid, ribs and wings along with piles of zesty Carribean-style salads.

It's such fun having James and his friends with us, and everyone seems to be getting on brilliantly. So much so, that my mind glosses over one important aspect of the evening.

'Are you ready for your personal development feedback, Emma?' Amber's eyes are twinkling a bit too mischievously for my liking.

'*Ah shit.* I forgot about that.' I set down my knife and fork despairingly. 'Any chance we can do it in the morning? We're having such a great evening.'

Five expectant sets of eyes (including mine) land on Amber, waiting for her to call judgement. Unfortunately, it's clear that I'm the only one who really wants her to grant my request.

'Nope, sorry.' She shakes her head. 'There's still too much we need to do. We're already behind because of your hissy fit earlier.'

'Excuse me?'

'Well, I'd planned to do your feedback this afternoon, but it was obvious it would have gone down like a lead balloon – especially with Romeo here having made an appearance. No offence, James.'

'None taken.' He flashes her an easy smile.

'And according to the plan, we're meant to be doing your first round of presentation practice right now, but I've had to put that back, *so*... this has to happen now.' She raises her eyebrows at me, as if challenging me to go against her word.

Reluctant to cause another scene, I give in and accept my fate. James may have used the term 'endearing' to describe Amber's and my bickering, but I'll be damned if it's to become the main entertainment on this resort for him and his friends. Though saying that, I have a horrible feeling that they'll be treated to one hell of a performance imminently.

Amber pulls out what appears to a scoring sheet with notes scrawled all over it.

'Have you heard of Emotional Intelligence, Emma?' she asks.

'Sure.' I shrug. 'Who hasn't?'

'Good. How would you define it?'

'You're not honestly going to make me answer that, are you? We're not in a classroom, and you're not a blinking teacher. Will you get to the point so this can be over quickly?'

'OK, as Emma's dodged the question, does anyone else want to answer?' says Amber.

I scoff and sit back in my seat. There's no way the others are going to let Amber treat them like school kids.

Rob half raises his hand. 'Is it not roughly summed up as the ability to understand and manage your thoughts and behaviours, as well as understand other people's perspectives and build good relationships with them? Daniel Goleman coined the phrase and came up with the development model based on that definition, didn't he?'

My mouth gapes in disbelief that, not only has Rob played right into Amber's hands, the others look fully engaged with the conversation.

'Gold star for you, Rob.' Amber beams at him. 'That's spot on.'

Rob looks elated that he's now top of the non-existent class, while the others seem impressed with his knowledge. I let out an exasperated sigh, but no one even seems to notice.

'There you go, Emma.' Amber gives me an infuriating wink. 'Keep that definition in your mind while I explain the approach I took with this experiment.'

'I'm glad you refer to it as an "experiment",' I mutter. 'Because I certainly feel like your bloody guinea pig.'

James takes my hand under the table and squeezes it in what I interpret as a message of 'hang in there, there will be something good that comes from this'. I want to believe him and I want to improve. I just don't want to have to endure the inevitable humiliation that'll go with it.

'Anyway...' Amber ignores me and continues to address us as a group. 'I set up the task as per that exact definition, which gave me four areas of Emma's personal development to focus on. I then scored her on how she performed in each. Let's see how she did.'

To my horror, Amber pulls Cat's iPad out of her handbag and brings up a video still of me, nostrils flaring, looking like a raging bull.

'*You filmed me?*'

'It's the most effective way. Allows you to see where you're going wrong. And believe me, once you see some of this stuff, you'll want to work on your problem areas.'

'*What the shitting hell, Amber?* You've *seriously* overstepped. That stuff had better not appear online.'

Her face spreads into an impish grin. 'You sure? If we started a YouTube channel, we might get another holiday out of it. It's comedy gold.'

'I'm... I can't even... *I have no words*,' I splutter, covering my face with my hands and wishing I could disappear from what's about to become my worst nightmare: watching myself behave like a complete plank, alongside an audience that includes the man I'm dating and his best pals.

Chapter Twenty-Six

'Amber, *no way*.' My tone is desperate. 'You're not playing this in front of everyone.'

'It's better if everyone sees it,' she says. 'Means you can get more than one perspective. Kind of like three-sixty feedback.'

'*Have you completely lost it?* I asked you to help me prepare for this interview, not to become some crazed life coach.'

'Amber, you can't do that.' Cat looks equally alarmed on my behalf. 'Give Emma the iPad and let her watch it alone. We agreed we would put her out of her comfort zone to some extent, but this is taking the mick.'

Amber looks around for someone to back her, but James and his friends, quite wisely, are staying out of this one.

'*Fine*,' she grumbles and passes across the iPad. 'Be a baby. I'd be totally fine with it.'

'Good for you.' I shoot her a scathing look. 'You're also happy to throw yourself around a karaoke stage like a lunatic. We have different standards.'

'Now that I'd like to see.' James grins.

'Don't encourage her.'

I take the iPad from Amber, wander out of the restaurant

onto the nearby grass and hit play. The three-minute video, which is basically a montage of all the key events of my crappy afternoon, unfolds in front of me while I die a little inside. *Thank god this wasn't played in front of the others.* It's like one of those highly exaggerated 'how not to do things' training videos. I watch with dismay as one scene melts into the next: my reaction to being soaked by the water guns (each time it happened); my inability to stand my ground politely with the woman who stole my lounger; me taking off across the poolside in furious hot pursuit of the kids; and my reaction when Amber told me about us being moved to another resort.

How did I not notice she was filming that – or any of it? The only slight saving grace is the footage of me consoling poor Fiona, who I'm sure would be equally mortified if she knew she'd become an unsuspecting on-screen 'reality star'.

Once the video has finished, I sit for a few moments to gather myself, and as I do, I land in a place I really don't want to be. As much as I could murder Amber for this stunt, I can already see exactly why it's a useful exercise, and how it's going to help me not just with this interview, but with how I handle stuff in life generally. And that's before we've chatted any of this through.

I return to the table and hand the iPad back to her without saying a word.

'You OK?' says James, grasping my hand under the table once again.

'Yeah, fine,' I reply. 'Thank you.'

'So?' Amber fixes her gaze on me and our audience of four follows suit.

I take a deep breath and cast aside my pride. 'It was... awful to watch. I hate seeing myself on screen, but I can see where you were coming from with your approach.'

'And?'

'And what? If you're looking for an apology or a declaration that I was wrong, you're not going to get either. I still don't agree with your methods.'

'I meant what are your observations? I want to hear your thoughts before I give you mine.'

'Oh. Right.' I'm suddenly hyper aware of everyone around me. This must come through clearly to James because he springs to action.

'Hey, guys...' he says to Tyler and Rob 'I'm really full after that starter. How about we take a short breather on the beach before the main course?'

Not only is it obvious what he's doing, James's friends look like they've been sent to bed with no supper. They were clearly looking forward to the show, and to be honest, I can't blame them. Who doesn't enjoy a laugh at someone else's expense? That's what every bloopers show ever has been built on. I feel my tension dissipate as James gives my hand a final supportive squeeze under the table and gets up to leave, forcing Tyler and Rob to reluctantly trudge out of the restaurant after him.

'That was *so* sweet of James,' says Cat, the moment they're out of ear shot.

'He's a good one all right.' I eye Amber disdainfully for her lack of being 'a good one' herself at this particular moment.

Of course, she ignores my comment and bulldozes on. 'Shall we get started then?'

'OK, let's get this over with.'

'Great. What are your thoughts after seeing the video?'

I rest my elbows on the table and rub my weary face. 'Mortification, humiliation... temptation to walk into the sea and never return.'

Cat chuckles at my joke.

'Very funny.' Amber rolls her eyes. 'Come on, take this seriously.'

'You never take anything seriously,' I throw back at her. 'And you're definitely no role model in this respect. Makes me wonder how you're remotely qualified to deliver this feedback.'

'I know exactly what I'm doing all the time. I push the boundaries by choice, not because my actions are uncontrolled. Plus, I'm not the one trying to secure their dream job.'

'Point taken. OK... here's what I got from it. I overreacted massively to the kids with the water guns and to hearing that we were moving resorts. And I bottled it with the woman who stole my lounger.'

'And what does that tell you?' She puts her scoring sheet on the table so I can refer to the different areas she's scored me on. 'Don't read my observations. Make your own judgements.'

I quickly read through the headings and the descriptions for the four areas she's mapped out. 'I reckon it means that I think before I act. That I lack a bit of emotional self-control.'

'Why do you think that?'

'Because I let my instincts drive me. Sometimes they're right, but sometimes they're wrong or not helpful, even if I'm justified in how I'm feeling.'

'Great. What else?'

'I'm not sure where it fits in here, but I didn't stand up for myself when that woman nicked my lounger. As soon as she got a bit tetchy, I wimped out.'

'Well observed.' Amber adopts an uncharacteristically gentle tone. 'Now I'll give you mine. I completely agree with what you've said so far and these issues go on the list for you as areas for improvement. We already knew about your weakness when it comes to being assertive because of what happened with your ex-boss and Dave the wanker, but it's useful to see it play out on screen, so we can pinpoint what's going on for you in the moment and work out how to approach things.'

'*Wow, where's Amber gone?*' I joke. 'Now you sound like a professional trainer.'

'I do this stuff with my team at work.' She shrugs. 'It's really helpful.'

'Just wouldn't have had you down as being into it. Thought you'd see it as too fluffy.'

'What's fluffy about learning to conduct yourself in a way that earns you loads of respect – and therefore, success?'

'Nothing, I guess.' I can feel myself getting invested in the conversation. 'OK, what else did you pick up on?'

Amber consults her notes. 'Your ability to keep things in perspective.'

'Meaning?'

'In the grand scheme of things, was it that big a deal that you got soaked?'

'Not really. Though in my defence, those kids were really annoying. And they did it *three* times.'

'I told them if you didn't react, not to soak you again, but if you did, to keep winding you up. They simply responded to *your* behaviour.'

'*Oh.*' This revelation is quite stark and I find myself pondering how often I've inflamed situations by having an unnecessary negative emotional reaction.

'"Oh", exactly.' Amber chuckles. 'And would it really have been the end of the world if we'd had to move resorts?'

I frown, considering this. 'I guess not. It would have been super disappointing though.'

'*Super* disappointing? Or just disappointing. Thinking about it in comparison to the likes of Lottie's accident, for example.'

'I see what you're getting at. It wasn't a big deal at all compared to that. Kind of first world problems really.'

'You see? You're really getting this. Let's add "keeping things in perspective" and "dealing with setbacks" to the list.'

'Sure.' I purse my lips thoughtfully and sip at my wine. 'Was there *anything* I did well?'

'Yes, there was.' says Amber. 'Cat, over to you for this one.'

'There was something you did really well, honey,' says Cat. 'How you dealt with the situation with that woman who was upset.'

'Fiona, right.' I nod with interest. 'Amber said that wasn't set up.'

'It wasn't. It was as natural a moment as they come, and you handled it perfectly. You showed such amazing empathy towards that woman: taking the time to listen to her, seeing things from her perspective and offering her the support she needed right then in that moment. And in the process, you built trust and a rapport with her. You also helped her find a way forward. So big thumbs up for that.'

My face spreads into a smile. 'I did do all that.'

'You did.' Amber nods. 'You have great skills in that area, and you're a natural relationship builder. The new friends you picked up during your week of living like a millionaire is a perfect example of that. You need to capitalise on that when you're hit with difficult questions during your presentation. Read the behavioural signals coming from the person who's asking and tailor your answers towards what you think matters to them. Not in a dishonest way, but in a way that lets them feel heard and respected. It's much easier to find common ground with someone if you show you care about their point of view rather than jumping into defence mode.'

'That's genius – and so true.' My eyes light up in comprehension. 'Wow, this is really helpful.'

'I told you it would be,' says Amber.

'I'm sorry I doubted you.' I reach across the table and put my hand on her arm, and she gives me an uncharacteristically affectionate smile.

'I get why it was uncomfortable, and in hindsight, maybe I should have briefed you on my approach, but it was worth it, yeah? People pay hundreds of pounds for this kind of developmental support, you know.'

'I know. Thanks, Amber. So how do I work on my other weak areas?'

'How do you think you could work on them?' she asks.

'I knew you'd throw that question right back at me. I guess... if my issues are with my reactions and keeping things in perspective, I would say... maybe I need to find a way to catch myself in the moment and change course – *before* I have a "hissy fit".' I smile at my friends, who seem to enjoy my self-deprecating humour.

'*Bingo*. You hit the jackpot.' Amber gives me an enthusiastic high five.

'Ooh, what do I win?'

'A steamy night with your hot man.'

'Would I not have got that anyway?' I raise a cheeky eyebrow.

'Yeah, I just wanted to say it out loud. I'm going to have to order him not to keep you up all night though. You've got a long day of prep again tomorrow.'

'And... she's back.' I laugh. 'Shall we let the guys come back now?'

'I already messaged James while you were talking,' she says. 'They're on their way.'

Chapter Twenty-Seven

After dinner, we head to the cocktail bar for our evening of 'company research'. According to Amber, there's a Caribbean steel drum band playing there this evening, which sounds divine. James and his friends, not yet put off by our dysfunctional friendship group, decide that they'll join us for this.

While wandering along the path towards the main resort building, James slips his hand into mine, sending a lovely, tingly sensation through my arm. I look up at him and he gives me a little wink: one that seems to say 'how amazing is this, you and me here together'. Suddenly, it's as if the stars are shining brighter and the air is fresher and more wonderful. It's such a beautiful intimate moment that I almost don't want it to end.

We reach the cocktail bar with its lively evening buzz and I have no choice but to shift my attention to the night ahead, which isn't exactly a chore. 'Company research' is my favourite part of my interview preparation schedule – other than when it involves standing behind the reception desk looking like a deflated beach ball. *Ugh*.

We grab a free table overlooking the pool, and James and Rob go hunting for extra chairs. Amber manages the drinks order, which has somehow expanded by six tequila shots, a salt shaker and a pile of lemon wedges by the time it arrives at our table.

'This is your initiation, lads,' Amber declares, as James, Tyler and Rob groan loudly, but are too polite to decline. 'Emma, Cat...' She then looks at us expectantly.

'Did you not say you wanted me in good form tomorrow morning?' I say.

'One won't do you any harm. You can go onto water after.'

'I'd rather just sip some wine and not have to switch to water so early.'

'Fine. Emma gets a pass. The rest of you, get it down you.'

Seeing me let off the hook, Cat tries her own escape strategy. 'Amber, I need to be in good form tomorrow too for helping Emma—'

'Not a chance, Cat. Emma's got a proper excuse. We're just the support team. Ever been to work with a hangover?'

'Well, yes, but—'

'Then you know how to do this.'

Cat looks gutted as I sit back, relieved at having dodged the alcoholic bullet. The rest of our group obediently shake salt on the backs of their hands, clink their tiny glasses together, and go through the motions, making pained noises as they do.

'*Yuck, I hate that stuff,*' Cat complains.

'You know what they say: a tequila a day helps the holidaymakers play,' singsongs Amber, her eyes glinting wickedly in the artificial light.

I frown. 'That's not a saying.'

'It is now.'

'So, when is this band playing, Amber?' James asks.

'Think it said nine on the entertainment timetable.'

'It's nine now.'

'*Huh*. That's weird.' She illuminates her phone screen to double check the time, and as she does this, the sound of distant steel drums carries across the breeze.

'I can hear them,' I say. 'Have we maybe got the wrong venue?'

'No, it definitely said here,' says Amber. 'And listen... The sound is getting closer.'

I crane my neck in the direction of the music and gasp with delight. 'There they are! They're coming this way.'

We stand to catch the action and watch, hypnotised, as the steel drum band rhythmically circles the pool and climbs the steps to the cocktail bar. The wonderful soothing yet cheerful sound grows louder the closer they get until the group of perfectly synchronised musicians emerge onto the terrace, drums hanging in front of them, held up by wide leather straps around their necks. They deposit their instruments onto waiting drum stands that we didn't spot before, barely missing a beat in the process. Then, less than a minute later, they wrap up the tune they're playing to rapturous applause.

'They're so slick,' I holler to my table mates over the clapping and cheering. 'I'm really going to have to be at the top of my game on Monday.'

'I thought you had an interview, Emma, not a scheduled performance,' says Rob.

'I'm presenting to staff and guests as part of it,' I reply and his eyes widen. 'I know. I'm as terrified as you think I should be.'

'You're braver than me. How are you going to win them over? Fire eating while playing rake and scrape on a banjo?'

'There's an idea.' I giggle. 'Nothing quite as impressive as that, I'm afraid.'

'No point in asking her about it,' says James. 'I tried earlier and got palmed off. Apparently, it's on a need-to-know basis only.'

'*Ooh, burn.*' Tyler chuckles. 'You'll make it into the inner circle yet, James.'

'I can hope.'

'Aww, don't take it to heart.' I pat James's shoulder affectionately. 'It's not personal.'

'Do we get to come to your presentation at least?' Rob asks. 'Would be great to see you in action.'

'Sorry, no. Sébastien – that's the guy that owns the resort – is managing the attendees list and I expect it'll be in a conference room of sorts.'

'I'll be filming it so you can watch it later, Rob,' says Amber.

'*Eh... no you won't.*' I pierce her with warning stare.

'Not like you can stop me. Plus, it's another great learning opportunity. Think how much you can gain from watching back your own presentation.'

'That is true, and it did work before, as excruciating as it was... OK, fine. But it's my call whether it goes into wider circulation. That's not your decision.'

'Deal.' Amber reaches across and shakes my hand to lock in the agreement.

We fall silent as the steel drum band starts up again. They really are incredible. It's an experience I know I'll think about in the future when I'm back home in beautiful-but-not-remotely-tropical Scotland. And it's made all the better by James clutching my hand tightly throughout, while we intermittently steal infatuation-filled glances at each other.

After about thirty minutes of performing, the band announce a short break.

'Perfect timing,' I say, getting up from my seat. 'I need to make a trip to the ladies.'

'I'll come with you,' says Cat.

We weave our way across the terrace and into the main

atrium by reception to the same ladies 'powder room' I changed in that morning ahead of my slot on reception.

'How are things going with James?' Cat asks, when we reach the safe haven of the toilets. 'You guys looked so cute together in the pool earlier.'

'*So great.*' A dreamy smile blossoms on my face. 'We can barely keep our eyes off each other. He's so easy to talk to. And he's so considerate too.'

'Totally. I loved how he took his friends away so you could do the feedback session with us without feeling under the microscope.'

'*Right?* He really is a good one. I... um... told him about my win earlier.'

'You did?' She seems surprised. 'Gosh, you must feel comfortable with him.'

'I do, and I just know I can trust him.'

'Normally I'd say to be careful, but in this case I agree with you. It's partly his parents being Lottie's neighbours, but there's something else: he's so genuine and he never played any games with you. Made it clear he liked you and that was it.'

'That's it exactly. Crazy, isn't it? Especially as only a week or so ago, I thought he was an idiot.'

'Love moves in mysterious ways.' She gives me a knowing nudge and I laugh out loud.

'*Steady.* We're miles away from that. You'll reach that point with Mike well before we do.'

Instead of assuming a similarly misty-eyed expression to mine, Cat looks deflated all of a sudden.

'Hey, what's up?' I ask. 'Are things OK between you? He's not done something shit has he? Because I'll kill him if he has.'

'No, it's nothing like that... It's... Is it bad that I really wish he was here? Don't get me wrong, I'm *loving* this trip, but I miss him way more than I thought I would and seeing you with

James is making me a wee bit...' She trails off, not wanting to use the word I know she's meaning.

'Envious.'

'Yeah.' She winces as if she's insulted me in the worst way possible.

'Cat, don't feel bad about that. It's perfectly natural.' I swoop in and hug her. 'Between you and me, I was bursting with envy seeing all the loved-up couples smooching in this place. Still can't believe my luck that James is here. Though it would have been better if I didn't have the biggest interview of my life looming.'

'Of course. That'll take the shine off. Thanks for sharing that you were feeling the same way. Makes me feel better.'

'I'm glad. Because you have nothing to feel guilty about. Actually... have you got your phone on you?'

'In here.' She holds up her pink clutch. 'Why?'

'How about you FaceTime Mike right now? Tell him how much you're missing him – and before you do that, maybe I could say hello? Although, it's what... half two in the morning in the UK so maybe it's too late.'

'No, that's a great idea.' Cat's face lights up. 'He was going out for a big one with friends tonight so he should still be up.'

'And you're looking hot to trot, so it'll be a nice reminder of what he's missing.'

Cat gets her phone out and brings up FaceTime. She's about to hit dial when I pluck the device from her hand.

'From the toilets? Really?'

'Good point.' She giggles. 'Got a bit excited there.'

'I still need to pee, so why don't you grab a seat in the atrium and I'll be out in a couple of minutes.'

She heads back out the door while I make my essential pit stop, then I join her on the comfortable cream sofa she's commandeered.

'This is so exciting, getting to meet your new man for the

first time.' I fluff my hair as if I'm about to go on camera in a different way. 'OK, go.'

Cat hits the 'call' button and moments later Mike's handsome face appears on the screen. And he *is* handsome. He also looks exactly as I'd imagine a boyfriend of Cat's to: honest, friendly, boy next door, with messy sandy coloured hair and kind eyes. I can already tell he's perfect for her.

'Hi there, lovely.' He seems elated to hear from her. 'How did you know I was thinking about you?'

'You were?' Cat's cheeks flush with embarrassment-slash-delight.

'I haven't stopped thinking about you since you left.'

I put my hand to my chest and fake a swoon, which makes Cat laugh.

'I haven't stopped thinking about you either.' Her tone is shyer than his. 'Mike, there's someone here I'd like you to meet.' She extends her arm so that I can get into the frame at the bottom of the screen. 'This is my best friend, Emma.'

'Hi.' I give him a goofy wave. 'It's so lovely to meet you.'

'*Emma*, it's great to finally meet you.' Mike grins back at me. 'Is Cat behaving herself?'

'She is and she's pining for you big time.'

Cat pokes me in the ribs, clearly mortified by this statement, but it doesn't deter me. The truth shall be spoken.

'That's good to know,' he says. 'I was concerned that she might find herself a hotter, richer man on that fancy resort you're at.'

My mind flits to Sébastien and our collective salivating over him during the last couple of days. It's obvious that Cat has the same thought because she turns beetroot.

'Not at all.' I wave his worries away. 'There's only one person who has Cat's heart – and that's you.'

I make a mental note to reassure her later that appreciating Sébastien's magnetic qualities is not her being unfaithful on any level. The man is a god. Even Mike would probably fancy him to a certain extent.

We enjoy chatting for a few minutes longer, then I excuse myself to give Cat and Mike some 'alone time' – and return to my own hot man.

Chapter Twenty-Eight

By eleven p.m., the steel drum band has long wrapped up and Amber's impatience at us not yet having moved on is evident.

'*Can we go already!*' She dings her glass to get our attention and succeeds in silencing half the bar in the process.

'Amber, where would you like to go?' James asks.

'So kind of you to ask, James. I want to go to the resort club.'

'There's a club here?' Rob seems surprised by this.

'Think it's more a bar with a dance floor. Can't confirm that though – thanks to these two boring bastards.' Amber jerks a thumb at me and Cat.

James looks to me and I shrug. 'She only asked once and we weren't in the mood that night.'

'And tonight?'

'I guess we could go. Although I don't want to have a late one for obvious reasons.'

'How about we head to the wine bar for a couple of drinks, then those who want to can go for a dance after that?' he suggests. 'Tyler and Rob will probably be up for it, right lads?'

'Sure, why not,' says Rob,

'Few glasses of champers and I'll be *owning* the dance floor.' Tyler mimics some dance moves.

'*Awesome!*' Amber punches the air. 'Glad I'm finally with people who know how to have fun. Let's go.'

We vacate our table and amble through the gardens to The Cave. Amber walks ahead with Rob and Tyler, the three of them having a right carry on as they go, while James, Cat and I follow behind.

'It's nice that Amber's found some playmates,' I muse.

'You sound like a proud mum,' says James.

'It *can* feel like parenting with her sometimes. Right, Cat?'

'Sure can,' she says. 'Amber can be hard work, but her heart is in the right place – though sometimes it requires the skills of a code breaker to work that out.'

'She's certainly a character.' James chuckles. 'If she wasn't married, I'd have been trying to pair her up with Tyler. He has a devilish sense of humour as well. Though maybe that would be too dangerous a combination.'

'Probably.' I nod.

We round the last bend to The Cave and discover that the others have already gone inside.

'Good evening,' the same hostess from our previous visits greets us. 'It's lovely to see you again. Your friends are being shown to your table and Ashwana will return for you shortly.'

Moments later, we're collected by Ashwana who chaperones us to the outdoor terrace.

'I *love* this place,' I say James. 'I mean look at the moon and the stars. They're so bright and visible from here because of there being less artificial light around us. And the décor. It really makes you feel like you're in the opening of an actual cave.'

'It's very cool.' He looks around him, appearing impressed. 'I've seen photos but they don't do it justice.'

We perch ourselves on the tall chairs and join the others in staring out across the seascape. It may be dark but the sense of openness to the elements, the noise of the waves lapping on the shore and the idea of there being nothing but water beyond us is still mesmerising. The only person who's not hypnotised by the experience is, of course, Amber.

'Will we start with two bottles of the stuff we had last time?' she says.

'Maybe the guys would like to look at the drinks menu?' I suggest.

'No, that's fine,' says James. 'We're easily pleased, right guys?'

Tyler and Rob nod casually.

Amber relays the order to the waiter when he reappears, and within minutes, we're toasting to good health and amazing holidays.

I take a sip of my fizz, the fruity bubbles of which are like crystalline pearls on my tongue, leaving me giddy with happiness. I then steal a glance at James, who looks even more gorgeous in the half-light, and he obviously senses this, because his free hand seeks out mine and our fingers intertwine. It's an almost perfect moment – other than the fact that we're not able to enjoy a deeper level of intimacy together. Well, that, and the sight of Amber making rude gestures as she banters with Tyler, likely telling him one of her many inappropriate stories. He seems riveted, guffawing loudly, which backs up James's observation that they would be a perfectly suited couple – or a very dangerous combination.

Cat, Rob, James and myself have settled into a more palatable conversation about excursions we could go on once my interview is over, when Sébastien materialises next to us. His dark eyes sweep the table, taking in each of James, Rob and Tyler, then land on my hand in James's. Feeling uncomfortable,

I instinctively release it, attempting to disguise the movement by adjusting my necklace.

'*Mesdames, messieurs, bonsoir*.' Sébastien makes his way around Cat, Amber and myself with his signature greeting. 'How is your evening?' His gaze land on me and stays there.

'It's... good, thanks.' I shift in my seat. 'Managed to bag the last table out here.'

'I see this. You have also "bagged" yourself some new friends, it seems.'

'Oh, sorry. I'll introduce you. Sébastien, this is James, Tyler and Rob.'

'*Enchanté*.' Sébastien nods politely at each of them in turn. They offer similar responses though I note that James's smile doesn't shine quite as brightly as usual.

'James works at Archer & Crombie, a luxury travel agency,' I say.

'Ah, yes.' Sébastien's face lights up with recognition. 'I am pleased to see you here, James. Your company sells a lot of holidays to our resorts. I hope you will enjoy your stay and continue to recommend the resort after.'

'So far, so good.' James gives a polite nod.

'I am glad to hear this.' Sébastien's eyes shift from James back to me. 'You are looking well this evening, Emma. Your eyes have the shine of the stars in them once again.'

I feel myself colour from this comment, despite knowing that Sébastien doesn't mean anything by this. It's a reference to my 'funny turn' the previous evening. It also seems to be his way, to be open and say whatever is in his head, however, this isn't common knowledge, and I'm hyper aware of the look that's exchanged between James and his friends.

'Oh... thank you... yes...' I stammer. 'As I said this morning, I'm in much better form today. It's been a productive day of interview preparation.'

'*Bien*. I am looking forward to Monday, as I am sure you are too. Not only for the interview, but for being able to finally relax and enjoy your holiday.'

'Absolutely. Some rest and relaxation will be well overdue by then. Although I'm still getting some – in small doses.'

Sébastien's eyes crinkle in what appears to be acknowledgement of my comment, before his gaze sweeps around the group once more.

'I will bid you goodnight, then,' he says.

'You don't want to join us for a drink?' says Amber. 'The more the merrier.'

'*Ah, non*. Thank you for the kind offer, Amber, but I will be rising early tomorrow. I will take what I think you call a "rain check".'

'No probs.' She smiles at him. 'We'll expect to you to join us at another point then.'

'I will look forward to this.'

Sébastien gives us one final polite nod, his gaze lingering slightly longer on me, then makes his way inside. I glance at James and it might be that my radar is too sensitised, or I'm feeling weird about the attention Sébastien was showing me, but I get the sense that something's going on with him. He wasn't quite as friendly as I've known him to be just then with Sébastien. But then I don't know James that well. Maybe it's a guy thing. Maybe they cool things a little around other guys to come across as laid back and smooth.

'So, that was Sébastien,' I say unnecessarily.

'We saw,' says James. '*He's* all man, isn't he?'

I'm unsure how to answer this. Or what James meant by it.

'He's... a nice guy. Been very kind to me.'

'Seems like it.' His tone is light, but the affection he was displaying so plainly before is now distinctly absent.

As the others resume chatting, I consider whether to slip my hand back into James's, to pick up where we left off, but I'm not getting the right vibes to feel comfortable doing that. Instead, I try to engage him in conversation.

'Such a great place this, isn't it?' I say. 'What do you think of the resort so far? Now you've had a chance to experience some of it.'

'It's a cracking place all right.' He shrugs. 'Won't be a struggle to enjoy a good break.'

I continue to make what can only be described as 'small talk' with him, until I can no longer take the stark contrast between how he was with me before Sébastien appeared, and this odd sense of formality that's settled over us like a cloud. It's too reminiscent of how he was earlier in the day. Instead, I involve myself in the group chat, which I note that James is still heartily engaging with, so whatever is going on with him, it has to be about me and Sébastien – again.

By the time the fizz is getting low, Amber's lobbying heavily for moving on to the resort club. I have no intention of taking the night any further from a drinking and dancing perspective, so I stay out of the conversation. Cat does the same. Having caught her stifling several yawns, I know she's ready to call it a night. Tyler and Rob have already signed up to joining Amber, which only leaves James. A big part of me is hoping he'll come with me, so that we can enjoy some time just the two of us. But as things have cooled between us since Sébastien swung by, I'm not sure that experience would live up to my expectations.

He holds back from signalling his intentions at the table, and no one questions him on it. It's only after leaving the bar and reaching a fork in the path, which will send us in opposite directions that the decision can no longer be put off.

'Hey, Emma,' says James. 'I'm thinking I'll join the others in the club. You'll need a good sleep ahead of your prep tomorrow, so best I give you peace.'

My heart sinks at this announcement, which for me is a certain sign that something's badly wrong. It's dressed up as concern for me, but James's strange behaviour in the bar, as well as the lack of an offer to at least walk me back to my suite, is screaming that there's a problem – and he's avoiding dealing with it.

'Right, sure. I guess that makes sense.' I try not to let my disappointment show.

'I'll see you tomorrow, yeah?'

'Fine. Maybe see you at breakfast?'

'*If* we make it.' He laughs loudly, drawing attention from the others.

I make eye contact with Cat and I can tell that she's tuned into the situation.

'Shall we?' She offers me her arm and I gratefully thread mine through it.

'Have fun,' we call to the others, who are already gravitating in the direction of the club, with Amber so caught up in her boisterous chat with Tyler and Rob that she barely notices us go. She certainly hasn't clocked the awkwardness between myself and James, who jogs after them to catch up.

'You OK?' Cat asks, as we meander through the beautifully lit resort gardens, the faint sound of music from one of the many drinking establishments cutting through the quiet darkness. 'What's going on with you and James?'

'You tell me.' I look at her with hurt in my eyes. 'He's been weird with me ever since Sébastien came by our table.'

'How so?'

She gestures to a bench and we sit down. I explain how things were before and after, and she listens intently, then frowns.

'I'm no expert, honey, but maybe James is feeling threatened by Sébastien. Sébastien *does* pay you a lot of attention. We know he has no romantic intentions towards you – at least that's what he's told you – but James might still be worried that he does. And that you might respond to them. All he's seeing is this rich, charismatic, god-like man who he probably feels he couldn't compete with, so he's withdrawing to protect himself.'

'Could be,' I say. 'But I feel it's more than that. Also, James has never been backward in coming forward before. He's normally so confident, yet he's backed off twice now because of Sébastien – when there's no reason for him to do so.'

'*No* reason?' Cat raises a sceptical eyebrow and I wince.

'OK, maybe the first time when he saw us dancing looked bad. Especially as he didn't know what was going on. But I explained the situation.'

'Then maybe you've discovered his Achilles heel. Maybe James is super confident provided there's no competition. For all you know, he may have had a bad experience in the past.'

'I guess.' I bob my head in acceptance of this possibility. 'I never thought about it like that. What should I do then? I need him to know that there's nothing between me and Sébastien.'

'Are you completely sure there isn't?' Cat asks.

I'm thrown by this question. 'What do you mean? Of course there isn't. Why would you ask that?'

'Because I sense some chemistry between the two of you, and if I do, so will James.'

The memory of me dropping James's hand the moment Sébastien's gaze landed on us crashes into my consciousness.

'*Shit*. You're right. I messed up.' I quickly explain what happened.

'There you go,' says Cat. 'That's the problem right there. You doing that must have caused James to feel insecure and think that you have feelings for Sébastien.'

'That would hurt any guy's ego.' I screw up my face, annoyed at myself. 'But I only did it because Sébastien could end up being my boss. It felt weird him seeing me having a "holiday romance". It wasn't because I have feelings for him.'

'Then James needs to know that.'

'Yeah, he does... *Oh no*... I've just realised something else.

The night I went for dinner with Sébastien, I told him – somewhat misguidedly – that nothing could happen between us because I have someone special at home. Now he's going to think I've hooked up with some random guy on the resort and question my previous excuse, because he doesn't know James is that "someone special".'

'Why does that matter?'

'It matters because... I don't know. Why the hell *does* it matter?'

'Actually, I have an idea why.' Cat fixes me with a knowing look. 'Because as much as Sébastien said he wasn't interested in you that way, how he behaves around you suggests the opposite.'

'You've noticed it too?'

'Yes. To me, it seems like Sébastien's pretending not to be interested in you because it wouldn't be appropriate to pursue you romantically while you're a candidate for a job with him – and because you already fobbed him off. But he'll sense if there's chemistry between you. Perhaps he's hoping something will develop between you if you get the job, or indeed if you don't.'

'*Oh hell*, that's all I need.'

'Because you like Sébastien as well as James?'

'*No*. Well, yes. Who *doesn't* like Sébastien? But I want to be with James.'

'Then, once again, he needs to know that.'

'He does.' I nod resolutely. 'Shall I go to the club and tell him that?'

'You could... but you've both had some booze, and it's easy for alcohol fuelled arguments to blow up, no matter how much you want to resolve the issue. Maybe you could leave it until the morning instead.'

'That's good advice. Thanks Cat.'

Getting up from the bench, we continue our walk back to

our accommodation block, and on reaching Cat's suite, which is less than a minute's walk from mine, we say goodnight. I then wander along the corridor to my own room, caught in a cycle of indecision. What Cat said makes a lot of sense, but I'm concerned that not dealing with this quickly might do more harm than good. Although, with the mood James was in when we parted ways... *Oh, I don't know.*

While continuing to switch back and forth on whether to go and find him, I round the corner to my suite and my breath catches in my throat: because James is leaning against the wall by my door.

Chapter Twenty-Nine

'Hi there.' I approach James with a hesitant smile. 'I thought you decided to go to the club.'

'I did go,' he says. 'But it turns out I forgot something,'

'Oh.' I'm disappointed to that this unexpected appearance is for practical reasons. 'What did you forget? I don't think I have anything of yours.'

He looks pained for a moment. 'I forgot... how to behave.'

'Um... OK...'

'I acted like a sulky teenage boy back there at The Cave. Amber just gave me bollocking for that – which is unfortunate, because I was intending to drink my bodyweight in beer to forget about it.'

I use my key card to unlock my suite and beckon for him to follow me inside, which he does. But instead of making himself comfortable, he stands awkwardly in the middle of the room.

'Why don't you sit down?' I suggest.

'I don't want to sit until I know whether I'm staying or leaving,' he says.

'OK, let's work that out then. Is this to do with Sébastien?'

'Yes.'

'About the fact that I dropped your hand when he appeared?'

'That. And the way the two of you look at each other.'

'*Wait, what?* I don't look at Sébastien in any *way*.'

James sighs. 'You do, Emma. And he sure does in return. That might as well have been a table of one he rocked up at earlier. The rest of us were practically invisible to him. It's ridiculous if you can't see it yourself.'

I look at the floor. There's no point in denying that I sense some level of chemistry between Sébastien and I. James is smart and he's picked up on it. I must be respectful of that.

'Look, James... I admit that I find Sébastien attractive, and I am aware that there's some kind of connection between us, but there's no substance to it. I already told you about what happened when I went for dinner with him. I—'

'I know. You made it clear you weren't interested and so did he. But the problem is: that's all bullshit. You might have indicated to him that you like someone else, and he might have glossed over his interest in you and thrown the job interview into the mix, but—'

'*Hold on.* Are you suggesting Sébastien's only interviewing me for the role to get in my knickers?' I narrow my eyes at him. 'Do you have the slightest idea how that sounds?'

'*Fuck*, sorry.' James rubs the back of his neck in frustration. 'Don't even know why I said that. I'm not—'

'Good at this kind of chat?'

'You could say that.'

'Where's the articulate, self-assured James I've come across at almost every turn over the last few weeks?'

'We all have off days, eh?' He offers me a shameful smile and this is all it takes for my hackles to disintegrate.

'Please will you sit down?' I ask again, and this time he does and I sit beside him. 'How about *I* go first, because you're making an arse of this, and I wanted to talk to you anyway.'

'Fine by me.'

'All right. You might have been behaving like a sulky teenager – your words, not mine – but I understand why and I want to apologise.'

'You don't owe me any apologies, Emma. You can't help how you feel. I'm the one with the issue here.'

'I thought *I* was speaking?' I nudge him affectionately.

'Sorry. Yup. Go.'

'Thank you. I want to apologise for dropping your hand and undermining what we have in doing that. To be clear, I didn't do it because I *fancy* Sébastien, I did it because he might end up being my boss – and it felt weird showing that side of me to him.'

James's expression clears. 'I didn't think about it like that.'

'That's why it's good to deal with things rather than go off in a huff.' I give him another playful push and he smiles sheepishly. 'Anyway, what's really important is for me to reassure you that *nothing* is going to happen between me and Sébastien.'

'You can't guarantee that. Feelings can develop quickly and things can happen in the heat of the moment, especially if you end up working for him.'

'Are you talking from experience?'

'If you're asking if I've been cheated on, the answer is yes, but I'm not sure that's the issue here. All I know is that I like you – a hell of a lot. Sure, I'm normally more confident, but can you blame me for losing it a bit when I'm competing with a super human specimen like Sébastien. I'm not into men, but I can see what I'm up against – and I don't like my chances.'

I smile at his honesty. 'Well, *I* do. I like your chances very much, because to me, you're every bit as appealing as Sébastien – and more.'

'OK...' He seems doubtful.

'I *mean* it. You need a lot more than raw chemistry to make things work with someone. You need to click at a deeper level, and I think *we* do.'

'Me too.' James's gorgeous deep chestnut brown eyes finally meet mine. 'I think that's why I haven't dealt with this so well. You're the first woman I've seen any real potential with in a long time, and I don't want to get into something if there's a chance it might blow up in my face.'

'So instead, you turned into adolescent James and froze me out.' I give him a teasing wink.

'Any chance you can let that slide?'

'I already have. Just couldn't resist a wee jibe. James, I really like you too, and I already know I want this to go somewhere. I can't believe I'm even able to say that to you. In my experience, most guys would be halfway down the corridor by now, but I can tell you're different. I love that you've been so open and up front with me. Let's keep being that way, yeah?'

'I'd like that.' He leans in and kisses me softly.

'And when we bump into Sébastien again, I'll introduce you properly – as the guy I'm seeing from back home.'

'Good plan. Then I can scope him out, find his superhero weakness and hit him where it hurts.' The sexy grin I'm used to seeing finally returns to James's face.

'There's the man I'm falling—' I cut myself off, turning crimson as I realise what I've almost said.

Sharp as a needle, James eyes me mischievously. 'Falling...?'

'Off the interview prep wagon for.'

'Good save. So, we're official then – I mean in a holiday romance sense?'

'It's a solid "yes".'

This time, it's me that leans in, planting a smacker of a kiss on his lips. It quickly turns into a steamy snog with roaming hands and items of clothing flying left, right and centre, and the good sleep I'm needing ahead of tomorrow's prep is looking *very* unlikely indeed.

Chapter Thirty

The next morning, I'm awake before James and my mind switches straight into interview prep mode. Discreetly disentangling myself from him, I climb out of bed, grab my presentation notes and quietly open the patio doors, forgetting that the whoosh of the air conditioning powering down could wake him. He stirs momentarily, but doesn't come round.

Outside, the morning air is less humid than it's been, which suits me because if offers a refreshing start to my day. Between that, the paradise sea view and the sound of the waves crashing rhythmically on the shore, it's really quite a pleasant 'alfresco workspace'.

Sitting down at the table, I finish off my presentation content, then I spend some time quietly reading it aloud to get used to saying the words.

Once I'm satisfied that I've made some progress, I peer through the patio doors to see if James is awake and I'm surprised to see that the bed is empty. I then go inside and check the bathroom but he's not there either.

A mild panic stirs within me: has he got what he wanted and done a bolt? No, can't be. He's not the type. Returning to the bedroom, I look for some clue as to where he's gone and spot a handwritten note on my bedside table.

Morning, gorgeous. I saw you were working on your prep and didn't want to distract you. Hope it went well. Can't wait to see you later. x

My stomach does a skip and a jump: partly out of irrational relief that he hasn't cut and run, but mainly because of the tone of the note. It's peppered with positive signs for our budding relationship, and it was really thoughtful of him to leave me in peace while I was 'in the zone'. Of course, a tiny part of me is also disappointed that he's gone, but I can easily sweep that feeling away when I know I'll be seeing him again in a few hours.

Because last night was *unreal*. After all the weirdness and confusion, it was just me and James, getting to know each other in lots of different ways – and it was nothing short of spectacular. My insides fizz at the memory of his touch and the unmistakable physical and emotional connection between us. It was electric. And my god did he know how to satisfy me. I'm getting hot again just thinking about it.

Checking the time on my phone, I discover I'm running late for breakfast, so I get ready at lightning speed and canter along to the buffet restaurant.

'Was he a good lay then?' says Amber, before my backside has even hit the seat.

'*Amber, ssshh.*' I glance around me self-consciously. 'Can you keep your voice down?'

'Sorry... *how was the sex?*' She puts on a theatrical whisper, attracting more attention from our fellow diners than her original question did.

'That's not really what I meant.'

She snickers while Cat pats my arm sympathetically, shooting Amber a look of 'stop it, please' and pours me a cup of tea.

'Did you sort things out?' she asks me. 'Amber told me how she sent James to your room with his tail between his legs.'

'Yes, we're all good now.' My face spreads into a wide smile, my embarrassment already forgotten. 'That I will thank you for, Amber. Wouldn't have got much sleep otherwise.'

'You're welcome. You still didn't get much sleep though, right?' Her eyes twinkle devilishly.

'Oh, for god's sake. *Fine*. As you helped me out, I'll throw you a bone. We had sex, Amber – as grown-ups do when they have feelings for each other. He even stayed over in my suite.'

'So technically it was *him* who threw *you* a bone,' she hoots with glee.

I give a withered shake of my head. 'You're a sad woman. Makes me wonder if you're not getting any yourself.'

'*Huh-uh*. I've no complaints in that department. I could teach you two a few tricks to—'

'We're good, thanks.' I hold up a hand to silence her. 'Shall we get some food?'

'Yes, please.' Cat puts down her tea and scrambles to her feet.

Leaving Amber chuckling to herself, we make our way across to the breakfast buffet.

'I'm so glad you and James made up,' says Cat. 'How did it happen? After he turned up at yours, I mean.'

I quickly fill her in while we pile fruit, deli items and toast onto our plates.

'I really hope that's going to be the end of the Sébastien issue,' I say, once she's up to speed.

'Fingers crossed, honey.'

We return to our table to find James occupying the fourth seat and chatting away to Amber.

'Good morning,' I slide into my own seat, which is beside him. 'How are you?'

'I'm good.' He leans in and pecks me on the lips. 'And you?'

'*Eh*... I thought you two woke up in the same bed this morning,' says Amber.

'We did, but not at the same time.' I beam at James, while tucking into my plateful of food.

'Emma was studiously prepping on her balcony when I woke up,' he says. 'So I sneaked out to avoid interrupting her.'

'He did. And he left me a little note.'

'Aww, that's lovely,' says Cat.

'I'm more impressed that Emma was taking the initiative,' says Amber 'Which reminds me, you're meant to be doing your presentation run through right now.'

'I know.' I nod. 'I was practising it this morning.'

I look expectantly at James, but he doesn't seem like he's going anywhere.

'Where are your buddies?' My eyes roam the restaurant, hoping that'll encourage him to move on.

'Still in bed. Couple of lightweights. Amber wins the prize for the best stamina.'

'Damn right.' She fist bumps him. 'James, how do you fancy being panel member number three this morning? Emma needs to get used to having an audience, so bringing you into the fold will be a good start.'

I eyeball Amber, trying to reach her with the message of 'no, send him on his merry way', but she's either oblivious or intentionally ignoring me. Finding no help there, I lock eyes with Cat, and with one look, her thoughts are clear: I do need to get used to presenting to others, and do I really want to rock the boat with James again so soon?

'That OK with you, Emma?' James, at least, has the decency to check in with me. 'I'd like to see what you can do and hopefully offer some support and encouragement.'

'Eh... yeah, sure. Why not.'

Though I've managed to keep my tone casual, my heart is hammering like I've downed three double espressos, because this isn't just adding another audience member into the fold. It's James: the guy I played bedtime gymnastics with last night, and who I hope is going to fall hopelessly in love with me. I don't want him seeing me stumble my way through my presentation content.

Gathering myself together as best I can, I pull my notes out of my handbag, clear my throat and start my introduction. However, three sentences in, I look at James and it throws me off completely. I begin to stammer and stutter, eventually casting my notes aside in frustration.

'I can't do it with you guys watching me like that.'

'Watching you like what?' asks James.

'Like... really intently.'

'Emma, everyone on the day is going to be watching you intently,' says Amber. 'That's the whole point. *You're* delivering it.'

'I know that. But you're literally right in front of me. It's off putting.'

'Would you like to stand over there and do it.' She points to an empty spot about six feet away. 'Because I'm happy with that if you are.'

'*What? No.* Then *everyone* will be watching me.'

'Exactly. This is the best you'll get, so quit your whining and get on with it. You need to do this or you'll totally flake this afternoon.'

'What does that mean?' My ears prick up in alarm.

'Huh?' Amber looks at me innocently.

'You said something about this afternoon. What's happening this afternoon?'

'No, I didn't. *Go.*'

I'm reluctant to move on, given what I've just heard,

but she's gesturing for me to get on with it, and neither Cat nor James are reacting to what she said. Putting a hand on my churning stomach, I take a deep breath and start again, but within a minute I'm stumbling once more.

'Emma, stop,' says James and I happily oblige. 'I think I know what's going on here. You're faltering whenever you make eye contact with us.'

'You're right, she is,' says Cat.

'Eye contact always seems to be my downfall.' I sigh. 'It's the same when I try to assert myself with difficult people, that kind of thing.'

'Here's a tip for you,' says James. 'Don't make eye contact with any of us.'

'OK, but I can't do that tomorrow, can I?'

'Yes, you can. Look here.' He points between his eyebrows. 'If you do that, everyone will think you're looking them in the eye, and as you're not, you should be more comfortable. Try it now.'

'OK...' I launch into my introduction once more, and this time I get right through it. 'Wow, that worked. Great tip. Thanks, James.' I blow him a little kiss and he grins back at me.

'Good one. But you weren't meant to stop for self-congratulations.' Amber hurries me along, killing my moment with James. 'Go again, and *keep going*.'

I restart my presentation and this time I manage all the way through. I'm still a bit rusty with the flow, but it's better than this morning in my suite, and as I wrap things up with a theatrical gasp of relief, my audience of three give me a mini-round of applause.

'*Well done, honey*.' Cat keeps clapping after the others have finished. 'You got right to the end. That's brilliant for your first dry run with us.'

'Yeah, good start, Emma,' says Amber. 'We'll have you slick as they come by tomorrow.'

'Thanks,' I say and turn to James. 'What did you think?'

'I think you're making great progress and you deserve a walk on the beach as a reward.'

His gorgeous dark eyes are almost hypnotising, and the idea of a romantic stroll with him couldn't appeal more right now. However, I'm aware that today's prep schedule is tightly packed, so I look to Amber and Cat.

'Is there time for that?'

'Meet us by reception in an hour,' says Amber. 'Think you've earned yourself a break.'

'Amazing, let's go, James.'

Chapter Thirty-One

James and I leave the restaurant and make our way along one of the meandering paths towards the beach, enjoying the warmth from the sun while we walk. He slips his warm hand into mine, and I smile up at him shyly.

'You did incredibly well there,' he says. 'Presentations are tough, but you seem to have nailed the content.'

'You think?' I'm pleased with this unsolicited feedback.

'I do. Are you planning to use your notes tomorrow?'

'Yes, why do you ask?'

He seems to consider his response. 'Well, overall you did great, but there was one thing that I thought let you down slightly.'

'Which was?'

'You seemed to be reading some of the sections word for word from your notes.'

'Ah, right.' I nod. 'That's because there are some parts I don't know as well yet, but I'll learn them off by heart by tomorrow.'

'So, you're learning the content like a script?'

'Is that not essential? I need to know it inside out.'

We're about to step off the path onto the beach, so I stop momentarily to take off my sandals and carry them by the straps.

'It's certainly important to know what you want to talk about and when,' says James. 'But the problem with learning it like a script is that you could lose your place and struggle to get back on track. And you might end up using your notes as a crutch, meaning you're not looking at your audience enough.'

I know I should be grateful for this feedback, which I acknowledge is really on point, but for some reason, it makes me bristle.

'Right. Well, I guess I'll need to be super prepared then.'

'Or you could try having cue cards with just your key points on them? That would allow you some flexibility and help you come across as someone who really knows their stuff.' James takes my hand again as we walk across the powdery white sand.

I frown at this comment. 'I do know my stuff. Are you saying you think I don't?'

'No, not at all. I know you do. I'm talking solely about perception. People will judge you on what they see because that's all they've got to work with. They don't know you... know how you performed in your last job, or how experienced you are.'

'I suppose.'

Though I know James is right, I'm still bristling from this feedback, and I don't know why. Probably best then to change the subject to avoid getting into it any further. I scan the seascape and point at a paraglider in the distance.

'You ever done that?'

'No,' he says. 'And I want to tell you it's because I've never had the opportunity, but—'

'You're scared of heights?'

'Does that make you like me less?'

'Uh-uh. It just means I don't respect you.'

'*Oh, what?*' He blanches from my ambush.

'I'm kidding.' I smile up at him. 'I like that you're comfortable sharing things like that with me.'

'*I was*. Now I'm not.'

'*Aww... no*. Don't say that. I was genuinely messing with you.'

'So, what are you scared of, Emma?' James lets my hand go and slips his arm around my waist.

I wrinkle my nose. 'Too many things. Amber calls me a wuss.'

'I'm sure Amber has her own fears.'

'If she does, she's damn good at hiding them. Sometimes I think she's fearless to a dangerous level. She doesn't care what anyone thinks of her. And you should have seen her out here the other day: she tried every water sport available. I do wish I could have some of what she's got though.'

'You seem pretty solid yourself.' He cocks his head, seemingly surprised at my statement. 'You were certainly able to tell me to back off when we first met.'

'Yet here you are.' I chuckle.

'What can I say? I'm a sucker for punishment.'

James laughs too and draws me in for a delicious lingering kiss that sets my senses alight. It's an embrace so filled with desire that I wonder if we should hotfoot it to my suite. Then he breaks apart from me abruptly, leaving me worked up and wanting more.

'Seriously though,' he continues, as if the kiss never happened. 'How come you could do that with me – tell me what's what – but you can't do it with others?'

I consider his question. 'I guess I wasn't intimidated by you in in the way that I can be with some people. It's only the more aggressive, elbow-you-out-the-way types that I struggle with.' I gaze longingly at the breaking waves. 'Let's go down to the water's edge. I'm dying to get my feet in the water.'

'Sure.' James shifts trajectory but unfortunately sticks with the current topic of conversation. 'Has this issue held you back in your job then, Emma? There are a lot of bad behaviours in workplaces.'

Karla, my ex-boss and queen of intimidation, floats into my head, taking the shine off the moment when I finally reach the tide and paddle in the cool, crystal-clear water. This irks me a little. I don't want to be thinking about her right now. I want to splash in the sparkling sea and flirt with James. Why is he pursuing this stuff?

'Yeah, it has.' I shrug, wading ankle deep through the water. 'But that's par for the course. Some people want to climb the career ladder as quickly as possible and they'll tread on others to get there. It's a simple fact of life.'

'But that's the thing, Emma. You don't *have* to live with it. You can learn to stand your ground in a way that means people respect you and won't mess with you. It's about not showing weakness.'

My irk morphs into irritation. Why is James suddenly trying to play mentor? The tip about eye contact was great, but then there was the comment about my notes for the presentation and now this. He's obviously trying to help – but I don't want another interview coach on top of Amber and Cat. I told him this already. I also want my time with him to be the fun part of my day.

'I'm aware of my weaknesses, James,' I say. 'And Amber's already said she'll help me with that particular issue before I start a new job. Now, can we change the subject before I decide you should address your own fears by signing you up to a paragliding course?'

'Fair enough.' He shrugs easily, then points to the beach bar. 'Don't know about you, but I fancy continuing with our walk with a refreshing drink.'

'Ooh, yeah, that sounds perfect.' I'm pleased to have finally deterred James from Operation: Let's Fix Emma.

'Race you there? Last one gets the drinks in.'

'You're on.'

We take off up the gentle slope from the water, which is a lot tougher to run on that it looks, and within fifteen seconds I've given up. I'm more than happy to get the drinks in, given that everything's already paid for.

~

After the remainder of my beach walk with James, which was filled with the flirty banter and movie-style kisses I was craving, I feel like I've had some proper downtime. And to my relief, there was no more well-intentioned-but-at-this-point-unwanted advice from him.

After swinging by reception to get a loan of a laptop and USB stick from Charnice, I meet Cat and Amber in the resort's Business Hub, where I'll be creating the visuals for my presentation. As with my main content, they leave me to do the work myself and just chip in here and there when I ask for opinions.

'And... that's it. *Done*.' I close the PowerPoint file and pull the USB stick out of the laptop when I'm finally finished.

'Well done, honey.' Cat claps her hands excitedly. 'You've done an incredible job.'

'I've done my best. I'm no graphic designer or anything, but hopefully this will hit the mark.'

'It looks boss,' says Amber. 'All you need to do now is nail your presentation content and you're ready to roll. Right, let's go eat. I'm starving.'

We head to the beach bar, where we enjoy burgers and fries for lunch. It's the perfect setting, gazing out across the turquoise water to where the darker sea meets the azure of the sky on the horizon.

After we've eaten, we spend some time doing interview practice like the day before. Amber fires questions at me like a spray of bullets in an action movie, and I'm pleased to find that I'm much quicker off the mark with my answers this time.

'*Well done.*' She slaps me on the back once we're done. 'Your answers were great and you came across well. Do that tomorrow and you'll blow them away.'

'I reckon, after that, I could survive an MI5 interrogation.' I mop the sweat from my brow with my napkin. 'You're a hard bloody taskmaster, Amber. Being serious though, I think I am ready – on the interview side. The presentation still scares the living crap out of me though.'

'I know you're nervous,' says Cat. 'Most people would be. But you've got fantastic content. Believe in yourself, be as natural as possible – as you've done here – and you'll do amazing.'

On digesting her words, James's comment about me reading from a script floats into my mind – an unwelcome but relevant reminder that my presentation style is anything but natural. This stirs up a nauseous feeling in my gut. He may be right, but I'm not confident enough to freestyle it.

'You OK, honey?' Cat seems to sense my discomfort.

I force a smile. 'Yeah, I'm fine. Just nervous about my presentation, as I said.'

'You'll be glad to know then, that we're doing more presentation practice this afternoon,' says Amber 'We'll have you knocked into shape by this evening.'

'Hmm...' I grimace. 'Why does that worry me more than it reassures me?'

Chapter Thirty-Two

An hour later, we've retrieved our beach gear from our suites and trekked across the sand to claim three empty loungers, shaded by large parasols. They're located on a section of the beach with a cluster of towering palm trees, giving us some extra protection from the afternoon sun. We unpack our things and get comfortable, then I look around me and sigh.

'I may be dreading whatever you have in store for me this afternoon, but I am happy that I get to do it here.'

'It *is* stunning.' Cat follows my gaze. 'This view... the powdery white sand and that water. It's mesmerising. I could never get bored of it.'

'Me neither.'

'Are you ready for your next task then, Emma?' Amber terminates our moment of zen.

'Sure.' My reply is empty of any enthusiasm.

'Honey, before we start...' says Cat suddenly. 'I want you to know that your instinct about this activity is right. It's not going to be comfortable for you, but I've agreed to it because I genuinely think it's going to help you. Please keep that in your mind.'

'There's a statement that fills me with confidence... and *it* is...?'

'We'll get to that in a minute,' says Amber. 'First, let's go back to your personal development stuff that we talked about the other night. What were your areas for improvement again?'

She's testing me rather than asking me to help her remember, and this time I know better than to back chat her while she's in coach mode. I close my eyes to divert my brain to where it needs to be focused.

'We talked about... building my assertiveness... working on my impulse control... keeping things in perspective...what else?'

'Getting over setbacks quickly and making more of your natural skills in empathy and relationship building,' she fills in for me.

'Ah, yeah, that was it.'

'Any thoughts on those since we discussed them?'

'Not really. But I've been busy with other stuff.'

'That's true, but try to keep them in your mind, so you can catch yourself in the moment and avoid continually making the same mistakes.'

'OK, sure. I'll give that a go.'

'Great, then let's get to it.' Amber puffs herself up like she's about to announce the winner of the BAFTA for Best Supporting Actress. 'Emma, this afternoon, you're going to do a presentation, but not the one you're doing tomorrow. I want you to pick a subject – anything you like – and prepare ten-minute's worth of content. Then you're going to deliver it to Cat, myself and some of the people on this beach.'

'*What?*' I sit bolt upright. 'You're kidding, right?'

'I'm not kidding.'

'But... I can't do that.'

'Why not?'

'Because it's *terrifying*... and *humiliating*.'

'Emma, do you want to get that job tomorrow?' Amber's

tone is calm and reassuring, which tells me she was one hundred per cent expecting this reaction from me.

'Yes... but—'

'Then you need to do this. A dry run with a crowd will let you feel all the unpleasant feelings you're going to experience tomorrow, which means you'll be ready for them and you can manage them.'

'Or it'll be the single most humiliating moment of my life.' I cover my face with my hands. 'What the hell are all these people going to think of me?'

'That you're brave and someone to admire,' says Cat.

Amber gets up from her lounger and sits down next to me. 'Emma, you need to care a lot less about what others think of you. You don't know these people, and you'll never see them again after this holiday, so who gives a shit what they think?'

'What if they film me and I end up as a meme online? I'd die.'

'They won't do that. I'll ask them not to, and we've picked this part of the beach on purpose, so that the trees provide some privacy. No one will be able to film from a distance, and I'll be watching your audience like a hawk to make sure there are no phones out.'

With Amber already having thought of everything and Cat supporting this activity, my only remaining option is to hurl my toys out of my adult-sized pram – something I'm not prepared to do, given all the effort my friends have put into helping me. I'm going to have to suck it up and try to reap the benefits I'm assured it will provide.

'Fine. Let's get it over with.'

'That's the spirit.' Amber pats my knee. 'First thing then: choose your topic. It's totally up to you what you talk about.'

'OK... um... I have no idea. Why do I suddenly feel like I don't know anything about anything?'

'Because you're panicking, honey.' Cat adopts a soothing tone. 'There are lots of things you know about.'

'Like?'

'You just bought a new car. You could talk about that experience. Or you could cover a subject like report writing. You did lots of board reports in your last job.'

I grimace. 'That sounds boring as hell. But then I do know that stuff inside out.'

'Think of your audience,' says Amber. 'Do you think a bunch of holidaymakers are going to be interested in report writing?'

'Ugh, no.'

'What about something light-hearted that you can have a bit of fun with?' she suggests. 'It's not about the content, it's about your presentation skills. You could talk about why street food is the best thing since McDonalds fries, or what you'd do if you ruled the world?'

'Don't think I could talk about street food for ten minutes, but I guess I could do the one about ruling the world.'

'Excellent, that's sorted then.' She grins at me. 'We'll leave you in peace for an hour to prepare.'

'*An hour?*' My eyes widen. 'That's not long enough.'

'OK, ninety minutes. That's all you're getting.'

'But—'

'Clock's already ticking.'

'*You're so cruel!*' I wail after her, as she and Cat leave our spot and approach a sunbathing couple nearby.

They appear to have a quick conversation with them, then move onto a small group, and it dawns on me what they're doing: they're recruiting my audience. My heart starts pounding. *This is awful.* No, it's worse than awful. It's borderline my worst nightmare. Karaoke now seems like a breeze in comparison.

After working myself up into a substantial lather, it dawns on me that I need to pull myself together or I'll find myself in front of an audience in – I check the time on my phone – eighty-four minutes time with nothing to share.

Fixing my gaze on a point on the horizon, I take some deep breaths – resurrecting the self-help approach I used when I was having anxiety attacks after Dave dumped me. This helps a little, but I'm still a long way from being able to focus. Then I have an idea. I quickly slather on some sun cream, grab my notepad and pen, and make my way down to the water's edge.

The moment my feet are immersed in the cool, clear water, the heat of my panic is extinguished. I wade in up to my knees, and the deeper I get, the more in control I feel. Within minutes, I'm capable of coherent thought, and I start to play with ideas in my mind, noting down the those that appeal the most.

Twenty minutes later, I'm back on my lounger, scribbling furiously. The content isn't a problem once I get going, but I need as much time as possible to be confident presenting it. Every time I think about my impending audience, I feel nauseous – and also tempted to do a rain dance in the hope that a tropical storm materialises and we have to call the whole thing off. Who am I kidding? It's a perfect cloudless day, and even if that were to happen, Amber would make damn sure to mobilise the troops somewhere indoors. *Man, I hate her sometimes* (in a really loving way).

By the time my friends return, I'm nowhere near ready to do this – but given that that time would be *never*, it's probably irrelevant.

'You all set?' Amber gives me an encouraging nudge that nearly knocks me on my arse because I'm feeling so faint.

'How about some water?' says Cat. 'You're looking a bit peaky... and damp.'

'No shit.' I look at her glumly. 'I think I've sweated out the entire water content of my body.'

'It'll be over really soon.' She hands me a bottle of water and I take a sizeable glug.

I catch her giving Amber a look to move things along, and without warning Amber puts her fingers in her mouth and gives a loud piercing whistle. Then, like a scene from *The Walking Dead*, about two dozen people get to their feet and start moving in our direction. And I feel a crushing dread like I've never experienced before.

Watching the sea of people gather around us, some chatting and laughing while others are talking in hushed tones, I feel an urgent urge to take off up the beach towards my suite. But I know I have to see this through, so I fight it and focus on my breathing.

'Hey, everyone,' Amber greets them. 'Thanks so much for agreeing to this. This is Emma... and as I said, she's got a big interview coming up, so she'll be presenting to you to get some practice in. She'll talk for about ten minutes, then you'll have the opportunity to ask her some questions.'

They'll what? My face drains of any remaining colour. Amber didn't mention there would be a Q&A session as well. No doubt on purpose, because she knew it would send me over the edge.

I'm on the verge of hyperventilating, when a calming hand makes contact with my waist, and Cat pulls me into a squeezy side-hug.

'You've got this,' she whispers in my ear as Amber says 'Emma, you're up' and gestures for me to take 'centre stage'.

After (too) long a pause, where I'm willing my body to move but it's refusing to cooperate, I step forward on Bambi legs and smile weakly at my audience. Clearing my throat a couple of times while rustling my notes (more for the security of knowing that they're there than anything else), I take a shuddering breath and let out what can only be described as a cross between a croak and a squeak.

Mortified at this being their first impression of me, I dare a sweeping glance around my audience, expecting to see impatient, bored or amused faces, but all that's reflected back at me are encouraging and interested looks.

'Let's give Emma some, shall we?' a smiling grey-haired American woman wearing a pink sequined T-shirt calls out.

She starts to clap and whoop, and like a landslide, my whole audience joins in, creating quite a ruckus. They're so enthusiastic that before I know it, I've joined in – until I realise that means I'm clapping for myself and I quickly drop my hands by my side, hoping nobody's registered that moment of idiocy. I continue to smile at them though, hugely grateful for the support.

As the applause dies down, I know I've got to catch the moment and not to allow the tumbleweed to roll in again.

'*Ahem*... thank you for that,' I say. 'Think it was needed. I'm also wondering if the lady who started that would like to take my place?'

There's a collective chuckle, which almost takes the edge off my terror.

'Sure, anytime,' the American woman calls back to me.

'OK, then...' I look down at the sand to ground myself, then back up at the forty-odd eyes on me. 'As you already know, I'm Emma, and I'm going to talk to you about the very important and enlightening subject of "If I ruled the world".'

I pause briefly and look down at my notes.

'The first thing I'd like to say is that, if I ruled the world, I'd definitely ban presentations at interviews...'

My audience laughs again, and I notice a couple of them giving each other approving nods. Feeling slightly more in control, I check my place and continue.

'My friend Amber here, encouraged me to keep this subject light, and while there must have been plenty opportunity to get some jokes in, I discovered that I'm not funny... well, every day is a school day as they say...'

There's a ripple of sympathetic amusement and a few more approving looks. Encouraged, I stand taller and keep going.

'This means I'm going to address some of the bigger stuff, because I reckon most people would want to do that if they ruled the world. Right the wrongs, eradicate hunger, end conflicts, see that no child ever went to school hungry or had to walk miles every day for water, while missing out on an education. Jim Carrey certainly did.'

Briefly looking up at my audience, I see a mix of amused faces from those who have clocked the *Bruce Almighty* reference and more sombre expressions from audience members who appear to be connecting with the bigger message in what I'm saying, some of them even nodding agreement. I continue my monologue for what feels like forever, and when I eventually wrap up, my onlookers break into yet more cheers and applause. And this time I feel like I've earned it. I smile back at them self-consciously, wondering why I can't recall any of the last ten minutes, then a fresh dose of fear floods through me on remembering that the Q&A is next.

'Well done, Emma!' Amber's voice breaks through the clapping, causing it to peter away. 'Now, who has questions?'

A few hands raise.

'Yes. The lady with the pink and blue sarong.'

'Thanks, Amber,' she says. 'Emma, loved the pop culture reference. Which is your favourite – *Bruce Almighty* or *Evan Almighty?*'

I catch Amber rolling her eyes, but I'm delighted by the ridiculousness of the question.

'*Bruce Almighty*. No question.' I beam at her. 'I'm a massive Jim Carrey fan.'

'OK, who's next?' Amber moves things along. 'Yes, man with the Hawaiian shirt...'

'Thank you, Amber,' he says. 'I'm wondering, Emma, given that you mentioned saving the planet as being high on your priority list, what approach would you take with reducing carbon emissions globally?'

I ponder this for a moment. It's a challenging question, but surely I can come up with a reasonable response. I'm willing my mind to hand me the perfect answer, but unfortunately it does the opposite and goes completely blank.

'I... eh...' I feel myself start to panic. 'I think...'

I glance helplessly at Amber and she mouths the word 'governments' at me. Thankfully, this is enough to kick my brain back into gear.

'It's a great question... I think national governments are the answer. They have to care enough to make it a priority and make real change happen. So, I'd put people in power who would do that.'

The man with the Hawaiian shirt seems satisfied enough with my answer and I breathe a sigh of relief that I've made it through.

'Who's next?' Amber looks around for any more raised hands. 'Yes. Lady with the flowery sunhat.'

The woman Amber has indicated to steps forward to address me. 'Emma, you mentioned that you'd end conflict and create world peace...'

I cringe. That line sounds like the stereotypical beauty contestant response. The problem was, at that point, I'd lost my place in my notes and was trying to fill the silence while I found it again.

'I'm just wondering how you'd do that?' says the woman. 'Humans, by their very nature, are hardwired to come into conflict: it's a survival instinct. How would you suppress that biological urge in the pursuit of world peace?'

This question almost floors me – literally. Having only made it through the last one thanks to Amber, my legs begin to tremble. I have no clue how to answer this question – perhaps another reason why I should have kept the subject light. I'm so out of my depth on this one, it's not funny.

'Gosh, right... that's a toughie...' I'm floundering, my brain has crashed again and this time it's shut up shop. No amount of coaxing or being prompted by Amber is going to help. 'I... eh... gosh, it's really hot isn't it...'

I put my hand to my forehead and glance across at my friends, then at my group of onlookers, who suddenly look very blurry. Then the next thing I'm aware of is everything closing in around me and the world turning black.

Chapter Thirty-Three

I come around on the sand to Amber and Cat kneeling beside me talking urgently to each other and a hazy group of people watching from a few feet away.

'Emma, honey, can you hear me?' Cat's voice sounds distant and tinny. 'Amber, we need to get some water in her.'

'Come on, Emma. Let's sit you up.' Amber sounds similarly far away as she and Cat hoist me into a sitting position onto a lounger.

Once I'm more with it, I take the bottle of water being offered to me and glug at it thirstily. The crowd of onlookers is thankfully dispersing, but it does little to ease the sting of humiliation as I catch up with what's happened. Tears prick at my eyes.

'I messed up.'

'You didn't mess up. You passed out.' Cat strokes my hair. 'The heat must have been too much for you. Especially when you were sweating so much. I'm so sorry. We should have thought of that and done it indoors.'

'Yeah, our bad.' Amber trickles some water down my face to cool me down.

As much as I want to believe that my faint was due to the heat and dehydration – and it may well have been a factor – the truth is that I was in a blind panic because of the question that woman asked. And the one before it I only managed to answer because Amber bailed me out. Which begs the question: how will I cope tomorrow when it's going to be ten times harder?

My friends continue to fuss around me, checking I'm all right and not going to pass out on them again.

'Probably best we get you out of this heat,' says Cat.

'Do you feel up to walking?' Amber asks me.

'Maybe we could get one of those golf cart things to come and get her,' suggests Cat.

'*No way.*' I hold up two hands to halt them from taking that idea any further. 'I *do not* want Sébastien hearing about this. I'll be fine to walk. The water has helped.'

'OK, honey.' Cat resumes stroking my hair protectively. 'As long as you're sure.'

'I'm sure. Let's go. I can't take any more people staring at me.'

'Nobody's staring at you.'

'They are. Trust me.'

Cat and Amber are braced to swoop in and rescue me while I get to my feet, but I wave them away. If I couldn't end my presentation with dignity, I can at least try to leave the beach with some. They flank me on either side while we trudge across the sand towards the pathway that leads to our suites, passing some people I recognise from my 'audience' as we go. A few of them offer sympathetic nods and comments of 'take care.'

I'm almost at the walkway and feeling like I've redeemed myself slightly by not being carried off the beach, when a young couple pass us.

'That's her.' I hear the man mutter under his breath to his partner. '*What a flake.* No way I'd hire her.'

His partner scoffs by way of a response, and I stiffen, their cruelty rattling through me like a pinball, reinforcing the self-doubt that's been tearing through my mind.

'Ignore them.' Cat threads her arm through mine. 'That comment says a lot more about him than it does about you.'

'*Arseholes*,' Amber mutters. 'I should go after them and show them what's what.'

'Please don't,' I say. 'I don't need any more drama today – particularly not you getting arrested.'

We walk the rest of the way back in silence, the mood more muted than it's been all holiday. Cat convinces me to go to her suite so she can keep an eye on me, and I reluctantly agree because I don't want to worry her, but all I really want is to be left alone.

I lie out on her bed while she and Amber try to get some more upbeat conversation flowing, but it falls flat. This leaves me certain that what's going through my friends' heads is the same as what's going through mine: is this interview such a good idea after all?

Before long, my exhausted mind can no longer cope with juggling my worrisome thoughts. I feel my eyelids drooping and I'm drifting off to sleep.

~

Sometime later, I wake with a pounding head to an empty room. At first, I wonder if Cat and Amber have gone out to avoid disturbing me, but then I hear faint voices outside on Cat's balcony terrace. Getting up, I walk across to the patio doors, which they've left open a crack – probably so they can check on me without waking me – and I'm about to step outside to join them, when I hear a male voice: James. He's out there with them, which means they've told him what happened and he's seen me out for the count. I smart a little at this.

Should it not have been up to me to tell him what happened? If I even wanted him to know.

In my hesitation, I pick up the thread of their conversation.

'I think it's all been too much.' I hear Cat say. 'She's been through a lot in the last month. Maybe we shouldn't have encouraged her to go for the job.'

'You might be right,' says Amber. 'She didn't cope well at all with the practice Q&A session on the beach. I'm now thinking that's why she passed out, not because of the heat. She did better on the presentation itself, but she was literally reading it like a script, same as at breakfast. I didn't say anything earlier because I had hoped I'd see something more dynamic this afternoon and that I could offer her some helpful feedback then.'

'I tried to talk to her about that,' says James. 'Don't think she was in the place to hear it, but who can blame her? The interview's tomorrow.'

I feel a stab of hurt as they continue to talk about me like I'm a lame pet.

'This is a big job,' says Amber. 'I've no doubt she's got the potential to do it in the longer term, but it might be too soon. I haven't had the chance to work with her on her confidence and her other weaker areas yet.'

'I'm also a bit worried about who might be at that presentation tomorrow,' says Cat. 'If that horrible bloke who's had a go at her twice already is there, he could tear into her again. I really don't want that to happen.'

'What guy?' James asks. 'Emma never mentioned him. He shouldn't be getting away with that.'

Tears brim in my eyes. They really have no confidence in me. Would they be this forthright to my face? Maybe Amber would, but Cat and James? It all feels underhand them gathering like this to discuss me.

For a moment, I consider going out there and confronting

them, but I just don't have it in me. Instead, I quietly gather my stuff together and slip out of Cat's suite, accidentally slamming the door behind me.

Cursing myself for that error, I rush along the corridor, removing my sandals as I go, so I can get away faster. The last thing I want is them catching up with me. Aware that my suite is the first place they'll look, I scurry past reception and out the front entrance of the main resort building. The lush tropical gardens that frame the long driveway from the main road are plentiful, so I can easily stay out of sight here. With my sandals dangling by my side, I miserably make my way along one of the meandering paths, barely noticing the vibrant flowers and plants or the towering exotic trees.

I pass a large pond and a building that has a sign on it saying 'staff only', eventually settling down on a bench that's well enough concealed to give me the privacy I need. I'm struggling to process what I heard back in Cat's suite. Their care and concern for me was evident, which, if that's all it was, would be fine. That's not what's bothering me. It's their lack of belief in me, and how they seemed to think they needed to form a committee to assess my fitness for the interview. It was hard enough having Amber playing coach with Cat in a supporting role, but James deciding to muscle in on things as well – it's too much. And I'd never doubt them like they're doubting me. That hurts more than anything.

But they have good reason to, an unwelcome voice in my head pipes up. I've might have shown that I'm great on paper. That I can evidence my skills and experience, create top quality content and build strong arguments. But I can't seem to carry that through when presenting to and being challenged by others. Without the safety blanket of detailed notes, I'm skittish and lacking in self-belief, and I clearly suffer from imposter syndrome in that respect. Why wouldn't they doubt me?

Regardless of whether Cat, Amber and James are justified in their lack of faith in me, there's only one logical conclusion here: I need to pull out of the interview. I can't bear the thought of them – or Sébastien and the audience at my presentation – cringing and pitying me. It makes me feel physically sick.

Decision made, I walk back through the gardens, into the atrium of the main resort building and across to the reception desk.

'Emma, how are you?' Charnice greets me with her usual bright demeanour.

'Hi, Charnice.' I give a feeble smile. 'I'm... not so great actually. Could you pass a message on to Sébastien for me?'

'Yes, no problem.'

'Please can you tell him that I'm really sorry, but I need to pull out of the interview tomorrow.'

'Yes, I can pass that on, Emma. No problem.' She regards me with concern, and under her scrutiny, I feel the need to justify my request.

'I'm just... not up to it.'

'You are unwell? I'm sorry to hear this. I can arrange for you to see a doctor if it would help?'

Although this is not quite what I meant, it's not altogether untrue. I did pass out on the beach, and I'm not in the best form right now – physically, mentally or emotionally. Charnice could also hear about what happened through the resort grapevine, so it may as well act as my cover story.

'Thanks for the offer, Charnice. I haven't been well this afternoon, but there's no need for the doctor.'

'All right, Emma. I do hope you feel better soon, and I will pass your message on to Monsieur Dumont straight away.'

I thank Charnice and take the route via the busy poolside and garden back to my suite in the hope that I'll blend into with the other holidaymakers. I do feel guilty that Cat, Amber and James are possibly looking all over for me, but right now I need to be left in peace.

On reaching my suite, I shake off my sandals and cross the room to the huge bed, suddenly feeling quite home sick. I pull back the sheets and get under the covers, where, as expected, the tears come thick and fast. This holiday was supposed to be perfect. It was meant to be about three friends relaxing and having the time of their life: my treat to Cat and Amber on the back of my lottery win. It should have been *that* simple. *That* good.

I could point the finger at Amber: she was the one who 'prodded' Sébastien and who set off this whole chain of events. But it's not really her fault. She's a chancer – an opportunist. I could have said no when Sébastien offered me the interview. It was my hunger to find my dream job, not just her and Cat's encouragement, that made me gun for it.

And then there's James. He's amazing and so damn gorgeous, and the thought of not continuing things with him makes my heart shred like that Banksy painting at the auction, but he's another fixer. I kind of knew that from when we first met that he was a helper – though at that time I mistakenly thought it was that he had an ego-driven hero complex. But he's not just a helper, it seems he likes to fix things (and in this case, it means he's trying to 'fix me'). Is that what *I* need in my life? Between my parents and Amber, I'm not sure I can cope with any more people trying to improve me. I want to build-a-better-Emma, but too many voices will beat me down, not lift me up.

I lie there, staring up at the ceiling, for what seems like an eternity. I have no idea what time it is and I don't care. I'm still exhausted and just when I'm at the point of falling back asleep, there's a loud rapping at my suite door.

Chapter Thirty-Four

'*Emma! Are you there?*' Amber shouts from the other side of the door.

'*Honey, we're worried about you!*' calls Cat. 'If you're there, please answer.'

My overriding instinct is to stay silent so they give up and go away, but if I'm off the radar for too long (particularly given the fact that I passed out earlier), I know they'll get worried and set up a search party, or worse, call the police. That would take my loss of dignity to a whole new level.

With a defeated sigh, I get up and open the door to my visibly relieved friends, noting to my own relief, that James isn't with them.

'We had a feeling you'd be back here by now, so we sent James to have another look on the beach,' says Amber. 'Figured you wouldn't want to see him right now.'

'Or either of us,' Cat adds with a shamefaced expression. 'We know we've upset you, but we can't stand the thought of you being miserable and alone when you're so far from home... well, I can't anyway.'

I say nothing. All my efforts go into stemming the tears that are welling in my eyes.

'Can we come in?' she asks.

'OK.' I pull the door wider and return to my bed, leaving them to close it behind them.

They follow me inside and sit down on the sofa.

'We're so sorry that you overheard us talking about you like that.' Cat does seem genuinely gutted. 'I imagine that wouldn't have been nice to hear.'

I glance from her to Amber, then avert my gaze, unable to trust myself to keep it together.

'It wasn't. I thought you guys believed in me, but you don't at all.'

'That's not true,' says Cat. 'We *absolutely* believe in you. There's no doubt you're heading in that direction with your career—'

'But only if I fix myself. Because the truth is: I'm a flake who's not up to it, right?'

'Wrong.' My bestie shakes her head. 'We don't think that at all. That label was used by someone who knows nothing about you, or what you're capable of. It came from a thoughtless—'

'Arsehole.' Amber finishes Cat's sentence for her.

'You might not have used the label, but you clearly don't think I'm up to tomorrow – or that I have any chance at that job. And neither does James. You even formed a bloody committee to rule on it.' I swallow thickly, still fighting to keep my composure.

'It wasn't quite like that, but in hindsight, I can understand how it felt that way,' says Cat. 'We had some concerns, especially after what happened at the beach, but as long as you're feeling up to going ahead with the interview, we're behind you and we believe you can do it, right Amber?'

'Yeah.' Amber nods. 'We do.'

'Thanks, but that's kind of hard to believe, given I heard you all discussing how I read my presentation like a script and I can't cope with a Q&A session.' I wring my hands anxiously. 'Anyway, it doesn't matter because you didn't say anything that wasn't already running through my head. I was kidding myself going for that job and the three of you helped me realise that. I've called off the interview.'

'You've called it off?' Amber shares a pained and somewhat regretful look with Cat.

'Yes. I asked Charnice to pass on the message, so Sébastien will know by now.'

'Oh, honey.' Cat joins me on the bed, enveloping me in a hug, which I give in to instantly. 'We're so sorry. We never wanted to ruin your big opportunity – or destroy your confidence.'

'It's fine. It's for the best.' I give a half-smile. 'Let's just try and salvage what's left of our holiday, yeah? Have the R&R I came here for in the first place.'

'And James?' asks Amber.

I chew on my lip. 'I don't know. He's amazing but I'm now questioning whether I've jumped into that too soon as well. I'm not sure if I'm ready for another relationship yet. Plus, do I really want a guy in my life who doesn't think I'm enough? He should like me for who I am, right?'

'Emma, I think James...' Amber starts, then trails off as she meets Cat's eye.

'You don't need to think about that right now,' says Cat. 'But it is dinner time. Do you feel up to going for some food?'

'If it's OK with you guys, I think I'll just get some room service and an early night. I'm exhausted.'

Cat seems reluctant to leave me, but she respects my decision. 'OK, sure, honey. We'll probably take the opportunity for a quiet one as well, right Amber?'

Amber nods, quite unconvincingly, which makes me think

she'll be out partying with Tyler, Rob and James until the small hours.

'If you need anything, message us,' she says.'

'I will, thanks... Oh, would you...' I cringe a little.

'We'll tell James we've found you and that you need some space,' says Cat.

'Thanks.'

I don't like asking them to do my dirty work for me, but I can't face James this evening after everything that's happened.

After seeing my friends out, I pull the curtains, climb back into bed and settle down for the night. All I want to do is to sleep. Missing one meal when I've been eating like a pig for the last few days will hardly be the end of me.

Chapter Thirty-Five

I sleep right through the night, and having gone to bed so early, I also waken very early – I know this because there isn't a hint of light peeking through the curtains. Rubbing my eyes drowsily, I reach for my phone on my bedside table, before remembering that it's still in my beach bag from the day before. I throw back the covers, pad across to retrieve it, and on illuminating the screen, I see that it's awash with new message notifications. Mostly from when Cat and Amber were looking for me, but there are also a couple from James and one from my mum offering me yet more unsolicited advice on staying safe abroad.

In addition to the messages of concern from the girls, there's one more on our group chat from Cat, letting me know they'll be at the beach bar – which doubles up as an à la carte breakfast spot – at nine a.m..

I'm about to reply to say I'll see them there, when I clock the time on my phone – it's 5.03 a.m.. With Cat and Amber having told me the night before to call or message if I needed anything, I fully expect they'll have kept the ringers their

249

phones switched on overnight, which means it's way too early to message back.

Abandoning that idea, my eyes are drawn to the unread messages on my Messenger app from James. The oldest is from yesterday afternoon, expressing similar concern to that of the girls' messages, and apologising for the conversation I overheard. Then there's one more, obviously sent after he'd been told that they'd found me.

Hi again. I hear you're back in your suite and that you want to be left in peace. I will obviously respect that, but I need you to know I'm sincerely sorry for what happened. I only ever wanted to help. I think you're an amazing woman who's capable of so much, and I'm gutted to hear you've pulled out of your interview because of this. I hope we can still fix 'us' because I miss you already. x

Guilt pricks at me. James will have seen that I didn't even read his message last night. He's probably wondering what that means – though maybe not. I don't yet know him well enough to understand how he thinks, but if it were the other way around, I'd have convinced myself that he was going to ditch me. My hope is that Cat and Amber told him I was going straight to bed. Because as much as I now have big doubts about us, I do have feelings for him, and I don't want to hurt him any more than I have to. I'll reply at a more reasonable hour (just in case he also has the ringer switched on on his phone) and ask him to meet me in the afternoon. That will give me some time to figure out where I'm at and what I want to say to him.

Now fully awake and alert, my brain hands me another unwelcome bone to chew on: the fact that I should have been going to my interview in several hours' time. But I'm not. Because I pulled out.

I pace around my room as I try to work out how I feel about this. There's a strong sense of cowardly relief fighting a competing chunk of disappointment, but there's also something else: the feeling that I've let myself down. I consider calling Lottie, but having not told her anything about my interview in the first place, I decide against it. She doesn't need me crying to her about the latest cock-up I've become embroiled in – especially as I haven't followed her advice about having some proper downtime. No. This one I have to work through myself.

Pulling back the curtains, I open the patio doors and step out into the early morning air – and a monsoon style downpour, which has been masked by the (clearly very effective) soundproofing of my suite.

One day too late. I laugh ironically, remembering my desperation for something to hijack my presentation practice the previous afternoon.

Remaining by the patio doors to avoid getting soaked, I breathe in the moist air, expecting to at least feel a sense of freedom from having thrown off the shackles of my impending interview. But it doesn't come. Something's niggling at me, and it doesn't take long to work out what it is: the feeling of failure. I guess that was always going to come. But I *have* done the right thing pulling out of the interview.

Haven't I?

The rain subsides and I nip inside to grab a towel and the novel I'm reading in the hope that it will distract my troubled mind. After drying off one of the patio chairs, I settle myself down but I can't seem to get into the story, and before I realise what I'm doing, I've made another trip inside and picked up my presentation notes. Shrugging to myself, I make a cup of green tea, then I head back outside and do exactly as James suggested:

I re-write my notes, but this time with key points to replace my scripted approach.

Once I've finished, I set my old notes aside and try delivering my presentation out loud with this new approach. At first, it feels impossible. My mind constantly blanks, and I hesitate, stutter, stumble (and curse) until I almost give up. *Almost, but not quite.* Because a fire has been lit inside me, and I can't let it go. I can't let this be a wasted opportunity. If I can at least come away from this experience having achieved something, then I won't have unnecessarily stolen away everyone's time – and ruined our girls holiday.

After a short break to clear my head and second cup of tea, I take another stab at it, and this time it's not a complete car crash. More of a bumper-to-bumper collision. But it's the glimmer of progress I needed to see. Encouraged by this, I keep going, and by the time I stop to get ready for breakfast, I'm feeling quite proud of myself. I'll never be asked to do a *Ted Talk*, granted, but I can see how much better my presentation flows – and how much better *I* come across – all thanks to James's suggestion.

Half an hour later, I'm on my way to meet Cat and Amber with what could almost be described as a spring in my step. I may have squandered the biggest career opportunity of my life, but at least I've redeemed myself enough to hold my head high. And I have something positive to report to them.

'Morning.' I slide into my seat while admiring the sea view, which, even with the ominous clouds rolling across the horizon is still amazing. 'This is nice. A lovely change from the buffet restaurant.'

'How are you, honey?' Cat clutches my hand, her face etched with concern.

'I'm OK. Better than I expected.'

'That's good. Did you sleep well?'

'I did. I was out for the count within minutes of you leaving my suite. Meant I woke up stupidly early, but I feel refreshed, and I've been using the time productively.'

'Oh yeah?' Amber looks up from the breakfast menu. 'What have you been doing? I'm assuming not James.'

I wince at the mention of his name. 'Correct. I've actually spent the morning practising my presentation.'

'You have?' Amber shares a look with Cat. 'Emma, you *do* remember what happened yesterday? That you pulled out of the interview?'

'Of course I remember. I haven't completely lost it.'

'Do you have any regrets?'

I thank the waiter who has just served us tea, coffee and toast before considering her question. 'Yes and no... It's mixed. The pressure being removed is a relief, but I also feel like I've let myself down... that I've failed somehow.'

'You haven't *failed*.' Cat squeezes my hand to punctuate this point.

'I know that – sort of. But it did feel like I'd wasted everyone's time, so when I got up this morning I felt the need to redeem myself. To have *something* to show for this whole experience.'

'Now you're thinking like a kick-ass professional,' says Amber. 'And?'

'And so, I worked on my presentation skills.' I butter a piece of toast as I talk. 'I re-wrote my notes with key points instead of a script, as James suggested, and I spent some time practising my delivery with that approach.'

'*Go you.* And?'

'It went OK. I'm no Michelle Obama, but I've gained a new skill – one that I can hone over time.'

'How about you hone it this morning?' says Amber, who raises an eyebrow in Cat's direction. Cat puts her hand to her mouth and seems to hold her breath in anticipation.

'*Huh?* What are you on about?' I ping pong between them,

bewildered by their strange behaviour. 'I feel good about the progress I've made, but why would I want to spend my morning doing prep when I've pulled out of the interview?'

'Maybe because there's a parallel universe where you haven't?' says Amber and I shake my head in utter bafflement.

'Um... OK...'

'Amber, *please* get to the point,' says Cat. 'There isn't enough time for this.'

'What's going on?' I look from Cat to Amber again, suddenly suspicious.

'*All right, fine.*' Amber sniffs in mild annoyance. 'Emma, your interview is still on.'

Chapter Thirty-Six

'*What?*' I just about fall off my seat at this revelation. 'Amber, you need to explain what's going on – *right now.*'

'I'm about to. Chill.' She rolls her eyes at Cat, as if I'm the one causing the issue here.

'No, I will not *chill. Explain.*'

'All right. When we lost you yesterday, we split up to look for you and I passed by reception literally about thirty seconds after you spoke to Charnice.'

'Right. And?'

'You forget that I know you. I figured there was a high chance you'd act impulsively and pull out of the interview. After a bit of coaxing, I managed to get it out of Charnice that you'd asked her to contact Sébastien – she had the phone in her hand, about to do it – and I convinced her not to pass the message on because I thought you'd regret your decision by this morning.'

'You did *what?*' I'm aghast (though if I'm honest, not altogether unsurprised) by Amber's meddling. 'You mean Sébastien's still expecting me to show up this morning? *Amber, what have you done?* I need to get Charnice to contact him straight away.'

'Or... you could go ahead with the interview.' She raises her eyebrows suggestively.

I hesitate. 'No... *no*, I can't. I'm obviously not ready for that job. You even said it yourselves yesterday.'

'And we were wrong. Because despite everything that happened, you got up at five this morning, and instead of having a little pity party yourself – which is something you might have done even a week ago – you stuck two fingers up to the situation and decided you were a winner. That's a clear sign of someone who's determined and one hundred per cent deserves this job.'

I look to Cat uncertainly and she nods agreement with Amber.

'Honey, if you hadn't spoken to Charnice yesterday, do you think you would have wanted to go ahead with the interview this morning?' Cat asks. 'After a good sleep and some distance from things?'

I puff out my cheeks. 'I'm not sure. I guess... with the humiliation of yesterday's disaster having dulled, I probably would have gone ahead with it – because I committed to it more than anything else. I'd still be terrified and thinking I'd got ahead of myself though.'

'And now that you've sneaked in that extra prep, and the interview's still on...?'

'I think... it's a ridiculous long shot, but as Amber has stuck her oar in yet again, I need to do it, for the experience and feedback if nothing else.' I blink at my two friends in semi-shock while I digest what this means.

'*Boom.*' Amber simulates a mic drop. '*And... she's back.*'

'She sure is.' Cat beams at me across the table.

'Right, well, I'd better get some food in me and go get

ready.' I clutch my face in disbelief. 'This is a curve ball I did not see coming. Thanks for believing in me, you guys.'

The waiter approaches to take our order and Amber holds up a finger to stall him for a second.

'Once last tip for you, Emma: if at any point you blank, or there's a question that feels impossible to answer, do nothing other than count to five slowly in your head. Don't think, just do it. That will give your brain the chance to offer you something useful before you let the panic set in.'

I nod slowly, committing this nugget to memory. 'OK, thanks, I'll try to remember that.'

~

Ten minutes before my interview is due to start, I'm seated in the atrium, jangling with nerves. I've dressed in the most appropriate outfit I could find – a sophisticated (and not revealing) black evening dress paired with a cropped jacket and black heeled sandals.

Fiddling with the strap of my handbag, which is housing my new improved presentation 'cue cards', I self-consciously glance across to the reception desk and meet Charnice's eye.

'Good luck,' she mouths to me with an encouraging smile.

'Thank you,' I mouth back.

'Emma, *ça va?*' A smiling Sébastien appears from nowhere, as is his style, looking devastatingly handsome in a dark grey suit, but with no tie and his top shirt button open.

I waver. Now we're doing the interview, I don't know how to play things with him. It's not often one has an intimate (and borderline raunchy) dance with their possible future boss. Or has unmistakable raw chemistry with them. I get to my feet and extend my hand.

'Hello, Sébastien. I'm very well, thank you. How are you today?'

He looks at my hand with amusement, then steps forward and plants a kiss on each cheek, giving me that same heady feeling I get every time he does it. And with today's pre-interview nerves thrown into the mix, it almost ends me. I shift backwards to steady myself.

'I am well too.' He smiles and with a wave of his hand he guides me out of the atrium along one of the long corridors. 'Please relax, Emma. There is no need for you to change how you are with me. How was your breakfast this morning?'

We chat lightly while we walk and thankfully my nerves settle a bit. Sébastien is in the middle of telling me about his morning when he brings us to a stop outside a door with a sign that says 'staff only'. He opens it, gesturing for me to go inside ahead of him, and I find myself in another, much shorter corridor that leads to three meeting rooms.

'In here.' He points to one of them, the door of which is propped open. 'Please make yourself comfortable.'

There's not much in the room. Just a long table surrounded by twelve boardroom style chairs, which take up most of the available space, and a large monitor mounted on a metal arm so it can be moved and adjusted. With it being such a tight space, my presentation audience will have to be very limited. *Thank goodness.*

I pull out a chair and sit down while Sébastien takes the seat opposite me.

'Are you doing the interview alone?' I ask.

'*Ah, mais non,* Emma. Did I not mention that my colleague will be the second interviewer? Pardon me. We will be joined remotely by my Director of Strategy, Eloise Lefebvre. Eloise and I, we go back a long way, as you might say, and I consider her to be one of the most capable people I have had the pleasure of knowing.'

My insides squirm. I'm going to be on trial with Sébastien's right hand woman. No pressure or anything.

'She is also a very kind and understanding person, Emma.' He has clearly read me like a book, making my squirm even squirmier.

Before I can respond, the room is filled with an electronic ring tone and an incoming video call flashes up on the screen. Sébastien grabs the remote control from the middle of the table, and moments later, the head and shoulders of a beautiful woman around Sébastien's age appears on the screen. She has long dark hair and a warm smile.

'*Salut, Eloise, ça va?*' Sébastien greets her fondly. 'I am sorry to have you interviewing on your day off.'

'*Salut, Sébastien. Pas du tout.*' She smiles brightly. 'With a *bebé* who wakes me up at the fifth hour every morning, I am never on a day off.'

'How is he?'

'He is nearly walking already. How has this happened so quickly? I cannot keep up with him.'

Sébastien's eyes crinkle as he chuckles at this comment. 'Eloise, may I introduce you to Emma?'

'*Bonjour, Emma.*' She gives me a little wave. '*Enchantée. Parles-tu français?*'

Having learned some French at school, I'm quick to pick up that she's using a familiar tone with me like Sébastien does – which is nice – and she's also asking if I speak the language. However, I find myself grappling for a response.

'*Bonjour, Eloise... Enchantée.* I'm afraid I don't speak much French anymore. Maybe just... *un petit peu?*'

Eloise doesn't seem fazed at all by this cop out. In fact, she looks delighted by my use of these three simple words.

'You can pick it up again, Emma,' she says. 'It is like skiing. You never really forget once you learn – some practice and you will be gliding again.'

I gulp, sincerely hoping that the use of French is not a requirement for the role. In skiing terms, my aptitude for foreign languages is the equivalent of opting for the kiddie slopes and still ending up arse in the air at the end of it.

'Shall we get started then?' says Sébastien.

'Sure.' I give a nervous nod. 'Ready when you are.'

'*Bien*. I expect this part of the interview will take an hour, then we will move elsewhere for the presentation...'

My heart sinks on hearing this. It undoubtedly means there will be a much bigger audience than I was hoping for.

'Eloise and I will both ask you questions,' Sébastien continues. 'These will relate to our company values and how your previous work experience relates to the role. Is that all fine with you, Emma?'

'Absolutely.'

Sébastien kicks off the questions and he and Eloise alternate between them in a very natural way. It's a far more relaxed experience than I had with Amber's 'interrogations'. However, I'm still grateful that she grilled me to that level and got me 'ready for anything'. Fortunately, in this case, 'anything' has turned out to be a rather pleasant surprise.

Sébastien and Eloise go out of their way to make me feel at ease, to the point that the whole experience feels more like a pleasant chat between like-minded professionals than an interview. If it weren't for the fact that Amber tested me with some values-based example questions, I might even have wondered if it *were* an interview. But the tell tales signs are there, and I'm pleased to note that I do feel a natural alignment with what the company is about.

'Thank you, Emma,' says Sébastien, after what feels like about ten minutes. 'Those are all the questions we wanted to ask today. Shall we move on to the presentation?'

'Sure.' I try to look enthusiastic, while my stomach feels like it's taken a dive into a cement mixer.

He turns his attention to the screen. '*Merci bien, Eloise*. I will take things from here and call you later.'

'*De rien, Sébastien.* It was nice to meet you, Emma. Good luck with your presentation.' Eloise waves goodbye and disappears from the screen.

We leave the meeting room and make our way back along the corridor to the atrium, where Sébastien leads me out of a door into the close humidity outside. We walk in the opposite direction to where the main facilities of the resort are located, and it's not long before I spot why. In the near distance, I can see an altar-slash-stage with a canopy roof and a huge AV screen positioned at the back of it. And as we get closer, rows of seats with an aisle running up the middle come into view.

Under different circumstances – a wedding, live act, anything – I would consider this set up, with its stunning backdrop of powder white sand and turquoise sea, to be an idyllic event location. But seeing the seats fill up with people, knowing that *I'm* the 'entertainment' kind of takes away the shine.

'Here we are.' Sébastien's tone is matter of fact, as if this set-up is something interview candidates across the world are faced with every single day. 'This is where we host weddings, and we also use it as an outdoor cinema sometimes in the evenings.'

'What if it rains?' I look up at the sky. It feels like we could be in for a downpour at any moment, and this time I'm not wishing for rain to stop play. I want this damn thing over with, once and for all.

'I am hoping it will stay dry, but if not, we can bring the canopy roof across the audience. It offers some protection and the electrics are encased, but in the event of a heavy downpour, we would, of course, move inside. You will find everything you need on the left side of the stage. I assume you have your presentation on a USB stick?'

'I do... yes,' I croak, then clear my throat.

'Please relax.' He puts a calming hand on my arm. 'I know this is a pressured situation – more so than you would experience on the job – but I also know that you can do this. I have seen your superstar *chanteuse* karaoke skills, remember?'

I chuckle nervously, taking it as a measure of my anxiety levels that my stomach doesn't flutter with desire at the physical contact.

Sébastien is approached by a member of the audience and excuses himself to speak to them while I give myself a silent pep talk, straighten my shoulders and walk down the aisle to meet my fate.

Once on the stage, I'm pleasantly surprised to find cool air being pumped out of air conditioning units above me. This at least gives me hope that I won't be a sopping mess by the end of the experience – which would be a distinct improvement on my previous practice sessions.

I busy myself with setting up my presentation so that the title slide is displayed on the screen behind me. Looking up at it and then out at my ever-growing audience, the reality of the situation hits me, causing my legs to wobble and the cement mixer in my stomach hit turbo power. *Oh god, please let me get through this in one piece.* The only thing that would be worse than yesterday is to throw up all over the stage *before* I pass out.

In desperate need of some reassurance, I scan the audience for familiar or friendly faces. My eyes land first on Charnice, who's clearly been waiting to catch my eye. She gives me a huge encouraging smile and silently brings her hands together in what I think is a message of 'you'll be great'. I nod gratefully in response. My gaze then shifts to two people approaching Sébastien: Cat and Amber. He greets them with his signature kisses, before they claim two seats right at the back. I keep my eyes on them for a moment, but they're busy chatting with the people next to them.

Once the rows are full – totalling about sixty people – Sébastien makes his way down the aisle and joins me at the side of the stage.

'Ready?' he asks.

'Probably shouldn't keep them waiting any longer.' I say, while trying to calm the raging protestations in my body.

'*Bien*. Perhaps you can use the headset to make sure the audience can hear you?'

I look across at the table where the laptop is and spot the headset. I feel a bit daft at the idea of using it, but it's the obvious choice over shouting my way through my presentation. Grabbing it and switching it on, I rejoin Sébastien and he greets the crowd.

'*Mesdames, messieurs*... ladies and gentlemen, good afternoon and thank you kindly for taking the time to join us today. As you know, at Paradis Resorts, people are the most important part of our business. That means you: our valued guests and colleagues. We live by our brand values, and we make sure that the colleagues we bring in live them too. So, today I would like to introduce you to Emma, who I am interviewing for a very important role within the company.'

Sébastien gestures to me and I feel a rabid heat creep up my neck, quickly followed by another wobble in my legs and a lurch in my gut.

'Emma has already shown an admirable level of dedication in how she came to be here on this stage today, but I will leave her to share that story with you. Emma will be presenting to you her plans for the first ninety days in the job if she is successful. This is where your role comes in. There was a feedback form on your chair when you arrived. If you would be so kind as to fill this out, but only once Emma has completed her presentation so you do not distract her...'

At this mention of feedback, I find myself fighting an irrational (and familiar) urge to flee the scene. Desperately seeking the support of my best friends, I look to the back of the audience for Cat and Amber, and this time we make eye contact. They're both grinning like idiots while giving me enthusiastic double thumbs up. It's enough to calm the worst of my anxiety, and I'm immensely grateful that they're there.

'So, I will not take up any more of your time,' Sébastien finally wraps things up. 'Thank you again, and please welcome... Emma.'

Chapter Thirty-Seven

There's polite applause as Sébastien steps off the stage and takes the only remaining front row seat, kept vacant by a 'reserved' sign.

All eyes are on me now. I shift under the collective scrutiny, then James's tip about eye contact pops into my mind and I alter my gaze.

It works.

I discreetly clear my throat and start talking, my voice projecting clearly through the headset.

'Thank you, Sébastien. Good afternoon, ladies and gentlemen, I would like to echo Sébastien's appreciation of you taking the time to be here this afternoon. How I came to be here myself today is not characteristic of how interviews go at Paradis Resorts. So I'm told anyway. I'm actually here on holiday, and I was lucky enough to be offered this opportunity. I won't bore you with the whole story, but I will share that it involved an appalling karaoke performance and the antics of a rather opportunistic friend of mine...'

A ripple of amusement dances through my audience, along

with some raised eyebrows, expressing what appears to be a mixture of surprise and intrigue.

'So, rather than spending the last few days soaking up the sun and devouring the beach reads I brought with me, I've been diligently preparing for this moment. You might be feeling pained for me. I've missed out on the much needed R&R I came here for – and I'll admit, I wrestled with that too at first – but it has all worked out well. I've been able to use my experience as a paying customer to help me prepare for today. And instead of taking a more predictable route with this presentation, I'm going to give you my plan for my first ninety days in the role through the eyes of a guest...'

I click the button on the wireless presentation remote I'm holding and the stage is instantly filled with colour and sound – a montage of photos and videos of the resort displayed on the huge screen, accompanied by lively Caribbean-themed music filtering through the speakers. I've also added a smattering of text in between the visual images with teaser lines of some of the key points I'll be highlighting over the next twenty minutes. The impact of this alternative approach is immediately apparent, with murmurs of interest, approving nods, even some people moving to the rhythm in their seats.

My intro video comes to an end with the music fading out, and I proceed to deliver a relatively smooth, upbeat, and at times, even humorous presentation. I also ensure I make plenty of 'eye contact' and encourage audience engagement. My presentation slides, which are mainly visual and quite whizzy (if I may say so myself), are the perfect enhancement to the experience, and I find myself feeling quite Ted Talk-esque with my fancy headset and gesticulating arms.

When I eventually wrap things up twenty or so minutes later, I can't help feeling a little bit proud – and amazed that I'm still in one piece. I also take it as a positive sign that my audience are clapping a good bit more enthusiastically than earlier.

Sébastien returns to the stage to join me, his presence quickly curbing the applause.

'Thank you, Emma, and well done. It is not easy to stand in front of so many people and deliver like that. Now we will move on to questions. Who would like to start?'

Several hands raise across the audience.

'Madam Sinclair. Please go ahead,' Sébastien addresses a smartly dressed mature woman.

'Thank you, Sébastien,' she says in a deep throaty voice. 'Emma, may I firstly congratulate you on an excellent presentation.'

'Thank you.' I beam at her in response.

'I've been a regular guest of Paradis Resorts for over a decade, and so far, I've seen little dilution of the quality of customer experience as the company has grown. However, I'm concerned that further expansion will have that impact. I'm wondering what your thoughts are on ensuring this does not happen?'

It's a challenging question, triggering yet another bodily protest, but I'm determined not to go to the same panicked place as yesterday. Amber's words from breakfast float into my mind and I find myself doing as she suggested.

One...two...three...four...five.

'Thank you for your question, Madam Sinclair,' I say. 'I think your concerns are very relevant, and there are many real-life examples of what you describe, especially when a workforce is inherited as part of an acquisition. I would say that, aside from ensuring the same quality of physical environment and produce, the answer lies within the company culture. There are two things for me that are key: making sure the right leaders are in place; and ensuring the employees are treated with respect and feel valued, so they care about the company and they fiercely protect what it stands for. For me, people are what make or break an organisation.'

'Thank you, Emma,' says Madam Sinclair. 'That's a very comprehensive answer.'

Sébastien opens up the floor again, and several times after that. It's a tough process, but with my secret weapons of not making direct eye contact and counting before I answer each question, I make it through relatively unscathed. The only hurdles I stumble at are a complex financial question from one of the resort accountants and a couple that are very specific to the hospitality industry. But I do my best to answer them as well as I can.

However, just as I think I'm out of the danger zone, things take a turn for the less amicable.

'We shall make this the last question,' says Sébastien. 'I am sure that Emma must be looking forward to a well-earned rest.'

This time only one hand raises. I look to its owner and freeze. It's Mr Miller – the unpleasant man from the bar and reception – and he's watching me with pure derision. Utterly intimidated, I scan the audience, willing someone else to raise their hand, but there's nothing. Sébastien appears to hesitate, before inviting him to speak.

'Monsieur Miller. What is your question for Emma?'

Mr Miller gets to his feet, clearly intending to make the most of being in the spotlight. 'Thank you, Sébastien. My question for Emma relates to guest privacy. Just days ago, I caught her eavesdropping on a private conversation my family and I were having in the bar. Therefore, I would like to ask Emma, as a potential senior member of staff within Paradis Resorts, where her morals lie in relation to privacy and discretion?'

An unsettled murmur snakes through the audience. Mr Miller doesn't have a question for me at all. He didn't even respect me enough to address me personally. He's done this to discredit me and sink my chances of getting the job, and whatever his agenda – power, sexism, simple arrogance – he may have royally screwed things for me.

After a moderate pause – this time I have to count to ten – I decide that even if my chance at the job is gone, I need to hold my head high and come out of this the bigger person. I take a long, steadying breath.

'Mr Miller, thank you for your question. Firstly, I would like to apologise if I in any way intruded on your family discussion in the bar. I can assure you that this was not intentional and that I consider guest privacy to be of the utmost importance. I have held positions of responsibility in the past with access to confidential and sensitive customer information, and I have always treated this with complete discretion, while also taking careful measures to keep it secure. As an employee of Paradis Resorts, I would absolutely treat guest privacy with that same level of respect and care.'

Mr Miller sneers at me, and looks like he's about to say something else, when Sébastien cuts in.

'Thank you, Monsieur Miller. And thank you, everyone, for your time today – in particular, our treasured guests. Perhaps we can give Emma one final round of applause for taking on this task today. And for giving up her precious holiday time for this process.'

There's another polite round of applause, to which I nod my thanks, then my audience turn their attention to the feedback form, before getting up to leave, chatting animatedly as they go.

'How was that?' Sébastien asks me. 'I hope not too painful.'

I bite my lip, desperate to say something about Mr Miller, but I know it's a bad idea. I can't change the fact that it happened, and by bringing it up, I could end up causing more damage.

'I feel like I did my best,' I say instead, searching Sébastien's face for any clue as to what he's thinking, but there's nothing. 'And it didn't rain.'

'That is true, it did not. Well, Emma, I must go and attend to some business. Thank you once again for your efforts. I will be speaking with Eloise this afternoon, and I will come back to you with a decision by the end of the day.'

'OK, thanks. And, Sébastien... thank you again for the opportunity. I've learned a lot these last few days.'

'I am glad to hear this. *À bientôt, Emma.*'

He walks swiftly up the aisle as Cat and Amber come rushing towards to me.

'*Honey, you did so well!*' Cat gushes.

'*That was boss!*' Amber slaps me a high five. 'So much better than your previous run throughs.'

'Well, I didn't pass out. That's progress,' I say. 'Though it doesn't really matter how well I did. It was always a long shot, but my fate is sealed now that horrible bloke, Mr Miller, has sunk my chances.'

'Yeah, he was a right tosser.' Amber frowns.

'He was *so* unpleasant,' says Cat. 'Guess we'll have to wait and see what happens.'

'Yes, we will,' I give a despondent shake of my head, still unable to believe that was how things ended. 'Sébastien said he'd be in touch later today, so I may as well forget about it for now. Can we go eat? I need some fuel after that experience – and maybe a nice, chilled glass of pinot grigio.'

Chapter Thirty-Eight

We head to Cucina, the resort's Italian restaurant, which is a tastefully decorated but minimalist space that claims to be 'an authentic taste of Italy in paradise'. Once our plates are piled high with antipasti from the starter buffet, we return to our seats, digging into delicious marinated mussels, pesto shrimp, cured meats, cheeses, bread, olives and chargrilled vegetables. It's a pleasant, companionable silence, until Amber obliterates it.

'So now your interview is out the way, Emma, what are you going to do about James?'

My fork clatters on my plate. '*Shit*. I never messaged him back. The whole interview-still-going-ahead thing knocked me sideways and... I completely forgot about him.'

'That's hardly a good sign.' She raises an appraising eyebrow.

'No... *no*. It doesn't mean anything, other than I've been distracted with other things.'

'So, is it on or off with him?'

'I... don't know. I was hoping I'd have figured that out by now.'

'Where's your head at, honey?' Cat asks. 'Maybe we can help.'

I spear an olive and chew on it while I think this through. 'What's in my head is that he's gorgeous, intelligent, so thoughtful and caring. He makes me feel all fizzy and excited when I'm with him '

'*Spew.*' Amber simulates sticking her fingers down her throat.

'That's all good, isn't it?' says Cat, shooting Amber a disapproving look.

'It is. But there's something that's really bothering me. One of the things that irritated me about James when we first met was how he kept playing the rescuer. It seemed like some kind of hero complex, and when I met his mum it finally made sense, with her being a retired nurse and all. She's a helper and so is he, and I found that quite endearing. But then with him playing third interview coach over the last day or so, I've realised that he's not just a helper – he's also a fixer.'

'Is that so bad, honey? It does seem to come from the right place – not manipulative or anything – and his tips were really useful.'

'I know.' I shrug, unable to refute this. 'Being cared for and supported in that way is good in theory – especially after Dave's self-centredness – but if it's all the time, and it has the impact of making me feel like I'm incapable, it'll chip away at my self- esteem. No matter how well intended it is. I'm just wondering if that makes us incompatible – at least for now, with my confidence having taken a knock recently.' I decide not to add that I've already got enough 'fixers' in my life, because that list includes Amber and I'm not up for that discussion.

'Ah, OK. I see where you're coming from.' Cat purses her lips, and if I'm not wrong, she looks disappointed.

'Also... I'm not sure I'm ready for a full-on relationship

again. I keep landing back on the question of whether it might still be too soon after Dave.'

'One question...' Amber holds up a finger, chews and swallows. 'Dave was a selfish materialistic arsehole, and James is the opposite.'

I wait for her to continue but she doesn't. 'That's... not a question.'

'Yes, it is.'

'Is it a *trick* question?'

'Two ends of the spectrum, Emma.'

I furrow my brow, trying to work her angle. 'Oh... I get it. If I don't want a selfish materialistic arsehole or a thoughtful and caring man, what do I want?'

'*Bingo.*'

'Aren't there shades of grey along that spectrum?'

'I wasn't talking about your sex life, but if you insist—'

'That's not what I meant, and you know it.' I shake my head at her, chuckling. 'But I suppose you're right.'

'I know I'm right,' she says. 'No man is perfect. They're all bloody infuriating at times, but so are we. Would you rather his flaws were being too into helping you, or too into helping himself?'

'All right, when you put it like that... *ugh*... Look, as I've already said, this is all fine in theory. It's how it'll play out that concerns me. *And...* as I've also already said, it might still be too soon.'

'Or you might have the relationship jitters?' says Cat.

'Could be... *oh, I don't know.*' I play with my food absently. 'I'm more confused than ever now, but I know I can't leave him waiting around. That's not fair. One way or another, I have to make a decision today. In fact, I'd better message him now.'

I pick my phone out of my handbag and type a message to James.

Hi there, sorry for leaving you hanging. Can we meet this afternoon? x

He replies in less than a minute.

No worries. Hope you're feeling better. 5pm in the cocktail bar? We're off the resort just now. x

I confirm that will be fine and give a loaded sigh. 'OK, ladies. I've got three and a half hours to make my decision.'

～

After lunch, we head to the pool for some rest and relaxation – my first proper bit of downtime since my interview brief appeared under my door three days before. Lying back on my sun lounger, I can feel the pressure of my interview shedding like down feathers. I'm free. *Finally*. And what's more – *I did it*. After all the sweating, stuttering and drama of the last few days, I stood up there and delivered a quality presentation to a sizeable audience – and I wasn't even regurgitating a script. *That* I can be proud of.

However, my moment of self-acknowledgement is short-lived. Mr Miller's contemptuous face materialises in my mind, alongside a tangle of worries. That man has a lot of power and influence. He could probably damage Paradis Resorts' reputation if he wanted to. And how will Sébastien view me now – after hearing how I apparently behaved? Will he think I'm a sneak? Someone who's not quite as trustworthy as she makes out? The idea of that makes me feel sick and angry.

'*Oh, stop it,*' I grumble out loud.

'You OK?' Cat asks from the lounger next to me.

'Sorry, yes. I'm winding myself up over that bloody man who hijacked my presentation. And I'm annoyed at myself for letting him get to me.'

'Try to put it out of your mind for now. You've only a few days left to enjoy yourself, so don't waste that time thinking about him.'

'I know. I need to make the most of what's left of the trip.' I stifle a yawn that suddenly creeps up on me. 'Think my early rise and busy morning is catching up with me.'

'Here, I'll put your parasol up, so you don't get burnt if you fall asleep.' She jumps up and wrestles with my umbrella until it's secured and spanning me protectively.

'Thanks, Cat. You're a star.'

I close my eyes and it's not long before I feel myself drifting into a comforting afternoon snooze. Then a few minutes later, I come round to someone nudging me.

'*Emma?* Emma, wake up.'

I open my eyes blearily to see Amber standing over me.

'What is it? I only just nodded off. Could you not have left me for a bit?'

'You haven't *just* nodded off. It's quarter to five. You're meeting James in fifteen minutes.'

'*What?* How can it be that late?' I leap off my lounger and start gathering my things. 'I only meant to have a quick shut eye.'

'You've been snoring your arse off for the last two hours,' she gleefully informs me.

'Great. And you couldn't have given me a poke to save me the embarrassment?'

'No way. Every time someone walked past, you'd let out this snorty noise, and they'd almost jump out of their swimwear. It was hilarious. I even managed to get it on video. Wanna see?'

'No, I don't "wanna see".' I bat away the phone she's

brandishing at me. 'I've got somewhere to be, remember? And *that* had better be deleted by the time I see you later.'

'*Grumpy guts.*' Amber trots back to her lounger, chuckling at what I assume is a muted viewing of my poolside inelegance and my unsuspecting victim.

Cat's fast asleep on her own lounger, so I leave her in peace and head to the poolside toilets to check my hair is presentable enough and my makeup is intact. Then, on arriving at the cocktail bar, I grab a shaded table with a view across the pool to the beach and wait for James to appear.

Thanks to my unexpectedly elongated nap, I've made zero progress with my decision on whether to shut things down or keep seeing him, so I attempt an on-the-spot analysis. It's really about weighing up my feelings for him and what he could bring to my life, against the reality of his 'fixer' personality and my state of mind following my break up from Dave. There's no doubt my confidence (generally, and in men) has been damaged. But does that mean I should focus on healing those psychological wounds? Or should I get straight back on the horse, so to speak, to avoid turning into a commitment phobe who's terrified of getting hurt again?

My inner musings come to an abrupt halt when James pulls out the chair opposite me. His hair is wet, and he smells citrusy and divine. My heart skips at the sight of his gorgeous melty brown eyes and his increasingly tanned skin.

'Hi, Emma.' His smile is faltering. He's clearly apprehensive about what I'm going to say.

I suddenly feel wracked with guilt that I didn't say something to put his mind at ease when I messaged him earlier – but then how could I have offered reassurance when I don't know what to tell him?

'Hi.' I try to sound as relaxed as possible, while my stomach shifts back into cement mixer mode. 'I'm OK. How about you? Where did you go today?

'We did an ATV tour of Nassau. It was great. How's your day been?'

'It's been... full on. A little terrifying... but all went well in the end... to a point.'

'Right...' A look of confusion appears on James's face. 'I was expecting something more along the lines of disappointment, regret... maybe even relief.'

Of course. James doesn't know that I went ahead with my interview. I had assumed Amber would have let him know but obviously not.

We order some soft drinks and I fill him in on the events of this morning. He listens intently, relaxing a bit as I talk, and when I finish my story, he gives an impressed clap of his hands.

'*Bravo, Amber*. What a move. And bravo to you too, Emma. *You did it.*'

'I did.' I can't help smiling proudly. 'Although I'm not feeling good about the impending outcome. I was always punching above my weight and that Mr Miller has likely scuppered any chance I had.'

'You don't know that,' he says. 'Anyway, you'll find out soon enough. I'm so glad you went ahead today, because I've felt bloody awful about everything that happened.'

I meet his kind, guilt-ridden eyes and feel myself melt. It makes me want to climb over the table and hug him – and then snog his face off. But I resist this urge. I need to get through this conversation without causing any further confusion. It's only fair.

'I know you have, James,' I say instead. 'And I'm sorry I left you feeling that way. You didn't deserve that.'

'Maybe I did.' He shrugs. 'I should never have got involved in that conversation yesterday. I also need you to know that I wouldn't have offered you advice if I didn't think you were up to the job. That's not my style. I guess with us not knowing each other that well, it might have come across a bit patronising, so I'm sorry for that.'

While I appreciate his apology, I can't help feeling uncomfortable receiving it, because everything he did came from a good place – and a good heart. How can I blame him for wanting to help me succeed? For wanting to look after me? I don't need looking after per se, but it's nice to know that he cares. Plus, who wants to be fighting their corner alone – ever? That would be a damn lonely place to be. I had three people fighting mine last night and while the way they went about it wasn't the best, it was well intentioned.

And anyway, who's perfect? Certainly not me.

'Thank you, James. I appreciate that.' I take his hand and squeeze it. 'I know you were only trying to help and I'm sorry I let you wander around looking for me. That wasn't fair.'

'Emma, you don't have anything to apologise for. Nobody wants to hear people talking about them that way.'

'Well, regardless, we've made our apologies and it's done, yeah?'

'You're the boss.' His face breaks into a relieved grin. 'So, now we're good, can we recommence our holiday romance?'

Ah shit. So much for not causing any confusion. I've wrapped this up too quickly. I still need to talk to him about us – and the fact that there possibly *isn't* an us.

Too sharp for his own good, James picks up on my body language and my hesitation and his grin wilts like a dying flower. 'We're not good, are we?'

Chapter Thirty-Nine

'James... I... I'm...' I search for the words but can't seem to find the right ones.

'Just say it, Emma.' He seems to brace himself.

'No, wait... there's no "it". But I do think we need to talk about where this might or might not be going between us.'

'I'm feeling an emphasis on the "might not" part.' He gently pulls his hand away from mine and my heart sinks at the symbolism of this.

'James, as you know I'm not long out of a relationship that damaged my confidence in men – and in myself. This is a timing thing. It's nothing to do with you, I promise.'

'Please spare me the clichés. I'd rather you went for the band-aid approach. Go on, rip it off.'

'I'm just trying to be honest. I genuinely don't know whether I'm ready to jump into something serious again so soon. You're amazing and attentive... someone who'll challenge me to be the best person I can be, and I'm worried that as you do that, my insecurities will bubble up and eventually ruin us. I need to rebuild myself and my confidence, and—'

'Figure out who you are, and what you want from life?'

'*No.*' I stifle a giggle. 'That's so "cheesy movie".'

'It seemed to fit the tone.' He gives a weak smile, but his gaze is fixed on the table.

I watch him trying to shield himself from the hurt of my words, and as I do, I visualise how this conversation will end: with a disconsolate James walking out of the bar and me looking longingly after him, wondering if I've made the biggest mistake of my life. This followed by three further days of bumping into him and feeling the agony of not being able to laugh with him or kiss him. And eventually heading off home to probably never see him again. Expect maybe awkwardly bumping into him with a beautiful woman latched on his arm, whom I greet with resentment, because... she should have been me.

In an instant, everything becomes clear. I can't let him go. I'm not going to lose him to that beautiful woman. Not unless he can't work with me on what I now realise I need from him – in which case, she was always going to get him anyway. But until I ask, I won't know.

'James, I promise I'm not blowing smoke up your arse. I do need to rebuild my confidence and my faith in men, but... I want to do it *with* you. Not without you.'

'You do?' He looks up at me in surprise.

'Yes.' I snatch up his hand again. 'But I need you to understand that I'm a bit fragile right now. I'm going to think you're trying to fix me because I (not you) see myself as broken. I'm also likely to wobble and overreact and read things wrong at times, so I'll need you to be patient with me, but ultimately, I think I'm going to fall for you... big style.'

James looks utterly bemused, but the corners of his mouth are twitching. 'So, you're not calling things off?'

'Well, no.' I feel myself redden. 'I guess I'm saying that, if you can deal with all that, then we're on. But I know that's a lot to stomach, and I'll understand if you choose to run out of here as fast as you can.'

'Are you done?'

'I'm done.' I scrunch up my nose while I wait for him to respond to my mad tirade.

He seems to take a moment to compose himself, and I'm pretty sure he's trying not to laugh.

'Emma, what you've said doesn't make me want to run. I actually respect and admire your honesty.'

'You do?'

'Yes. So, thank you for laying everything out like that. Now that I've heard your "terms" – which I wholly accept – can I share mine?'

'Go on.' I bite my lip coyly, basking in the magic of what he's said – that he still wants to be with me, despite me dumping my weighty baggage on the table with an almighty thud.

'All right, here goes... If I care about someone, I'm fiercely loyal. I'll do everything I can to protect them, support them, make them happy and help them succeed at whatever's important to them. It doesn't matter whether they're family, friend or partner, that's what you get from James.'

I giggle at his reference to himself in the third person and he gives a wry smile.

'What that means is that I'll be all of those things with you and for you, but it also means I'll sometimes miss the mark and get things wrong. All I ask is that you keep that in mind and give me the benefit of the doubt. How does that sound?'

I break into a grin. 'It sounds amazing.'

James gets out of his seat and comes round to sit beside me, gently taking my hands in his. 'Good. Because I *was not* looking forward to bumping into you on the street one day with some beefy bloke on your arm that should have been me.'

My hand flies to my mouth in astonishment. *'That's exactly what I was thinking*. But you with a stunning woman, obviously.'

'Really? Must be a sign.'

We both lean in and enjoy our most delicious kiss yet – symbolically sealing the terms of our agreement.

~

By early evening, I've reported the good news to Cat and Amber via our WhatsApp group. They're obviously delighted and Amber wastes no time in upgrading our dinner reservation to a table of six. I've also showered and changed, ready for my first fully relaxed evening out since Sébastien Dumont – the man who puts the 'hot' in hotelier – first appeared in my life. Though when I say 'fully relaxed', it comes with the caveat that I haven't yet heard the outcome from my interview, which I'm not taking as a good sign.

I'm giving myself a final once over in the mirror before heading out to meet everyone, when the phone on the bedside table rings. *Fuck*. This is it. Dashing across to answer it, I put on my best phone voice.

'Hello?'

'Ms Blake, this is Gizelle from reception. Monsieur Dumont sends his apologies for keeping you waiting. He would like to meet you in the atrium in ten minutes if this would be suitable for you?'

'Yes, absolutely. I'll make my way along there now.'

Replacing the handset, I quickly send a message to Cat and Amber to let them know it's crunch time (and that I'll be late for dinner), then I pull on my wedged sandals, grab my clutch, and hurry along to reception, overflowing with a fresh set of nerves.

Sébastien is already waiting when I arrive.

'Emma... *bonsoir*.' He greets me in the usual way. 'I am sorry to interfere with your evening. I will not keep you for long.'

'It's no problem,' I say. 'I told the others I'd be a bit late.'

'Shall we find a quiet place?'

'Sure.'

Sébastien leads me across the largely empty atrium to a seating area out of earshot from reception and any passing guests. He gestures for me to sit down before parking himself next to me.

'*Alors*... Emma, thank you once again for all your commitment to this process. The fact that you sacrificed your holiday in this way is a real measure of your dedication and potential – not because you will prioritise work over rest, I must add. You know I view rest time as extremely important. However, when grand opportunities show themselves, it is those with the most potential that grasp at them...'

Gosh, that's high praise. Maybe it's not bad news after all. Encouraged, I sit forward, ready for what's coming next.

'You are an impressive young woman and you have a bright future ahead of you. Which is why it pains me to tell you that you have not been successful in securing the role.'

My momentary optimism sinks like a stone. 'I see. That's OK. Other than a few moments of delusion, I was expecting that to be where things went.' I punctuate this statement with a self-deprecating chuckle.

'I am truly regretful that I am not able to offer it to you, Emma, especially when you were so keen for the challenge and you sacrificed your vacation time for this process.'

He does look like he means it, so as much as I'm disappointed, I can take comfort from that.

'Sébastien, it's fine, honestly. You gave me a fantastic learning opportunity, and for that I'm truly grateful.'

While my mind processes my 'unsuccessful' job candidate

status, the thought that's been haunting me all afternoon leaps to the surface, and I can't help myself. I *have to* put it to bed.

'Can I ask one question? It wasn't because of Mr Miller, was it? The man who asked the last question at the presentation. He was—'

'Rude and arrogant.' Sébastien frowns. 'You must not give him another thought. Monsieur Miller is a regular guest, and while some hospitality venues may allow their VIPs to behave in any way they wish, this does not apply at Paradis Resorts. He undermined the process for his own motivations – I was already aware of his complaints – and this I cannot accept. Please be assured that I will speak with him about this. I also have no doubt there is little substance to what he said.'

I wince. 'Actually... I did overhear his conversation, but I genuinely didn't mean to. He was being so loud and scathing about one of the housekeeping staff. I was shocked and it must have been clear from the expression on my face.'

'Emma, if Monsieur Miller is going to talk like that in the bar, it will be *very* difficult for anyone not to overhear him. I will say again only once – you must not give this another thought, and I ask for your discretion in what I have shared with you.'

'Yes, absolutely. Not a word.'

'*Merci bien.*' He nods his appreciation. 'Now, if I may, I would like to share some feedback with you?'

'Yes, please. I'm always keen to know what I can do to improve.'

'This is nothing less than I would expect of you. Your interview and presentation today were almost faultless, except for two things: you came across as nervous, which is perfectly understandable; and you showed a lack of understanding of some important strategic and financial aspects of the hospitality industry.'

'I know. I would need to learn about those areas.' I purse my lips thoughtfully, unsure whether to vocalise what else is on my mind. 'Sébastien, there's something I'd like to confess... No, wait, that makes it sound really bad. There's something I'd like to share.'

'Please, go on.'

'The night we met in The Cave, Amber exaggerated... well, everything really. She "bigged me up" – if you understand what I mean – and I was furious with her for that. At first, I was going to decline your interview invitation, but she convinced me to go for it, and I guess I stupidly thought maybe I had a chance. I always felt "kept down" in my previous roles, so I wanted a chance to prove myself – which it turns out I haven't. I'm sorry if that means I wasted your time.'

Sébastien scrutinises my flaming, apologetic face, and breaks into a kind smile. 'Emma, I knew that Amber was exaggerating.'

'You did?'

'Of course. She is your friend, your.... comrade. She wants to help you, but she is also.... mischievous.'

'She's definitely that.' I scoff.

'I did not give you the opportunity because of what Amber said about you. I did it because of what I *saw* in you. You caught my eye that night in the karaoke bar. You have a shine that makes people warm to you, and when we spoke in The Cave, I sensed your discomfort that Amber was "bigging you up", as you say. The more I see of you, Emma, the more I know you are exactly the type of person I want to work with. I hope we can keep in contact so that when the right opportunity comes up, we can talk again.'

As he's been saying all of this, my mouth has grown wider and wider in surprise – to the point that I eventually notice it and clamp it shut.

'*Wow*... Sébastien, I don't know what to say. I mean, yes, I'd love to stay in touch.'

'*Excellent.* Well, I must go. My wife is arriving at the airport in one hour, and I am going with my driver to meet her. She wanted to surprise me, but I am instead going to surprise her.'

His wife? This further revelation slams into me like a freight train. So much so, I almost lose my footing as we get up from our seats.

'Oh, how lovely,' is all I can manage.

'Emma, it has been a pleasure. I am sorry again that it is not better news, but I am confident that whatever you go on to do next, you will be a great success. Perhaps we will see each other around the resort over the next few days. I think you and my wife would get on well. She is one in a million, as you might say – and like you, she has a beautiful soul.'

His adoration of his wife is so clear that I'm amazed he's never mentioned her. But then we were strangers before. Why would he share information about his private life with me? *Oh, my god I'm such an idiot.* There was no spark between us. I really *did* read the signals wrong – but then we all did.

We part with me indicating that I would very much like to meet his wife, and as I walk away from Sébastien, my mind is a jumble of emotions: disappointment that I didn't get the job; enthusiasm from the strength of Sébastien's positive feedback; and pure shock at the revelation that he's happily married. There's also a sizeable wave of mortification as I wonder whether he's told his wife about my unsolicited (and slightly crazed) announcement on the beach that I couldn't have a holiday fling with him. Maybe best I avoid the two of them over the next few days just in case.

～

'So, he *definitely* doesn't want to sleep with you?'

'*Definitely* not, Amber.' I burn with fresh embarrassment at the memory of my conversation with Sébastien. 'He's one hundred per cent married, and super loved-up from the sound of things.'

'*Huh*.' She acquires the same perplexed look as the last time we had a near identical conversation – only this time we have the facts and we're sitting at a table for six in Zen Garden, the resort's Asian fusion restaurant.

'He did say that I caught his eye with my performance in the karaoke bar that night though.' I waggle my eyebrows at her.

'He liked your singing? That I find hard to believe.'

'No, not my singing. Nobody "likes" my singing. Apparently, I have a shine that makes people warm to me. Anyway... how about we kick that issue to the kerb once and for all, especially as we have company.'

'And because there's someone here who *does* want to sleep with you.' James gives me a cheeky wink across the table and I turn beetroot.

'Nice one, James.' Amber fist bumps him across the table.

A smiling waiter approaches us. 'Good evening, ladies and gentlemen. My name is Todd and I'll be your server tonight. I see you've brought your drinks through from the bar and that you already have menus. Can I get you anything else? And are you ready to order or do you need more time?'

We confirm that we're ready to order and he works his way around the table, noting down our requests before disappearing again.

Taking a sip of my coconut mojito, I sit back and let out a satisfied sigh.

'I'm glad you're OK about not getting the job, honey,' says Cat. 'You're taking it really well.'

'I second that.' James smiles across the table at me. 'Taking it like a champ.'

'It's funny...' I muse. 'I thought I'd be more disappointed

than I am. I'm almost relieved, because if I'd got it, I'd be bloody terrified.'

'I reckon you'd have coped way better than you think,' says James. 'From what I hear, you kicked the arse out of that presentation.'

'She really did.' Cat nods. 'It was impressive.'

I laugh out loud. 'I'm glad you have that recall. I can barely remember it, I was that nervous.'

'Well, in that case, you faked it well.' She slips her arm around me and squeezes me tight.

'I'm certainly leaps and bounds ahead of where I was a week ago, and I have a new business contact in Sébastien. That's something to celebrate.' I lift my glass and the whole group toasts this.

'How many days do you have left here?' James asks me, while Amber and Tyler kick off a very mature discussion about phallic shaped objects in nature, with Cat and Rob watching on.

'We leave on Friday morning, so three more full days, and I intend to make the most of them.'

'Fancy spending one of those "full days" with me – on a *proper* date? Maybe a catamaran cruise and some snorkelling followed by an evening just the two of us?'

I press my lips together to suppress my excitement. There's nothing I'd like more than having James to myself for a whole day.

'Sure. Sounds lovely.'

'Great, I'll get it sorted. Amber, Cat, you don't mind if I steal Emma away for the day tomorrow, do you? Promise I'll share for your remaining days after that.'

'Knock yourself out.' Amber barely glances at us. 'I've seen more than enough of her over the last week.'

'*Hey!*' I cast her an unimpressed look. 'Cat, is that all right with you?'

'Go for it, honey.' She blows me a little kiss. 'Think you've more than earned it.'

'You know, I think I have too.' I lift my chin proudly, while James gets to his feet and reaches right across the table to plant a smacker of a kiss on my lips – this attracting whoops, cheers and foot stamping from our table mates.

Chapter Forty

After another delicious night of snuggling up to James, exploring every bit of each other, I wake up slightly later than usual to find he's already in the shower. Stretching indulgently, I giggle at him singing away to himself. *This* is what holidays are about: relaxation, lying in, sexy men in your shower. Not intense interview preparation, nervous knots and sweating so much that you pass out from anxiety and dehydration.

Unfortunately, however, my brain doesn't appear to have got the memo that I'm happy as a pig in shit, because these sumptuous thoughts are chased closely by a now familiar feeling of disappointment over not getting the job. But it's fine. My slightly wounded pride will recover quickly. Because job or no job, I've 'hit the jackpot' for the second time in as many weeks by making a professional contact in Sébastien. Oh, and there's that sexy man in my shower as well.

A billow of steam escapes from the bathroom as the door is hauled open, and a grinning James emerges, looking super sexy with a towel wrapped around his waist.

'Ah, you're awake, finally,' he says.' I was thinking of pouring a glass of water on you.'

'That's how you would wake a sleeping woman?' I raise a judgmental eyebrow. 'And there was me wondering why you're single.'

'You should see what I do to you when you're asleep.'

I blanch and playfully hurl a pillow at him.

'Anyway, *am* I single?' He asks. 'Is the jury still out on that one?'

'No, I think we've reached the "seeing each other" stage. But the terrain's tricky after that, so mind how you go.'

'Noted.' He taps his nose. 'So... are you ready for our big day out?'

'Sure am. It's so good to be free from the shackles of my interview.' I hop out of bed and kiss him teasingly on the lips, then pad across to the shower – totally naked – knowing full well he's watching me as I go.

~

'*Oh wow*. This is incredible.' I gasp in awe, drinking in my tropical surroundings, which are even more incredible than those of the resort itself.

We're standing on the deck of a catamaran, which has dropped its anchor not far from the shore of a small, apparently unpopulated – and unbelievably beautiful – paradise island. The sparkling turquoise water around us is even more mesmerising than it is at our resort, fuelling me with an overwhelming urge to jump straight in.

'Don't know about you but I'm dying to get in there,' says James.

'Like I've never felt before.' I'm unable to tear my eyes from the hypnotising ebb and flow of the water.

We grab the snorkelling gear provided to us and 'suit up', laughing at how daft we look in our masks and flippers.

'Shall we step off together?' says James.

'Erm... yup. Let's do it.' I squeeze my eyes shut then quickly reopen them because falling blind will be worse than seeing where I'm going.

'One... two... three... *go*.'

We step off the side of the catamaran together and plunge below the surface before emerging side by side, laughing.

'That was *amazing*.' I beam at him while treading water.

James smiles back at me, then gently pulls me towards him, allowing me to float while he does the legwork (quite literally).

'How good is this, eh?' He kisses me softly, then turns me around so that he's behind me, his head resting on my shoulder while we take in the exotic view together. There's nothing man-made in sight, save for a few yachts and catamarans in the distance. It's all stunning shades of blue and green, from the almost indigo depths of the open sea in the distance, to the turquoise waters around us and the crystal clear shallows at the shore, where the powder white beach is framed by dense green shrubbery.

I let out a sigh of pure contentment. 'It's unreal. Like nothing I've ever experienced before.'

I pop in my mouthpiece and briefly duck my face into the water, letting out a peep of delight as I re-emerge. '*James, we've got friends.*' I point below the surface.

'Let's go under so we can see them then,' he says.

He adjusts his own mask and mouthpiece, and we swim along together, partially submerged, our periscope-like breathing tubes sticking proudly out of the water. The change to my breathing is weird and this distracts me at first, but as I get used to it, I'm able to focus on the clusters of tropical fish swimming curiously around us. There are loads of them in a kaleidoscope of colours with different patterns and markings. Some big, some small, some long and elegant, some short and stubby looking. But all so alive and utterly fascinating. It's way better than watching a David Attenborough nature programme and those are hard to beat.

We swim until our tour guide gives us the signal that it's time for lunch, and we reluctantly return to the boat.

'Can I ask you something?' says James, when we're halfway through our Bahamian fayre and a couple of Rum Punches, the catamaran gently rocking on the waves while we eat and drink.

'You can ask me anything you like.'

'OK. But this might be a bit too personal, so tell me to back off if it is. I was wondering, with you having that big lottery win, why you're keen to get a new job so quickly? I get that it's not enough to retire on – not once you've bought yourself an apartment or whatever. And I understand you still having ambition – I can imagine I would too – but could you not enjoy a *wee bit* more freedom before you get back on the hamster wheel?'

I set down my forkful of food thoughtfully. 'I probably could. If I didn't have parents who continually breathe down my neck.'

'Perhaps it's their way of feeling relevant. Maybe they're worried that if they let up then you won't need them anymore.'

'You know, I've never thought about it like that.'

'Here's a useful piece of wisdom that was once shared with me,' he says. 'Every interaction you have with another person is at least fifty per cent about them. Which means your parents probably have more going on in here than you might give them credit for.' He taps the side of his head.

'I like that. A fountain of wisdom you are. Is that what happens when you turn thirty?' I reach across and tweak his nose.

'*Cheeky.*' He tickles me and I wriggle out of reach.

'Seriously though. Maybe I do need to look at this differently. How many people get the opportunity to take some proper time out? Perhaps I should use some of the stuff I've learned through my interview prep to finally stand up to my parents and do things my way. Who's to say that a short career break wouldn't be a really good thing? Maybe I could go travelling and see more places. Learn about different cultures. *That* would be amazing.'

'There you go. That's one thing you could do. And maybe I could come with you? It's not long 'til I finish my course. We could take a few months away – *if* things continue to go in the right direction for us as a couple.'

'*Yes*. We could do that.' I'm suddenly filled with giddy excitement at the thought. 'I could pay for us both. We'd need to keep it affordable, but—'

'*Not a chance*.' James plucks my Rum Punch from my hand. 'Think the booze and the sun are going to your head. I'll be paying my own way. I've got savings left from my previous job as I said to you before, remember? And I'd been considering doing something anyway. My last bit of freedom before I embark on my own new career.'

'OK, fine. Even better then.' I snatch my drink back. 'So, it's a deal? We're going travelling – if this works out between us?'

'Looks like it.' James clinks my glass. 'We can start planning it and make reservations that are refundable just in case. Though let's see if you're still as enthusiastic when the booze has worn off – and after we've spent the next few days together.'

'I get the feeling I will be.'

'Me too. I like the idea of you as my travel buddy. Now, get some food down you to soak up the alcohol before you have any more crazy ideas.'

~

After what was undoubtedly one of the best experiences of my life, James and I return to the resort and get showered and changed in our respective suites. We've agreed to meet in the atrium at seven p.m., so we can go for a drink before dinner.

I take extra time getting ready to make sure I'm as irresistible as possible and I'm quite happy with the result. With a last look in the mirror, I admire my slinky burnt orange dress (which looks good with the hint of a tan I'm now developing), strappy sandals and shimmery eye makeup. *Perfect.* Even my hair looks good – so far. Hopefully this will have exactly the right effect.

'*Wowsers.*' James gives an impressed whistle as I totter across the atrium to meet him. 'You look... *wow.*'

'Thank you.' I offer him my cheek to avoid smudging my lipstick and he threads his fingers through mine.

Across at the reception desk, Charnice shoots me an awestruck smile and clasps her heart. I can't help but giggle, mouthing a friendly 'thank you!' back to her.

'You look great too.' I admire James's smart jeans, shoes and dress shirt as we head out of the side door into the gardens. 'Where are we off to?'

'I thought we could start with some champagne at The Cave. That work for you?'

'Absolutely.'

We chat easily while ambling through the resort gardens hand-in-hand, and as we pass the waterfront, I stop suddenly.

'Can we FaceTime Lottie? I think she'd love to get a call from the two of us together.' I open my clutch to retrieve my phone and blanch. 'Aww, no... I've left my phone in my room.'

'Don't worry, I've got mine.' James pulls his out of his back pocket and checks the screen. 'We're in luck, I've got a Wi-Fi signal.'

'But... do you have her info?'

'I do. Saved it before I left. I said I'd give her a call at some point so this is perfect.'

'You did?' My mouth drops open in shock and admiration.

He shrugs. 'Figured she'd get bored as she was recovering, so yeah.'

'You are *too* sweet.'

He gives me a little wink, then dials Lottie and holds the phone out so we can both be in the frame. She answers quickly, her smiling elderly face materialising on the screen in front of us.

'*Hello!*' we greet her in unison.

'Emma, James, how lovely to see you together. How are you both?'

We glance at each other coyly and laugh.

'We're great,' I say. 'We went on a catamaran cruise today. It was incredible. You should have seen the colour of the water we were snorkelling in. And all the tropical fish.'

'That sounds wonderful.'

'It really was.'

'And now we're going for champagne,' says James. 'It's a hard life this, Lottie.'

'Sounds like it.' She chuckles. 'And Emma, my love, how are you feeling? Your silence has pleased me because I assume it means you've been relaxing finally.'

'Erm... I've certainly been enjoying the resort.' I give James a side-glance and it's clear he's in agreement: I should wait until I get home to tell Lottie about my job interview. 'Anyway, how are *you*? You look like you're doing well.'

'I'd say I am. Even managed a short walk outside this morning with Archie and Eva's help.'

'That's *great* progress. You'll be running laps of your cottage by the time we get back.'

'Oh, I think my running days are well and truly over.'

'Running's overrated anyway,' says James. 'Here, look at this view, Lottie.' He flips the camera, giving her a panoramic view of the coastline.

'*Golly, look at that.* It's quite stunning, James.'

'Maybe we can take you somewhere like this at some point. Though perhaps a bit closer to home.'

'I'm not sure you'd want an old crow like me tagging along with you.'

'*Rubbish*,' he tuts at her.

'Yeah, *rubbish*,' I repeat James's objection. 'We'll have to make that happen.'

'Well... that would be divine,' says Lottie. 'Anyway, it's so good to see you together. You do make a lovely couple.'

James and I look at each other somewhat bashfully again, and he slips his arm around my waist.

We continue to chat to Lottie for a few minutes longer, before saying our goodbyes and heading into The Cave.

'Sir, ma'am, come with me, please.' The waiter leads us outside to the table closest to the water, which is perfectly situated for watching the upcoming sunset.

'How lucky are we?' I say, climbing onto my seat. 'I'd have thought we'd need to book ahead to get this spot.'

'I did,' says James.

'You booked it? When?'

'A few days ago.'

I suck in my cheeks to suppress my delight at the thoughtfulness of this gesture. Then I remember that I don't have to do that with James. I can show him the real me.

'That's so romantic. Thank you. I'm glad you didn't cancel it when I had my mini-meltdown.'

'I considered it.' His gaze locks on mine, and I can almost see the indecision he felt. 'But then I decided I should wait and see how things landed first. I'm not one for knee jerk reactions – unless some herculean creature is trying to steal my woman from me.'

'Oh, so I'm *your woman*, am I?' I raise an appraising eyebrow.

'*Ah crap*, sorry. I didn't mean it like you're my property.'

'I'm kidding. I kind of liked seeing your jealous side. It made me feel like I was worth getting in a tussle over.'

'You're worth all of that and more,' he says, and just as I think he's about to lean in and kiss me, the waiter comes to take our order, massacring the moment.

Within minutes, we're clutching two fizzing flutes and a chilled bottle of champagne is nestling in an ice bucket by our table.

'To the start of something amazing?' James holds up his glass.

'I'll drink to that.' My eyes flicker to his lips as we clink, and we barely manage a mouthful each before we're locked in a long sensual kiss across the table.

When we eventually pull apart, I look around self-consciously to see if any of our fellow holidaymakers are grossed out by our PDA. However, no one seems to have noticed us and there's an obvious reason for that. All I've done is join the ranks of the many loved-up couples here that I was watching so enviously before. Why would anyone bat an eyelid?

'Emma, look...' James points across the water, where the sky now resembles an impressionist painting: streaks of red, pink and orange mimicking brushstrokes across the sky, framing the molten sun which is now skirting the horizon.

'This just gets better and better,' I give a contented sigh while gazing at the fiery seascape.

James shifts his seat round beside mine and cuddles into me while we enjoy the dramatic sunset together, sipping at our bubbles.

'I can't think of anywhere I'd rather be,' he murmurs, kissing the side of my head, and though I say nothing in response, I feel exactly the same.

Chapter Forty-One

Departure day

'You got everything?' James asks, when I've completed a final sweep of my suite.

'Think so. But the good thing is... if I've forgotten anything, you can bring it home for me.' I pull a cheeky face.

'True. Provided it fits in my luggage.'

'I still can't believe I'm going home and you're staying here. I know me and the girls have had our holiday, and I'm being totally unreasonable, but it doesn't feel fair.'

'Life isn't fair, Emma.' James offers me a wise (and highly unwelcome) smile.

'That's not what I want to hear right now. You should be agreeing and ruminating over what a tragedy it is that we can't spend more time here together.'

'I'd say your use of the word "tragedy" is a little overkill.'

'Only a little?' I chuckle, well aware that I'm being a drama queen.

James sits on the bed and pats the covers next to him, inviting me to join him briefly. I plonk myself down.

'Would it make you feel better if I told you that, while you were snoring like a banshee last night, I was looking up how much it would cost to change your flights and have you stay on here with me?'

'*Really?*'

'Yes. So, there you go. I was in the same mindset as you.'

He ruffles my hair and I launch myself on him, covering his face with kisses. Laughing, he slips his arms around me and tosses me playfully across the bed, before straddling me and kissing me deeply and sensually. Had we had more time, this would no doubt have led somewhere hot and steamy, but as my airport transfer is arriving imminently, we have no choice but to exercise some self-control.

'No luck with that search then?' I say, once I'm back on my feet, readjusting my outfit.

'Unfortunately, not. There was nothing available on my return flight, or any other flights around the same window of departure.'

'Ah well, that was *really* sweet of you to check.'

'I'll be home before you know it. Then maybe we can move things up a level and go exclusive? Unless it's too soon for you?' He searches my face, probably to check I'm not freaked out by this suggestion.

'Hold on, mister... are you suggesting that for your return so you can "enjoy" your remaining days here?' I put a hand on my hip, feigning suspicion.

'Not for a moment. Why would I want to hook up with anyone else when I already have the most incredible woman waiting for me back home?'

'Nice save. And also... *aww.*' I pounce on him once more.

'So now I'm confused,' says James, as we half-cuddle, half-wrestle on the bed. 'I feel like you're sending me mixed signals. I've been trying to keep the pace slow out of respect for you and your recent circumstances. Does that mean you already want to go exclusive?'

'I'd say so, wouldn't you?'

'What the lady wants, the lady gets.' James kisses my nose and I beam back at him, delighted at this upgrade in our relationship status. 'Right, let's get your stuff along to reception.'

'Do we have to?'

'Do you want to shell out two grand for a flight home three days after I've left?'

'No.'

'Then we have to.'

I trail along behind James to the atrium, where Cat and Amber are already waiting for us.

'*Aww, honey.*' Cat puts her arm around me when she spots my pouty lip and subdued demeanour. 'It feels too soon to leave, doesn't it? Especially with everything that's gone on.'

'It really does.' I lean my head against her shoulder.

'You could always treat us to another holiday to make up for ruining this one?' suggests Amber.

'*Amber!*' Cat scolds her. 'That's so inappropriate.'

'I was joking. *Obviously.*'

'With you, it's hard to know.' I try to pull her into a group hug but she ducks away from me.

'*Mesdames, ça va?*' Sébastien appears out of nowhere, greeting us with double kisses as he always does. This includes James, who looks mighty uncomfortable, as he has done each time it's happened since I introduced him and Sébastien properly the other day. 'It is time for you to return home. That is sad.'

'It's very sad,' I say. 'I could go another week at least.'

'Such is life, huh? Félicité and I wanted to come and wish you well for your journey home.' He beckons to his wife, who's chatting to one of staff at the reception desk.

Despite having already met and had drinks with Sébastien's wife (my plan to avoid them didn't work out so well), I'm still cowed by her presence every time I see her. She's like a vision from an oil painting: a mane of golden-blonde tresses, skin as perfect as porcelain, curves in all the right places. Possibly the hottest woman I've ever clapped eyes on, which makes me feel *very* stupid indeed for ever thinking Sébastien was interested in me. A god and a goddess – us mere mortals would never get a look in.

'*Ça va*, ladies and gentleman James?' She smiles at us, her huge sapphire blue doe eyes glittering, while Sébastien looks on adoringly. 'I wanted to wish you all a safe journey.'

We respond to her with a variety of appreciative acknowledgements and I swear we all sigh a little in wonder.

'Well, I guess we'd better go,' I say.

'Before you do, may I speak with you for one moment in confidence, Emma?' Sébastien asks.

'Sure.'

We move out of earshot of the group, leaving the others to make small talk.

'I will make this very quick,' he says. 'Over the last two days, I have had discussions with Eloise and some other colleagues, and we have come to an agreement. We would like to offer you a role within Paradis Resorts – at a more junior level than the job you interviewed for, but in the same department.'

This comes as such a shock that my brain falters like a buffering video. 'Oh... I... um...'

'There is no pressure to make a decision immediately,' he quickly adds. 'I understand that you may wish to try for senior positions elsewhere, however, I want you to know that I see the role as a stepping stone to the one you applied for over time. Succession planning is a key aspect of how I operate the business.'

'Gosh, Sébastien, *sorry*...' I finally find my voice. 'I just wasn't expecting this. Of course I'm interested. I don't even have to think about that.'

'*Bien.*' His face breaks into a crinkly-eyed smile. 'I am very pleased to hear this. I will email the details to you, and we can talk more once you are home and rested.'

'Fantastic. I can't wait to hear more. Thank you *so* much for this opportunity.'

'The pleasure is all mine, Emma. You have earned your place with us and we will be lucky to have you join our team...'

As he's talking, I suddenly remember my agreement with James to go travelling together. *Sh-i-i-t.* I don't want to miss out on that, and I certainly don't want James heading off to god knows where alone and potentially finding himself an exotic goddess like Félicité to replace me. But then I don't want to miss out on the job either.

'Emma? *Ça va?*'

Double shit. I've completely zoned out because of this dilemma. Honesty is the only way forward here.

'Sorry, Sébastien. Yes, I'm fine, however... when I found out I didn't get the job, I made other arrangements. I was hoping to travel for a few months with James in the summer.' My gaze falls to the floor as it dawns on me how lame this must sound.

'That is not a problem, Emma,' says Sébastien to my surprise, and I look up. 'This job is new so we have flexibility. We can agree a start date in the autumn. How does that sound?'

I break into a relieved grin. 'It sounds perfect. Thanks so much again, Sébastien.'

'As I say, Emma, the pleasure is all mine.'

We return to the others and say goodbye to Sébastien and Félicité who head in the direction of the pool. Cat, Amber, James and I then make our way outside to the waiting people carrier, where the concierge is loading our luggage into the boot.

'What was that about, Emma?' Amber asks.

'Nothing really...' I adopt a sly expression. 'Except that Sébastien just offered me a job.'

'*He what?*'

I laugh at the three stunned faces blinking back at me and quickly fill them in. What follows is much cheering and whooping as we celebrate my surprise job offer – and the fact I can still go on my trip with James.

'We'll leave you to say goodbye properly,' says Cat when the excitement of the moment has passed.

'Yeah, we'll skip the face sucking,' says Amber. 'Bye, James. See you on the other side.' She gives him a little salute, then Cat hugs him and they get into the waiting taxi.

'I've been dreading this bit.' I say to James, wrinkling my nose.

'Hey, don't be so glum. I'll see you in about four days' time.' He lifts my chin with his forefinger so I'm gazing right into his eyes.

'I know that. It's more that it's the end of our time here together. It's been so wonderful and romantic – bar one or two hiccups – and I wish we could have longer.'

'Well, remember... all being well, we'll be going on our own trip soon – just the two of us.'

'I know.' I beam at him, my mood instantly lifting. 'I already can't wait.'

'Me neither.' He takes my face in his hands and kisses me tenderly. 'Safe journey home. Never thought I'd say this but I'll be looking forward to getting back to cold, rainy Scotland.'

'That *is* a rare statement.'

Keeping hold of his hand until the very last second, I reluctantly get into the people carrier, giving James one final wave as we drive off.

'You OK?' Cat takes my hand while the taxi crawls down the long driveway past the lush vegetation and towering trees.

'Yeah, I'm fine. But sad that our trip is already over.'

'You've got nothing to be sad about.' Amber eyes me from the other side of Cat. 'New boyfriend and a new job. I'd call that a bloody successful holiday.'

'I guess when you put it like that...' I give a sheepish laugh that's met with an approving wink from Amber and a hand squeeze from Cat. 'Actually, my new job will be the perfect sweetener for when I tell my parents about me going travelling for the summer.'

'That's true, it will be helpful,' says Cat. 'Hey, something dawned on me when you were saying goodbye to James. You've got another lucky number, honey.'

'Um... OK. Do you want to elaborate on that?'

'James's phone number was your first one, right? Because it won you the money.'

'Uh-huh...'

'And Sébastien said it was your karaoke performance that made him notice you. So... the song you sang is another lucky number. You know... like how a song can be referred to as a "number". As in "That's a great number".'

'*Yeah, grandma*,' hoots Amber. 'Nobody born post nineteen-sixty refers to music in that way.'

'Leave her alone, Amber.' I give her a stern look as Cat turns beetroot.

'*What?*' Amber's face is defiant. 'It's true. My Pops talked that way and he was practically from the Victorian era.'

'That's a bit of an exaggeration,' I say. 'But how cute that you had a "Pops". I can just picture you, all tiny, sitting on his knee. You'd probably still be able to do that.'

'*Shut it, Emma.*' She folds her arms and stares out of the window while Cat and I share a delighted look for having successfully one-upped her.

With one last look through the rear window at the resort, I

settle back in my seat contentedly, finally turning my thoughts to home – and all the exciting new beginnings that now lie ahead of me there.

Acknowledgments

I can't remember the exact moment that I decided to write a follow up to *Lucky Number* but one thing's for sure – I'm so glad I did. Not only was Emma's once in a lifetime holiday with her friends screaming at me to become a sequel, it was such a fun book to write. In fact, it's been my favourite writing experience so far, and I probably shouldn't say this with it being my own work, but I can't get enough of Amber's mischievous antics.

I started *Another Lucky Number* in 2016, but I had to shelve it a third of the way through the first draft to focus on writing something new to submit to publishers, and after that there wasn't much opportunity to get back to it. Then the pandemic hit, and like most of the world, I was stuck at home so I dusted off my partial manuscript and got to work. I've shared before that I find writing therapeutic – it provides a welcome distraction from the unpleasant symptoms that come with my long-term health issues – and it became an even more important support mechanism during that period. Physically, I was imprisoned in my tiny flat (apart from the daily walk we were allowed) but in my mind I was thousands of miles away with my characters, getting involved in their hilarious shenanigans while soaking up the Caribbean sun and enjoying great food and cocktails. It was the very definition of escapism and it helped me fare well mentally and emotionally during that challenging time.

Now it's confession time. I wrote the first draft of *Another Lucky Number* having never even been to the Caribbean (though I had been to another paradise island for my honeymoon), and I subsequently learned an important lesson: don't write a location you've never been to! I thought I had done a reasonable job until a friend and fellow author read it and fed back that the story was great, but the setting felt like a mish-mash of Cancun and various Caribbean islands. Well, at least I was in the right geographical area (sort of).

It had always been a dream of mine to go to the Caribbean but traveling long haul is almost prohibitive because of the symptoms I live with and I did wonder if I'd ever make it there. However, thanks to the support of my incredible husband, I was lucky enough to make my first ever trip there recently – to The Bahamas, where the colour of the sea and sand was every bit as amazing as I had imagined. That experience killed two birds with one stone, so to speak. I ticked off a big 'bucket list' item and managed to do the research I needed to do to make my story more authentic. That's what I call a massive win.

Anyway, getting to the point, the list of people to thank this time is shorter than with *Lucky Number*, which had quite the extended 'cast and crew' due to its long and winding road to publication. First up, as always, is the man of my world – my amazing husband, James, to whom I have dedicated this book. It felt fitting, given he has the same name as the male main character and love interest in this story, but I must reiterate (because I also mentioned this in the Acknowledgements of *Lucky Number*) that 'my James' is not the source of inspiration for 'story James' – although he is also incredibly supportive and helpful and I've totally lucked out with him. Thank you, 'my James', for everything. And that goes way beyond your support with my writing career and you making it possible to visit the setting of this book. I'm also well aware that, without you, my life could be so much more challenging.

On the book production side of things, a huge thank you goes to my brilliant author friends, Fiona Leitch, Sandy Barker and Andie Newton, who have once again offered me their skills, knowledge, insight and steadfast support and encouragement to help me get *Another Lucky Number* over the line. With this series being an independent venture, I don't have the might of a publishing house behind me and that has felt a bit daunting. Having the amazing support of these wonderful (and wonderfully talented) ladies in my life has made all the difference. I've said it before and I'll say it again: I appreciate you more than you could ever know. Another important thank you goes to illustrator extraordinaire, Jane Dunnet, for the utterly fabulous cover designs of both books in this series.

To my parents and all my family members, particularly my dad, who did some early editing on the first draft of this book back in 2018, my mum, who tells almost everyone she meets about my books, and my sister-in-law, Geraldine, who is an ardent reader of my novels, thank you once again for all your support with my writing career and in my life generally.

Finally, and as always, a huge thank you to my readers and avid supporters (you know who you are) for continuing to cheer me on. Every bit of support from you really does mean the world and it spurs me on to keep writing more.

About the Author

Nina Kaye is a contemporary romance author who writes warm, witty and uplifting reads with a deeper edge. She lives in Edinburgh with her husband and much adored side-kick, James. In addition to writing, Nina enjoys swimming, gin and karaoke (preferably all together in a sunny, seaside destination). Nina has previously published *The Gin Lover's Guide to Dating*, *Take A Moment*, *One Night in Edinburgh*, *Just Like That*, *Stand Up Guy* and *Lucky Number* (which is the first book in her Lucky Number series). She has also been a contender for the RNA Joan Hessayon award.

Printed in Dunstable, United Kingdom